ALSO BY JOSEPH O'CONNOR

Novels

Cowboys and Indians
Desperadoes
The Salesman
Inishowen
Star of the Sea
Redemption Falls

Short stories/novella

True Believers
The Comedian

Plays

Red Roses and Petrol
The Weeping of Angels
True Believers (adaptation)
Handel's Crossing

Film Scripts

A Stone of the Heart
The Long Way Home
Ailsa

GHOST LIGHT

Joseph O'Connor was born in Dublin. His books include six previous novels: *Cowboys and Indians* (Whitbread Prize shortlist), *Desperadoes*, *The Salesman*, *Inishowen*, *Star of the Sea*, and *Redemption Falls*. *Star of the Sea* became an international bestseller, winning the *Irish Post* Award for Fiction, an American Library Association Award, France's Prix Millepages, Italy's Premio Acerbi, and the Prix Madeleine Zepter for European Novel of the Year. His work has been published in forty languages.

www.josephoconnorauthor.com

JOSEPH O'CONNOR

Ghost Light

VINTAGE BOOKS
London

For Ciaran and Julia Carty

Published by Vintage 2011

2 4 6 8 10 9 7 5 3 1

Copyright © Joseph O'Connor 2010

Joseph O'Connor has asserted his right under the Copyright, Designs
and Patents Act 1988 to be identified as the author of this work

Grateful thanks to Faber & Faber Ltd and the estate of Sylvia Plath
for permission to quote from 'For a Fatherless Son'

First published in Great Britain in 2010 by
Harvill Secker

Vintage
Random House, 20 Vauxhall Bridge Road,
London SW1V 2SA

www.vintage-books.co.uk

Addresses for companies within The Random House Group Limited
can be found at: www.randomhouse.co.uk/offices.htm

The Random House Group Limited Reg. No. 954009

A CIP catalogue record for this book
is available from the British Library

ISBN 9780099481546

The Random House Group Limited supports The Forest Stewardship
Council (FSC), the leading international forest certification organisation.
All our titles that are printed on Greenpeace approved FSC certified paper
carry the FSC logo. Our paper procurement policy can be found at
www.rbooks.co.uk/environment

Mixed Sources
Product group from well-managed
forests and other controlled sources
www.fsc.org Cert no. TT-COC-2139
© 1996 Forest Stewardship Council
FSC

Typeset by Palimpsest Book Production Limited, Falkirk, Stirlingshire
Printed and bound in Great Britain by
CPI Bookmarque, Croydon CR0 4TD

SYNGE (pronounced 'Sing'), Edmund John Millington (1871–1909), the most influential Irish playwright of the twentieth century, co-founder with Yeats and Augusta Gregory of the Abbey Theatre, Dublin. His works include *The Well of the Saints*, *Riders to the Sea* and *The Playboy of the Western World*, which saw rioting at its premiere (Dublin, 1907) and during its subsequent American tour. Engaged at the time of his death to Molly Allgood, an actress, stage name Maire O'Neill. Associates, colleagues and both families disapproved. Her many letters to him do not survive.

A LODGING-HOUSE ROOM IN LONDON
27 October 1952

6.43 a.m.

In the top floor room of the dilapidated townhouse across the Terrace, a light has been on all night. From your bed it was visible whenever you turned towards the window, which you had to do in order to fetch your bottle from the floor. Most nights, the same. The bulb is lighted at dusk. In the mornings, a couple of moments after the street lamps flicker out, it dies, and the ragged curtain is closed.

You are sixty-five now, perhaps the age of that house, perhaps even a little older – what a thought. You approach your only window; it is shockingly cold to the touch. Winter is coming to England. The weather has been bitter. Last night a hurricane struck London.

You have never noticed anyone enter or exit that forlorn house, but the postman still delivers to it, stuffing envelopes through the broken glass in the door panel – the letterbox has been nailed closed many years. Men urinate in the porch. One of the street-girls plies her trade there, and the balustrade has long been splashed with obscene words. Many of the window embrasures are boarded. Buddleia sprouts from the façade.

You have a sense that the occupant of the room is a man. One midnight a fleeting shadow crossed the upper windowpane – so you thought – and there was maleness in how it moved. There was a time when you used to think about him – how can he live alone in a bomb-blasted old house? who sends the letters? what are they about? – for it helped to pass the brutal hours immediately preceding dawn. But this morning someone else is come to you again, out of the same light, somehow, out of an unseen room, out of a city you have lived in the last thirteen years but have never found a reason to call your own. This has happened to all of us: a coasting across the mind by one we had thought forgotten or purposefully banished. But today will prove him a wanderer reluctant to be exiled, an emigrant still attempting to come home.

He could be difficult sometimes. What use in denying it? Irritable, *unforgiving*, for a relatively young man. Because the whisperers and poke-bonnets and gossips and sniggerers always made such a *point* of the age difference between you. Envious vixens. Triple-chinned hypocrites, too deceitful to utter their true objection. What are years? Fictions. Ink-stains on a calendar. There are moments, of late, when yesterday feels a life ago, and tomorrow an unborn century, so unreachable it seems. And had he lived beyond his youth, the years would have contracted, because a married couple become the same age, grow to resemble one another over time, like bookends, their recollections in greyed bindings between them and neither bothering to read what once divided them. What's this he'd be now? Eighty? Something. A slippered old duffer. A shuffler. An auld bags. Hard to work the calculation through the fug of a hangover. Your reckoning of the decades keeps stalling, tripping up. After a few ruined attempts, you abandon it.

You take a small, sour sip. Medicinal. Just a settler. The reek of gin dampens your eyes, somehow intensifies his presence, but you grimace it away with a swallow. *The daily spite of this unmannerly town.* Wasn't it Yeats wrote that? Or my other lunk? Shaw. Dublin, he was whining about; but all towns are unmannerly, to the old, the poor, the collaborator. What is it in poets that must dress a thing up? Christ, they'd nearly call their dandruff 'the fairy-snow'.

Not long after dawn. The shadow-kissing time. Grey light at the window and the whistle of the kettle as you move about, failing to keep warm. Mittens flittered to ribbons. You wear a dead man's boots. Well, no point in wastefulness. A sin. Down below in Brickfields Terrace, a milk wagon is delivering. You wonder would the man advance you another month's credit but the fear of being declined dissuades you. Hoarfrost silvers the pavement, the telephone kiosk, the street, the wrecked colonnades of the house where the light burns all night, an awning over the grocer's on the corner of Porchester Road. Rooks are circling the chimney breasts.

Johnny Synge's bit of native. The proddy's little squaw. That Kingstown playboy's huer. Insults hurled long ago by the wags of witty Dublin, still audible after more than forty years.

You shuffle away from the window, to the cubbyhole by the cooking ring. The room smells of cabbage-water and dust. Somewhere below you a wireless is playing too loudly but you do not object to the interruption, find it oddly cheering sometimes. There are hours, late at night, when you miss its consolation. Silence can be frightening to the lonely. He always said you were over-imaginative, too given to fantasy. A Catholic trait, he would joke. These nights, you read Mills & Boons from the tuppenny library in Earl's Court Road. Sure you'd be lost for a bit of an escape only it wasn't for *True Romances*. How he'd have hated them, your dog-eared and tearstained bedfellows. 'Opium for spinsters,' he'd mock.

> *The sun would dry the oceans wide;*
> *Heaven would cease to be;*
> *The world would cease its motion, my love,*
> *Ere I'd prove false to thee.*

A song that would draw the heart out of you, Molly. That anyone ever felt such devotion.

A drop or two of milk would take the scald off the gin. This cheap stuff hits your throat like boiled sand. Eighty-one. His age. If he was alive today. *Were* he to be alive. Still correcting your grammar. The sense that you were an embarrassment to him has never quite surrendered. The difference was not only one of age.

The cupboard contains a tea caddy decorated with a transfer of a parrot, and an empty sugar bag that can be scraped for its few last grains. You are thinking about the milkman, who is old beyond his years. They say he was shell-shocked at Anzio. The children of the neighbourhood are afraid of him, call him names. It is whispered that he has queer obsessions, with dog-dirt, with blood, with immigrants, especially Poles, and the lack of public lavatories. He used to make a nuisance of himself with a pretty schoolgirl as she took the short cut to St Catherine's, and now no schoolgirls are ever seen on the Terrace. He has the grin of a corpse and the bearing of a soldier, but sometimes he stretches his stride as one negotiating stepping-stones, laughing the while through his teeth. Has he failed to understand that the gaiety of the passers-by is forced, is actually a peculiarly English kind of hatred? Perhaps an understanding could be reached. If one went to him with honesty. But no. It would not be seemly.

—*One does not ask for credit, Changeling. If appropriate, it is offered. One must always cut one's cloth having regard to proprieties. Anything less is the death of civilisation.*

The cat slinks haughtily across the sticky, bare floorboards and arches its back against a chair-leg. Of a sudden it appears taken by a leather-framed photograph that is propped between two empty candlesticks on the mantelshelf. The man in the portrait has been dead a long time. His clothes are Edwardian: a shabby plus-four suit and brogues, a loose varsity cap, a knotted kerchief about the throat. An ashplant cane in the gloved right hand and a book protruding slightly from the pocket. Sepia has made his garments the same colour as his hair, as his mother's chaise longue in the background. The picture has shrivelled over the years. It has seen many mantelshelves; many boxes and cheap hotel rooms, the greenrooms, the flophouses, the pouches of a cardboard suitcase. There is a stiffness in how he holds himself, as one braving the firing squad in an opera, and the eyes, martyr-sad, are very slightly blurred, as though he blinked or was weeping at the moment the shutter was opened. But that would have been so unlike him.

A medieval Scottish ballad on an unseen wireless. You'd be grateful for the coming of morning. The slowplodding clop of the milkman's dray. Someone's motor car grumbles into life, a bicycle bell trills, and the phantoms recede into the wallpaper. You seem to see yourself at a distance, as a character in a story, perhaps. Miss O'Neill shivers at the table, drinks the acrid black tea. An offcut of linoleum serves raggedly as tablecloth; it is spotted with candle grease and cigarette burns. Here and there on its surface appears a crest of crossed rapiers with the motto FIDES ET ROBUR. She has twice been married, once widowed, once divorced. Her only son, an RAF pilot, was killed in the war, shot down over northern Germany, never found. It has been a long time indeed since she last played a leading role, since the palaces of Broadway rang with acclamation for her brilliance, but in whatever life those riotous ovations still echo, if they do, the ghost of a curtain still rises. One St Patrick's Night they stopped a train in Scranton, Pennsylvania, for the townspeople had somehow heard Molly Allgood was on board. Irish immigrant families. Weeping and cheering. Lofting children on their shoulders. An old miner kissing her hand. Coal dust under his fingernails. Withered shamrock in his cap. You peer at your bony knuckles, see the fossil of a bird's wing. Can they remember they were once kissed in Pennsylvania?

> *Mother of Christ*
> *Star of the Sea*
> *Hope of the wanderer*
> *Pray for me.*

Somewhere in the room is a packet of old programmes all containing your name, but you wouldn't know where to find it among the clutter. Anyhow, the ones signed by the famous were long ago sold, with whatever books were worth anything at all. There is a little bookshop in Russell Square where they specialise in autographs. A kindly widower, a Jew, shy and scholarly, is the proprietor. A Communist, so they say – he denies actual membership. He lost an arm in the Spanish Civil War.

Does the body remember? When the mind has forgotten? Does Mr Duglacz dream that he is whole again, a sweat-stained revolutionary? If he stretched to pull an orange in the soporific heat of a grove, or groped towards some Annamaria's scarlet, mournful mouth, would he see his vanished hand and weep? And if dreams unmask our longings, as the wise have claimed since the Greeks, why is it that the dead are so often silent when we dream them? Don't we *want* them to speak? What would they say? Does Mr Duglacz ever dream himself a baby?

He always paid cash, more than fairly at that, was glad to see you coming, offered tea or a small sherry, showed you volumes he had recently acquired at house clearances in the shires, was perhaps even a little flirtatious in the abashed way of old men as he fumbled among his broadsheets and foxed aquatints. ('This might interest you, Miss O'Neill, the binding is exquisite. Not everyone could appreciate it as you would.') But you have almost nothing left to offer him and no pretext for calling. It has been more than a year. You think of him sometimes. His embarrassed, touching courtesies and mild self-deprecations; his cheerfulness only grief turned brave. At moments he suddenly arises like a rumour of himself, or as a reminder of someone else: the man in the photograph on the mantelshelf. Anyhow, you are glad. All that is behind you now. 'Bloom where you are planted,' your mother used to say. 'When sorrow sours your milk, make cheese.'

Life abounds with blessings. To *be* alive – even that. For the chances against our existence are incalculable, overwhelming; it would mesmerise you even to start considering them. So many you knew are gone. And the billions never born. Nobody should be here. Yet we are. And it is all such a beautiful and strange adventure; who would forgo it only the mad or the broken? This afternoon you have an engagement at the British Broadcasting Corporation, a part in a radio adaptation of a play by Sean O'Casey, one of the many Irish playwrights you once counted among your friends. You have never liked the piece. There are few plays you truly like. You wonder where O'Casey is now.

He would be old, even more bitter. His sweat would taste like the wince-making tea: metallic, like blood, only stewed. They say he lives someplace on the south coast of England (*Jaysus*), is grown shrivelled with his hatreds, has been blind many years. He wears a skullcap and sea-boots and a filthy Aran sweater he stitched from dead critics' hair. A face like an elephant's bollock, one of the stagehands once chuckled, and that was neither today nor yesterday, God knows. Poor Johnnybags Casey and his harem of perceived slights. What must they make of him, the villagers and their children, as he shambles the fogs like a poisoned old dosser on his way to sign fraudulently at the Labour? A Friday night fight-starter. A slum boy translated. Has he friends? Does he drink? You cannot remember now. Is he still at this end of the plank at all? You picture him facing out on the storm-lashed breakwaters, raging at the raucous gulls.

—*Napoleon the Third was exiled before dying in terrible agony on the south coast of England. Where a lot of people* live *in terrible agony.*

'Let me alone,' you whisper. 'I am not able for you today.'

The breeze comes back crisply, fricative, falling away, like a saxophonist playing sub-tones, full of breath. The cat pads towards the window and utters a famished mraow. From the cement factory in Paddington Dock, the alleluia of a siren. Men will be making their way from the estates of west London. The wind rising cinders. Wives in their milky happiness. Still the middle of the night in Manhattan.

You have nothing to eat. There has been little for two days. The hunger is dizzying, now groaningly painful, like the feeling that used to assail you when about to menstruate. Kindly, he was then. A womanly solicitude. It is so cold that you consider dressing over your nightgown and vest, but for pity's sake, Molly, there must always be self-*respect*. You cannot dander about London knowing you are in a nightgown. It would be a nice pancake if you had an accident and they had to cart you to the hospital. Imagine if you died in the street, girl. Naked, shuddering, your soles on cold boards. Quickly now, Molls, fetch a drawers and a shift. Don't be minding the lack of curtains for there's nobody gawping, and a nice fright he'd get if he did. A woman stalks across your memory, a dresser once assigned to you on an American tour, an astonishingly elderly Irishwoman – people said she was a hundred – but her name will not come, is kept at bay by the cold. She'd be dead these many years, you realise now. Was it Mary she was called? Born in Galway.

You have a rudimentary wash at the sink – the lavatory on the upper landing cannot be faced in the mornings – and dress quickly, fumblingly, blaspheming the cold, in your old black blouse and chestnut lambswool twin-set, and run a brush nine times through your hair. How he drowned in my ringlets. His mouth in my curls. Gone to spiderweb now. Old scuttler. The blouse is a little shiny but it is a pre-war Worth; good couture will always last, and proper tailoring. Taking your ancient box of numbered powders, you apply pan-stick and face pack in the little cracked shaving-mirror you inherited with the room: 2j with 3, a fingertip of 13, and yellow for an Italian warmth. After powdering, you dust your temples and cheekbones with terracotta dry rouge, a touch on the end of the chin, carmine lips for youthfulness. As you work, it is your fancy to imagine scenes the mirror has observed. Can it remember the man who first bought it, used it? Perhaps poor Mr Holland, the scaffolder's mate from Belfast who died in the rusting single bed you lie awake in. You sometimes wear his stiffened boots. You inhale him in dust. For months after you took the room, men would call to visit him, and it fell to you to tell them of his passing. Yes indeed, very sad. No, I myself did not know him. I am afraid I have no address for the family. I believe there is a brother, a priest in Chicago. No, I did not find any hammer. He borrowed it, you say? I am sorry, sir, I cannot assist you.

You had tried to give it dignity, your role as breaker of sad tidings. And you were good at it: poised, neither melodramatic nor too blunt. And it was better than having no role at all. It was how you had first realised you had somehow become old, for nobody is as skilled in the imparting of bad news as an elderly woman from Ireland. Once or twice you had gone so far as to proffer tea or a consoling glass of something – 'I rarely myself drink, sir, but I happen to have a bottle in beyond at the moment, which I was saving as a gift for a gentleman colleague' – but the offer had never been accepted. Perhaps it was improper. Some of them had looked frightened as they left.

No need to make your face but to do so is a rite, an act you have long believed brings luck with the doing, and like many of your profession you are unalterably superstitious. And what is *need* anyhow? We cannot live by mere need. The basest beggars are in the poorest thing superfluous. King Lear. Yes. There must always be more than need. Steam when you exhale. Ice on the window-pane, on the handles of the cupboard, the tap. Winter is closing on London and you have nothing to burn. Well, perhaps, on your walk, you will see something you could pick up. Broken twigs in the park, a lump or two of anthracite. Maybe try the coke merchant in the alley off Westbourne Grove. Wander into the yard where the navvies shovel the coal. But you would have to be careful not to be noticed, approached. There was unpleasantness the last time. Unwise to try again so soon. You are no beggarwoman, after all, but an artist.

Is it Joan Fontaine someone once told me I was the spit of? That part in the picture they made of the Daphne du Maurier novel, what's this was the name of it now? Jesus God, Molly. Laurence Olivier was in it. About the woman and the chap and the house and the drowned wife and the dreaming you went to Manderley again. You pout haughtily in the mirror. Fiercely narrow your eyes. '*I am Mrs de Winter now*,' you murmur.

Today you shall walk. That is the plan. There must always be a *plan*, girl; otherwise we pull into ourselves like snails, and the devil conjures thoughts for the untidy mind and you can lose thirty years in such a withdrawal. This is how time unfolds when you are old and susceptible. Wander into its spiralled shell and it is hard to escape. The glisten that looks inviting to age-bleared eyes has a way of suddenly liquefying and then coagulating around your heart, and the womb in which you find yourself so numbingly cocooned is too enveloping to allow you to resurface. You will walk from your room to Broadcasting House, through the grey, busy streets of a late October London, perhaps digressing through Hyde Park, for there is no need to hurry; the rehearsal is not until five o'clock. It will clear your jumbled thoughts to be away from this room. A change is as bracing as a rest. You might even kill an hour in the National Portrait Gallery, where it is always warm in wintertime and the porters are courteous, or perhaps light a candle for the poor in St Martin-in-the-Fields, a church whose strange name you love saying. It only costs a penny and sometimes there is music, the choristers practising Bach, or an organist at rehearsal. The great, fat pipes of the sonorous organ like giant bottles lined up on a bar. And the ground-bass rumbling through you, to the meats of your teeth. It is not too long to Advent. There might even be Handel. Better to light one flame than be cursing the darkness. And the store windows on Jermyn Street will be beautiful.

Was it stitched into a tapestry primer? *Bloom Where You Are Planted.* Because Sara was at the sewing of it all that summer I left school. Wasn't it Georgie had it framed and it hanging in Muddy's bedroom between the crucifix and the daguerreotype of Avoca. 'Jesus, come down and give me a rest.' Muddy's joke when she was wearied by a long day in the shop. Does he be looking and you naked, Mam? Sally red with laughter. Would he bother, child of God, he'd have better to be looking at. And the way she rubbed your back when you were poorly that time, and her legends of King Arthur and Cuchulainn. Poor Muddy, God rest her and the faithful departed. But don't be straying yourself into the glooms.

And so life abounds with blessings. It is only a matter of noticing them. You are grateful to have an engagement, a reason to leave the hungry room, an interlude of parole from the cat's grave stare, its reminder that man is not the Supreme Being. You will say to yourself, traversing the cold, great thoroughfares: *I am walking through London because I am busy, a professional. I have an appointment with people who need me.* Every role has its importance. London is full of actors. *But I have been chosen today.* And you will speak your few lines properly, with the austerity they demand, no bogus mellifluousness, no hamming or shamming, and the broadcast will be transmitted around the world like a wind, to India, Australia, Canada, South Africa, what a miracle, truly, when you think what man has done: airstreams of consolation engirdling the globe from a bunker in wintry London. And who can know what opportunities might result from today's performance? An impresario could be listening, a casting agent; a director. A little playhouse in the provinces or in Ireland someplace. Well, it is possible; it is *possible*. Stranger things have happened. Everyone has a slow year. It is the nature of the profession. Bad 1952 has not all that long to live. Maybe the better times are coming in. On such a full sea are we now afloat, and we must take the current when it serves, or lose our ventures. People have braved the Atlantic for less of a chance. All you must brave is London.

The producer, an elderly Dubliner, has remembered you at the last moment, has somehow dug up your address, when he could have chosen others, and to be remembered, for any actor, is a mercy. Such a cultured, benign man. Handsome as Ariel in a cardigan. You know what they say about him, Molly. Well, what business of theirs? Blessed Jesus, couldn't we do with more love in the world, not less. And if men wish the companionship and the beauty of one another, didn't God in His gentleness make us all? The pay is not good – it never is at the BBC – and they *always* pay late, but you have grown skilled at economising, as has everyone since the years of war. You will be able to make the two guineas last a fortnight, maybe more. Roll the pastry good and thin and you'll never grow fat, and hunger is the best sauce anyhow. And you could salt away a shilling or two for a Christmas gift for your grandchildren. A little comic-book, maybe; a bag of sherbet lemons. Perhaps you might even be able to redeem some of your costume jewellery from the pawn. ('Ain't so much of a market in second-hand eternity rings, love. Stands to reason when you reckon. The girls think it bad luck, see. I'll have a shufti if you like. But I couldn't give you much.') It will be a blessing simply to work, to see people again. Sometimes the younger actors are kind. They sense your fate to be the one awaiting most of them in the end. You have become for the young an example of What Could Happen. We should be merciful to those embodying our dreads, for the season of our own denouement will come, when we may embody the dreads of others.

I know
That my
Redeemer
Liveth

Your daughter lives in Aberdeen with her children and husband, an organiser for the Furnacemen's Union. Your twin grandsons are aged seven: James-Larkin and Emmet. You might go to them for the Christmas if you can somehow scrape the fare. Please God, some little job at the start of December. He is a good man, your son-in-law. But strict. Doesn't drink. Pegeen is a most fortunate wife.

She writes to you monthly, of schoolyard adventures, of head lice and hand-me-downs, second-hand furniture. They don't have much. Is her chattiness hiding something? Her handwriting is almost identical to yours.

To kiss the twins, smuggle them a sweet. So far away, Aberdeen. Five hundred miles from London, might as well be a thousand, for the night train is slow as a miser's compassion and it's rare you can afford the express. And the months tend to drift, and then tumble into seasons, and sure next thing you know it's gone a year since you've seen them. Now don't exaggerate, Molly. It is only eight months. And it shocked you, the last time, when she was waiting for you at the station, and hurrying towards your carriage with a smile would melt snow. It was like looking at your sister. For a moment, you couldn't speak. The twins tugging your coat, leaping around you like terriers, and the thunderstorm of family resemblance.

Your sister died two years ago, is buried in Hollywood. You and she had not met in some time. You did not attend the funeral – it was too arduous a journey, you had not been at all well. And money. Always money. The obituaries had been fulsome. Someone helpful had mailed them from Dublin. 'Greatest Irish actress of her noble generation.' 'The peerless heroine.' 'Academy Award nomination.' 'No character actress of her era would ever rival Sara Allgood. (A sister, Maire O'Neill, also acted.)'

—*Envy is unbecoming in a woman who is an artist.*

'Go and blast yourself' you say, aloud. 'It's all I have left me.'

The wind chuckles feebly as it gusts down the Terrace and the rattle of the bin-lids is the rack of his breathing. *You must not make me laugh so, with your scampish impertinence. You know asthma is made more distressing by amusement.*

Oh the cemetery is only *beautiful* – so you have been assured – and the funeral was a Cleopatran occasion. A dozen of holy priests and one of them in line for a bishopric and the others all as jealous as schoolgirls. Hitchcock read the lesson. Mario Lanza led the hymns. In a neatly wooded parkland overlooking Culver City. And a vineyard nearby. *Oh the little purple grapes.* Admirers are often witnessed placing lilies on the tombstone, or copies of play-texts, lighted candles. A half-mile of palm trees on an avenue of glittering quartz; a Roman temple of remembrance so impossibly white it would blind you to look at it in sunshine. Mexicans tending the orchids. Hoses spraying the lawns. Negro ladies in pink uniforms polishing the headstones till you'd nearly see your face in the marble. They give you a map when you visit, indicating all the movie stars' graves. It is whispered that Bela Lugosi owns a plot. So cool in the chapel on a blazing Los Angeles day. There is always music playing. Bach. Palestrina. A system of taped recordings. Onyx and porphyry. *O, les petits muscats mauves* . . .

And if I had emigrated to America. He and I used to speak of it. The brave young country where differences do not weigh and all must create themselves over. They love and respect the outsider. We have fought in their wars, constructed their cathedrals, bridged their savage rivers. A Republic will always treasure the newcomer, the rebel, the player of wild cards, the frontiersman. You and I shall truly feel we are come home at last. There is nothing in this heartbroken Ireland for either of us, Molly. It is a mirrorland of celibates and killers on bicycles, a Lilliput of Reverend Mothers and pittances and fogs and embarrassing stains on the mattress.

Rebecca. It was called. That picture.

Even after he died, in the rainfall of his mourning, you would imagine your newfound land. Him watching Niagara roar, or in the bird market at Baton Rouge, on the steamboat for Great Falls, Montana. Some go to Paradise, others to Purgatory, but the good to an eternal West. And in the years after his passing, the seasons of your American fame, you thought of him during every bow. To be a citizen of Brooklyn, of tall, stately Chicago. To gaze on Lake Michigan on an Illinois Christmas Eve, the faint smell of lakewater, and Lilliput far away, and the frost bitter-crisp as champagne. But the bags had been packed, the return sailing taken. There had never been a moment when you had decided not to defect. It was something you simply hadn't got around to.

The clunk of doors closing, of hobnailed boots on the staircase. London is outside in the rain. The house's barrenness looms at you, each partitioned-off room a stage in a theatre gone dark. Almost all who reside here are workingmen, labourers. No one in the house is married. It is impossible to imagine the laughter of a child ever lightening such corridors, or darkening them, for laughter can unease. And there would be no reason to imagine it, for it will never happen now. You hear them come and go; old men in their moleskins. Sometimes they pause on the landings conversing briefly of the weather, with the guardedness of men who do not like or trust one another and who have been hurt when they trusted or liked. Then the doors quietly close and someone switches on his wireless and there arises the stink of burnt frying. Pawned tools of a Friday. The pound sent home. The mail-boat on Christmas Eve. In your dreams the house screams with its murdered hungers. Its night-windows redden with lust.

To have someone to share the room with. A few words of an evening. Someone to make a pot of tea when you're sick. Lately you have caught yourself grumbling to the walls, to the turrets of broken-spined paperbacks that stand sentry about the floor-boards, to the lamp with its ripped shade, its dishevelled aplomb, the pegs on the coatless hatstand. The night-thoughts are the hardest. You cannot talk to the night. If you do, it might start talking back.

He is a good man, your son-in-law. Didn't mean what he said. Every family has these little disagreements, when harsh words are spoken. You are his children's only living grandparent, the mother of his wife. If you wrote and said you're sorry and you'd give anything to see the twins. It's been eight long months. If you promised.

Wind shrieks in the chimney as you open your tobacco tin and extract the makings of a poor cigarette. Little flimsies of paper, like torn pages of a bible, and fag-ends picked up in the street. But we mustn't complain. Haven't we health at the least, and the hurting comfort of smoke? My throat is a chimney breast, these lips a venting smokestack. Always he pleaded for you to quit the filthy practice, yet *he* never quitted, the great hypocritical *flue*, with his burblings and his *belchings* and his clouds of condemnation and his sermonising ridiculous smugness. *It is different for a man. You know that very well. Wilde said a gentleman must always have an occupation. It would be a nice pancake entirely if he didn't.*

Papers strewn everywhere, blown around the room like old leaves, for one evening last week you forced open the jammed window, forgetting the storm that was billowing across London. The season's weather has been violent, as though in overture to the hurricane, which struck last night as the street lights came on, with the bulb in the hermit's ruin across the Terrace. You lay awake in Mr Holland's bed listening to the wildness of the world, the racketing clatter; smashing roof slates. The bells of distant fire engines came borne on the storm. The house groaned like a ship in a cyclone. Around four in the morning there was a sudden brief lull and you realised that the public telephone on the street below was ringing. Who could it be? Would anyone answer? Should you yourself hurry down? Preposterous, dangerous. An insane notion came to you that it was Mr Duglacz in his bookshop, frightened among his Torahs and autographs and folios. Out of what junkshop of the heart do such yearnings arise? It rang almost twenty minutes. You let it.

———————

On the table is a letter from a postdoctoral student, a young Californian woman who intends visiting London 'in late January or February' and would like to conduct an interview. It would touch, naturally enough, on your recollections and impressions, your friendships and associations in the Ireland of those years, your time in America, especially on Broadway, your memories of your sister, her notable career in motion pictures, and of course on the question of Synge. The interview would be conducted with tact and sensitivity, as perhaps, if I may say so, without wishing to appear presumptuous or intrusive, only a woman could conduct it. Few of us, after all – I hope I do not trespass into the personal realm – have never been disappointed by a man.

—*Ignore it, Changeling. It is a ruse, nothing more. Tell them nothing about us. Do not even reply. We are too precious to be displayed before the rabble.*

I could offer a small sum as remuneration for your time. Would an amount of, say, $50 be acceptable? Alternatively I should be happy to send you anything you require to that value, since I know certain goods and foodstuffs are still quite scarce in England. There is another financial question I would like to broach, Miss O'Neill, and I hope I shall do so without offense. I understand that some years ago you sold to his surviving family all your letters of an intimate nature from Synge. My institution has authorized me to say, should other manuscripts having to do with JMS and his circle remain in your possession (scripts, revisions, juvenilia, notebooks, drafts, fragments, abandoned works, et cetera) we would be honored to acquire them for our archive. Our library has considerable funding for acquisitions. *['Considerable' is typed in red, Molly. That's the Yanks for you now. Subtlety is no Californian trait.]* American scholars take an avid interest in Ireland, as you know: her literature and history, her revolution and liberation, the lives of her great men of letters. Our collection is being developed and extended all the time. We like to think that there is little we are missing. I should have to see and appraise personally any material, of course. But we believe the proposal to be of mutual benefit.

'Liberation' is good, you think to yourself now. Liberation, my arse in parsley.

The letter arrived almost four months ago, among the reams of final demands and sundry threats of disconnection. ('Eviction is a recourse our client does not wish to pursue, but he shall have no alternative if the arrears remain unpaid.') You did not know what should be done with it, whether to throw it in the trash. Similar effronteries have come before, nearly always from America; you have ignored them, discarded them, forgotten them. And yet, might it be redemptive, after all this time – not pleasant, but healing, a settling of the ghosts – to allow yourself to speak of those years? But what is there to say? He lived. He died.

We wanted one another. He was afraid. A poor play it would make, with no hero or heroine, and all of its best lines offstage. And if it ever had a chronology – which it must have, it *must* have – the scenes are no longer in the right order.

'Mercia' she is called. The author of the letter. A name holy water was never poured on. You imagine her – Dr Mercia Vinson – a startlingly vivid picture. A capable piece of work with full lips and plum-sleek hair, who was almost pretty as a girl but too foostery, too nervous, and was always outshone by the louder, gayer classmates who liked her in a pitying way. ('Poor Mercia's teeth. Poor Mercia's *clothes*.') But men want her all the same. They court her with ironies. There is a certain type of man who admires intelligence in a woman, a windmill against which he can pit himself, a quality he can punish, a reason for a woman to have to apologise frequently, which is what men find most arousing in women. Ah Molly, that's not fair. Not all men are like that. Now Mercia sits in a library in hot California writing presumptuous, intrusive letters. But as suddenly as she forms, she vanishes into the odours of the room, for you have apprehended, in one of those moments of piercing clarity that can punctuate a hangover, that the young woman you are imagining is yourself.

You cross slowly to the scarred sideboard, kneel before it, knees creaking, and open the loose-hinged door. It falls out of its frame. The cat gives a start; approaches the interior's blackness cautiously, like a child encountering a waxwork of itself. A reek of mildewed newspapers and mothballs and old wood. Paper bags of ancient birthday cards, a sad-eyed dog in a deerstalker hat, cancelled ration-books, expired passports, redundant lengths of tinfoil. Because you have to save tinfoil, although you cannot remember why – a habit acquired in the war. The mice have been exploring; there are pellets in a broken souvenir ashtray someone brought you from a pilgrimage to Lourdes. You hear them scrabble late at night, especially now with winter coming, in the walls, beneath the floorboards, in the cupboard over the cooker. The cat makes occasional attempts, with infrequent successes. It sometimes seems to have grown frightened of its prey.

Empty jars. Divorced slippers. Long-abandoned attempts at knitting. A shoebox of yellowing reviews. The cat slopes lithely into the sideboard, purring, eyes glimmered, and scrobs at a stack of faded place-mats. You touch its scrawny tail, which makes to tendril round your knuckles. *Go way, you auld flirt*, you mutter. They used to rain the shredded foil from the Spitfires by the hundredweight. Wasn't that it? To bamboozle the German radar. Terrible what was done to those people in Dresden. They say that only the cathedral survived.

A chocolate-box of old postcards, none of them written. An Apache, Niagara Falls, the Opera House at San Francisco, Lake Pontchartrain, Boston Common, Times Square. At one point you had in mind to collect a postcard from every American town you played in, but after an eighth tour, or maybe the tenth, your resolve somehow evaporated. Yes. In New Orleans that time. Christ, what year would that have been? It came to you in the French Quarter, as you walked following rehearsal, through the windless heat of the sweltering noon and your own rattled thoughts and the aromas of strange food and the clouds of fly-filled pollen. What is the point? What does any of it matter? Just as well, you think now. You silly old mummer. Bundles of them in laddered stockings or tied up in lengths of twine. And who will ever want them? Nobody.

A stretch into the sideboard's deepest recess and you find the hidden thing you seek. A child's Sunday School bible, the ribbon frayed and tangled, the threads of its binding unravelled. Folded into Ecclesiastes is the only letter you saved. The first time he had ever written your name. Wrong to have secretly kept it when his family had wanted everything, but on the morning when they came to take away all the proof of your existence you had been unable to surrender the last you had of him. Here it is now, the only thing you have ever stolen. You open out the withered notepaper, its creases greyed by age, its inkblots like a mapped archipelago. It has not seen daylight in seventeen years. There were nights you hoped the mice would devour it.

Glendalough House
Glenageary
Kingstown
County Dublin
Thursday midnight

Dear Miss O'Neill: I hope that you will excuse the animated tone of my words to you earlier this evening at rehearsal. It was bloody of me and I am sorry. I allowed myself to become upset.

Permit me to add that I have had, since the moment I first observed them, the most earnest regard for your abilities. Moreover, I should like to state that I believe my respect to be shared by Mr Yeats and Lady Gregory. The thing not uttered may yet be felt. I should not like you to think of me as an enemy.

You must permit the words to lead you to the heart words come from. You requested of me advice. That is it.

In the hope that we have cleared the air and with apologies, again, I remain, very sincerely,

John Synge

His decorous handwriting, its elaborated loops, like the cursive of a Victorian governess so repeatedly jilted that she had time to perfect womanly accomplishments. Even to write a letter was a performance for him, poor owl — as though he felt, during its composition, that someone was observing from behind his shoulder, that from the fireplace in his study or the wardrobe in his bedroom some demon of disapproval might roar. The eyes of ancestral portraits gazing down on him as he wrote. That is not ink. It is our blood.

—*What a prig I was, Changeling. For Jaysus' sake, burn it.*

And you know, reading it now, that this is the last time. There is guilt. Yes. You had resolved always to keep it, to bequeath it to your daughter, whom you have not seen in a while but who is named for the heroine in the play that made him famous and is as fierily magnetic to men as her mother once was. But today, in the October of 1952, your pledge to yourself will end. One must eat, after all. It is not a matter of choice. You place the sentenced letter in the pocket of your only coat, a hooded cloak nobody wanted at the end of a pantomime's run; it had been worn by an ugly sister. Mr Duglacz will pay a fair price. You will not weep – no. It is what he would have wanted. And Pegeen will understand. I cannot bear the hunger any more.

Last night I dreamt I went to Manderley again. Vicious old hatchet of a housekeeper was in it. What's this was her name? Mrs Danvers. Yes. And the poor, brave bride and the sea and the shadows and the ghosts in the windblown curtains.

It seems important, suddenly, to clean and order the room. These illusions still arise occasionally. *Our home is our mind –* oh for Jesus' sake, stop it. But perhaps at least the scrags of tinfoil could be discarded. You screw them into a globe, stuff it tightly into the gas mask, whose eyes are grown so dusty that the wearer would be blind. A spider scuttles crablike from a gash in the windpipe, evicted from its rubberised world. A cracked snow-globe of the Matterhorn – what sophisticate gave me *that*? – and a dismasted ship-in-a-bottle *'From Ellis Island: Gateway to New York'*. You pour the last of the gin into the dregs of the tea.

Adultery comes the whisper of the chimney.

'Up your sanctified Kingstown hole,' you say quietly, raising the chipped delft cup to what you imagine to be his presence, or at least, the opposite of his absence.

—*I see there is no hope for you at all, Miss O'Neill. One is supposed to raise one's little finger while sipping.*

The leaden bell of St Mary Magdalene. So loud it hurts your

2

BRICKFIELDS TERRACE

9.05 a.m.

She hauls closed the heavy door behind her and descends the steps to the pavement, moving cautiously for the puddles are iced over. It is blowy, bitter; the air smells of smuts. The freeze moistens her eyes, makes her shiver. But the exhilaration of new morning in the glistered, busy city seems to shine from the whitened windowpanes. In the telephone box a man is shouting about someone being late. She places on her spectacles, lenses misting in the cold. A robin on the lamp of a chained-up bicycle regards her as she takes them off again to clean them.

'Hail fellow well met,' she says to it, smiling. 'You are dapperness itself today.'

Out of memory flows an old ballad, as a wavelet on a strand. It fizzes amid the stones of her mind. She drifts into it as she shuffles forth, for a song can be a companion, the helpmeet of a solitary journey. You can confide in it, hold its hand, wish it well, learn its secrets. A friend shortens the voyage, as her mother used to say. Would be a lonesome old sail without a song.

> *Go fetch to me a pint o' wine,*
> *And fill it in a silver tassie;*
> *That I may drink, before I go,*
> *A service to my bonnie lassie.*
> *The boat rocks at the pier o' Leith,*
> *Fu' loud the wind blaws frae the Ferry,*

Snakes alive, look at the street, thick with leaves and strewn rubbish. The dustbins all toppled, rotting contents disgorged. Lord, have people no shame? Do they not see their own filth? This socialism codswallop has taken root among the young. Someone else will sweep your leavings from cradle to coffin. And the things they discard, when there are Indians famishing. That heel of bread for instance, in its soggy paper wrap. Look at it. Idly tossed there. Profligacy at every turn. She wonders if anyone would see.

But a policeman is looking at her from the bombed-out school-house down the way. She continues towards Porchester Road. His boots scrunch boldly on the shards of mossy glass in the playground. He turns and peers up at the façade. Cornerboys assemble in the wrecked outhouse after dark, among the shattered, ghostly blackboards, the charred skeletons of desks. She has heard them fighting and howling, seen them weltering senselessly through the rubble. One night, she watched three of them capering like fops down the Terrace while their fellows clapped and shrieked and smashed bottles in some sort of contest. A shouting match had ensued between the roisterers and someone far above her in the house, a Connaughtman to judge from his accent. The vile taunts and competing threats had had for her a strange compulsiveness. She had imagined herself an eavesdropper at a door. Five constables had arrived and beaten the youths almost unconscious before dragging them into a Black Maria.

'Morning, ma'am.'

'Constable.'

'Everything quite all right?'

'Yes, thank you. That's a chilly one we're having.'

'Least the blow died down, eh? Believe the park took a pounding. I'm told one of the royal oaks was uprooted. Been there four hundred years.'

His eyes are glimmering with the particular excitement of men who have survived extreme weather. And she wonders, as she looks at him, if it would be cruel to point out that the storm of last night doesn't matter.

'Local are you, ma'am?'

'I reside here, yes.' *Give him your genteel accent, Molly. It could do with a rehearsal.*

'May I ask your name, ma'am?'

'Mrs de Winter. Rebecca.'

He advances her a look of collaborative candour, gesturing with his truncheon in the direction of something that must be clear to him. 'We've had reports,' he confides, 'of nocturnal goings-on. Neighbours being disturbed. If you get my drift.'

'I cannot say that I myself have noticed any ruffianism. Are you quite certain, Constable? This is a most respectable street.'

The proposition unnerves him. It is often thus with policemen. When dealing with them, she has learned, one has only two options: adamantine firmness or tear-smitten frailty. There is no room for anything in between.

'You are aware that number 41 was once the town house of Lady Bloxham?'

'I — wasn't aware of that, no, ma'am.'

'Heirs to the monarchy have dined on this street. Great love affairs have been conducted. Continents redrawn. The steam engine was invented at number 76. We often feel we are living in a sort of museum. Rather stirs the imagination, does it not?'

The constable's imagination, if stirred, throbs so deeply within him that no public manifestation ensues.

'Your carpetbag looks heavy, ma'am. May I fetch it for you a little way? My beat takes me in the direction of Bayswater Tube.'

—*Tell him Bayswater is Sodom. Go on. I dare you.*

'Oh. No thank you, Constable, you are chivalry personified, but I can manage quite naicely. I do not have all that far to go.'

—*The Whore of Babylon, 23B Bayswater Road. Next door to the Antichrist. I dare you.*

The cast of his eyes makes him appear apprehensive but his buff-coloured moustache is neat. You'd nearly want to lift him up by it. Dangle him in the air. Is he married? It seems likely. To a big-breasted woman. Amplitude would be important to him, somehow. She has noticed him lately, often early in the mornings, sidling along the Terrace in an underhand way, sometimes examining the parked motor cars or scrawling frenziedly in his notebook, *tucking* at himself now and again, as a man in second-hand underwear, always making time to clamber into the bombed-out schoolhouse whose fireplaces and chimney breast and staircases and blackened joists are obscenely bared to the elements. A signboard announces that the building and its immediate neighbour are CONDEMNED and must be avoided on pain of a fine. She has wondered what it is he is looking for. It occurs to her now to ask him, but to do so would betray that she had been observing his investigations and perhaps he would resent her curiosity. You don't want to make them resent you. You want to make them go away. Few situations are improved by the presence of a policeman, and many are made much worse.

'You've had no difficulties with – you know – the lodging house, ma'am?'

'I'm sorry?'

He comes closer, sucking his upper lip in a portentous manner. 'Lot of Irish, so I'm told. We've had numerous complaints. Apparently there's some female there too, old tramp sort of thing. Down on her luck I shouldn't wonder. Been seen begging now and again, bothering passers-by for pennies. Makes a nuisance of herself when she's drunk.'

Wind blows a newspaper slowly across the Terrace. A seagull alights on a hydrant and stares into her eyes for a long, unnerving moment. The shame feels like the beating of a huge wave against a hull. She fears she may vomit from disgrace.

'Gracious me,' she says, shaken, 'I have seen no person fitting that description. Perhaps you have been misinformed.'

'Never seen her myself. Told she stands out, poor old mare.

Spins a yarn she used to be an actress, needs a bob for the gas. You look out for her, ma'am, and don't be taken in by her nonsense. I'll let you trundle along. Don't listen if you see her. Better box on, myself. Good morning.'

'And the same to you, Constable, with my gratitude.'

The empty bottles clank in her carpetbag as she walks. Ice on the pavement, on the gratings and architraves, the street like a wedding cake in a dream. In one of the houses a pipe must have burst, for water is trickling down the steps and into the servants' area at the front and three hapless men with mops are looking at it. But touches of weak sun redeem the council-grown shrubberies and the trees in the tiny triangle of park. It is a day with a plan and any such day is a good one. And if the morning is cold it is also bracing, in its way. It is only the breeze that is raising tears.

> *The trumpets sound, the banners fly,*
> *The glittering spears are rankèd ready,*
> *The shouts o' war are heard afar,*
> *The battle closes deep and bloody;*
> *It's not the roar o' sea or shore*
> *Wad make me lainger wish to tarry.*
> *Nor shouts o' war that's heard afar –*
> *It's leaving thee, my bonnie Mary . . .*

If the young woman from America visited – if you permitted her to come – with her pryings and her lipstick and the jangle of bangles on her wrists and her notebook and her overly attentive eyes? Where would you meet her? What could be said of those years? Is there some way of ordering them as one would tidy a messy room, or would the clutter that has amassed merely be shifted about in conversation so as to create an illusion of neatness?

The day you first permitted an intimacy. Few had touched you there before. Heaven help us, you had hardly touched your*self*. There had once been a boy, and there was also a married man, but you had no feeling other than affection for either of them, in truth. To be touched by one you wanted was shocking. The bliss of it frightened you, his concern that you should be pleasured, the ardency of the obscenities he was gasping as you quaked, how he shook as he hardened in your hand. You had been walking Killiney Hill, near the memorial obelisk for the Famine. Grey light on the sea and the distant arms of Kingstown's piers. And afterwards, as you waited at Killiney station, there was a raincloud of silence between you. You were wet, still raw. His stubble had rasped your face. You could yet feel his fingertips and tongue. Frail smoke from burning weeds drifted unhurriedly over Dalkey Island. The music of a gypsy's hurdy-gurdy drifted up from the shore and you wondered why he was playing because there was hardly anyone to listen. The air smelt of seaweed and rotting vegetation. In the swells around the Muglins a green trawler was breasting. Its nets were black. You were eighteen.

'Is something the matter, Molly?'

You said nothing. Remember?

He approached. You stared at the damp strand.

'You think very little of me now, I am sure.'

He smiled confusedly. 'I – How do you mean?'

'You can have little regard for any girl who would allow herself to behave in such a way.'

'My dearest own sparrow . . .'

'Leave me.'

'What?'

'If you ever cared for me, leave me. You can take the later train. Or walk. But let me go. I do not want your company.'

'But – I cannot leave you standing here alone in a public place. What is – ? Are you upset? What has happened to make you cry?'

Horses cantering on the beach. You watched them a while. Stable-lads and romping dogs in the shallows off White Rock. Ecstasies of dirty yellow sea-spray.

The words of his letter of apology. You learned them by heart.

You silly, smitten schoolgirl, so besotted by womanhood that learning them seemed an act of faith. Would there be any point in confessing such an embarrassment to the young woman from America? Should you admit to her that you slept with that letter in your pillowslip for a year? That you sewed a pocket into your shift so as to carry it close to your breast? That the events for which it apologised, recollected even after a year, could still mist you to smoulders of arousal. A benefit, or maybe a hazard, of an actor's training, that texts can be memorised by repetition. Once committed to the loam of memory where important words are sown, they are incapable of ever being forgotten, for the part might be offered you again. Would she think it pathetic? His humble soliloquy. Oh my soft, sweet tramp. How I ached for you.

Dearest, most precious, my own most treasured friend.

She crosses by Queensway, where the buses cluster. A throng of Jamaican conductors sipping mugs on the pavement while the passengers comfortably grumble in the shelter. The morning has taken hold; the wind does not sheer quite so sharply as she turns down Pretoria Street, past the butcher's, the post office. That poor girl is on the corner, even though it is still so early, her dress too short, her face a mask of rouge. Does she have a room somewhere? Heaven help her, little mite. What is it in a man that could find solace in such a resort? Or does he merely pretend to himself that he enjoys it?

. . . You were upset and preoccupied when we parted today, and the fault is to my own account. I watched you from the Military Road as you paced and came and went and I wanted a dozen times to hasten to you again, to implore you from my secret heart to suffer me a moment or permit me to accompany you home to the city. But then came the train from Greystones and I watched you hurry onto it, and in a moment of smoke and thunder you were gone. It started to rain again. I stared at the sea. Its grey-brown was your eyes and there was smoke in the air, as though some great and

terrible violence had been done to something beautiful, and
everything in the world had been changed . . .

Every word, still. You are a professional rememberer. Dear Jesus,
how they touched you: those careful, vigilant sentences
masquerading as a flight of the heart. Oh yes. They were cautious;
you only came to see it years later. For which man can compose
a letter from the flames of his soul in neat, unedited paragraphs
and nothing crossed out? True desire, perhaps, but desire
redrafted. A thing to which you had to accustom yourself.

Away. Put it away. It is not worth recalling. He is not with
you now, as you turn down Marine Street. Perhaps he is back in
the room. Well, it is important to show gratitude. Thankfulness,
always. It is not easy for an actress once she has passed a certain
age to secure a role commensurate with her training. The parts are
too few. It is that simple and inescapable. Not in Shakespeare,
not in Ibsen, not in Shaw, nor in Chekhov. She wonders, re-
crossing Queensway, if any of the blockheads had mothers. Did
they never once glance up from their inks and their parchments,
their grubby little fingerprints besmirching the margins, seagulls of their own inadequacy flitting madly in the rafters, and
notice there was an elderly woman moving about in the room,
probably preparing their lunch? An old male actor will always
find something: a laird, a kindly king, the decrepit twit of the
village, a blacksmith with an announcement, a butler in Wilde,
the priest brought by night to marry ill-starred lovers whose
families would keep them apart. But for a woman, once she has
offended by outliving the age of childbirth, the roles disappear
as honeybees in winter. A jealous auld hag. An irrepressible
washerwoman. Some bitch to be bested in a pantomime.

Past the tobacconist's, the haberdashery, the ironmonger,
the fruiterer's, the door to the staircase leading up to the abor-
tionist's, past the Christian Science reading room, the Maison
Lyons Café, and the launderette with the sign in its window:

> CLEAN ROOM TO RENT
> SUIT COUPLE (MARRIEDS ONLY)
> NO BLACKS
> NO IRISH
> NO DOGS

And she comes to the World Turned Upside Down, an 'early house' for the Portobello stallholders. Truly, what a beautiful name for a pub, like the title of a morality play or a ballad. Poetry seeds itself everywhere. One has only to notice it. London's pub names often recall for her the reel tunes of her girlhood. The Mason's Apron. The Rights of Man. The Skylark. The Jolly Ploughboy. Carters are hefting kegs through a grille-hatch in the pavement and a boy stares up from the cellar as he receives them.

The fug of maleness and cigarette smoke, wet overcoats drying, belched beer, gin spilled over sawdust. Over there, behind the bar, leans the long-time proprietor. There is rather a lot of him but you couldn't call him fat. He is engrossed in a horse-racing newspaper, marking chances with a pencil whose end he intermittently gnaws. His cigarette is burning itself out in an over-full ashtray so spiked with discarded butts that it calls to mind a porcupine. In the browned mirror over the optics and the shelves of pale ales she observes that he has a bald patch, which she has never noticed before, and she finds herself wondering if it upsets him. He is surely not yet fifty. But perhaps he doesn't mind. It is like a monk's tonsure. You'd want to give it a little kiss. She has seen him at Speaker's Corner in Hyde Park, affably heckling the Trotskyites. It is rumoured in the neighbourhood that he has a fancy-woman in the Edgware Road. He has been witnessed buying carnations for no reason.

'Good morning, Mr Ballantine.'

'Lumme, Miss O'Neill. Didn't half give me a start.' He knuckles his left eye, which seems to be irritated by something. 'How's my best sweetheart today? Keeping well?'

'In the pink, Mr Ballantine. And yourself and your lovely wife?'

'Awake half the night with the wind in the willows, as it goes. You'd want to see my loft; half the blessed slates come down. Holes in the roof you wouldn't fit in your hat. But say not the struggle naught availeth. What can I do you for, my precious?'

'I'll tell you what it is, Mr Ballantine. A little mission of mercy. Some of us had a little party at the theatre the other evening. It was a last-night affair. Rather flamboyant in its way. All the critics were there, the Department of Broken Dreams as I call them, and some glamorous young adulteresses from the newspapers. Anyhow, I took the liberty of gathering up some of the empties afterwards. Seems rather a shame to waste the deposits when they could be put to good use. Would you mind awfully, Mr Ballantine? I should be most obliged to your kindness. Thing is, we always send the monies to a little charitable fund for India. Waste not, want not, and so on.'

'Many you got, then?'

She opens her jaded carpetbag and places them carefully on the counter. The count comes eventually to seven.

'I have rinsed them,' she assures him. 'They are something of an assortment of oddities. Rather like the critics in that way.'

'Quite the knees-up,' he says coolly, assessing the parade.

'Oh well. It *was* a last night.'

'You theatricals do seem to be fond of a shindig,' he says. 'Seems to be a hooley *every* night, as it goes.'

'Yes, it's scandalous, isn't it? We in the profession and our inveterate pleasure-seeking. But I know our naughty secret is safe with your good self, Mr Ballantine.'

'Well now, that's as maybe, you'll need to be good to me. Let's see; it's thruppence the piece is a bob and a tanner and sixpence on the large is two bob.'

'Is it so much? I had not counted. Well, that is excellent news. Father Fagin at the Fund will be delighted.'

'Don't mind the wages of sin, eh? They're all the same, clergy. Push comes to shove, they'll take a cheque.'

'Mr Ballantine, please. Father Fagin is a most reputable person.'

He fumbles in his cash drawer, which she has never seen closed. 'Oh, I ain't saying he ain't, love. Just pulling your leg. You be sure and have him say a rosary for us poor lugs as has to work. Coin of the realm. Cross your palm, my duck. That's true as Ripon rowels.'

One of the draymen trudges in now, bearing a docket to be signed, and Mr Ballantine banters with him suggestively for a moment or two about how tired he looks this morning, and the young man's recent marriage, and the tardiness of fellow-me-lads new to matrimony. *Been bringing you the bacon? I bet she has and all.* The carter is a puckish Scotsman, sallow, with bushy eyebrows, and he chuckles in such a sweet-natured and boyishly mortified way that Miss O'Neill experiences a throb of visceral protectiveness, which she assures herself is motherly solicitude of a most respectable kind, although actually it is mild jealousy towards his wife. Some entity calling itself 'The Spurs', a football team, apparently, is subjected to salvoes of baaing derision by Mr Ballantine, the better to be jovially defended by the chortling hauler, whose rolled r's the older man starts to mimic. And it is heart-warming, once again, to see how easily men talk to one another, about things that could not matter less.

Such fluencies they have. What wouldn't one give for them? These ways of asserting fellowship, a shared concurrence in the world, its verities acknowledged, its hard rains shrugged away, and to see two men conversing like Mr Ballantine and the carter is to be reassured that nothing will ever change. The young Hotspur lopes towards the door, still aspersing and hooting, and on a sudden she remembers an amusing phenomenon of New York theatrical life, whereby audience members wishing for taxis leave their seats at the very moment the play ends, applauding their way down the aisle, occasionally glancing back at the stage, but beetling like the furies for the lobby and the street: 'the walking ovation,' a colleague once termed it. If Manhattan catharsis occurs – and she was not always certain it did, for

Americans, unlike the Irish, do not like to be made gloomy by a night out – the tears are shed in motor cars crossing bridges for New Jersey, the true home of pity and terror.

'He wants learning, that boy. He don't half rabbit. He's come in here last Monday and no word of a lie if it ain't taken me an hour to get shut of him. That's your jock for you, of course. Talk the paint off the walls. May I offer you a libation, Miss O'Neill? As a guest of the house?'

'Oh. Well, I usually don't partake, as you know, Mr Ballantine. Not during the daylight hours anyhow.'

'Little nip to warm the cockles. You'll be glad of it afterward. That's a day I wouldn't send a beggar's bitch out and there's snow expected later.'

'Well, then, thank you, Mr Ballantine, so as not to give offence.'

'Take the weight off over there and I'll bring you a drop of Madeira and a pickle. The missus has a nice loaf inside if you'd have a cut off that?'

'Oh, but it is too much trouble. You have clientele to attend to.'

'No trouble for my secret sweetheart. Beauty's always welcome here, love. Take a pew over yonder; those are the ladies' seats as you know. Not that there's many of *that* species at large in London any more. Still, a little of what we fancy does us good, eh?'

She seats herself uncomfortably on the banquette in the window alcove, which commands a pleasant enough view of Queensway. Well, pleasant is not the word. Repellent is the word. But we see what we wish to see, usually. London, for Miss O'Neill, has an unkillable nobleness, even its less picturesque quarters. It is a town with a little dirt under its fingernails, perhaps, but you don't have to look at its fingers. Every Dubliner feels free here. She has noticed this, often. But perhaps only an immigrant would be able to perceive the broken grace that arises like a pea-soup fog. The arc of that railway bridge – has it not a stark *itself*ness? The chained gates of the derelict foundry are magnificently wrought: austere, crow-black, the massiveness of a portcullis, copper capitals in a trellis arching the arrow-tipped rails preach FORTITUDE WORKS – how beautiful. And if those workingmen's cottages are small, they are neat as a row of soldiers, the grey of the sky and the street and the faces making the wet redness of the brickwork lovelier. A pyramid of swept garbage disassembles itself as she looks at it, but the bar is too noisy for the wind to be audible. Hunting prints and regimental emblems alleviate the faded scarlet wallpaper; not the most womanly of decorations, poor dear Mr Ballantine, but an assortment of ladies' magazines several decades out of date has been arrayed on the table among the beer mats. The women in them look like boxers disguised as society flappers in a picture the Marx Brothers never made.

She leafs through the script, as though anything in it might be surprising. In her youth she played the lead. Today she will play the widow. Hunger flares fiercely, almost as an anger. She swallows it and reads on, but concentration dies, and anyway she knows the role already, its every pause and comma. She could play it in her sleep. She sometimes has. So kindly, Mr Ballantine. A gentle, mellow Englishman. As she thinks of him, the Gaelic word *caomh* unfurls in her consciousness: dear, mild, noble, restful. *Caomhnóir*: a protector, a guardian. Son died at Dunkirk. Never been the same. Sad to think of them all, the brave young boys, and the friends they never made and the girls they didn't kiss. She glances up and notices him talking quietly to his wife in the doorway that leads to the kitchen. The two of them look at her. Do they know?

Men barrel in and out, with their swearing and gruffness, and their ludicrous skittles and dominoes. ('Oi, Vernie! Ernie! Bernie McInerney! *Your* shout, you facking tart. Oy Oy!') Why can they never sit easy, must they always *emit noises*, and must the noises be deafening vowels? Heavens, look at that specimen of jailbird Lothario. Belly the size of the old queen's bustle and a face like a stevedore's armpit. To think he has a vote. It is appalling. If one handed him a copy of the *Complete Works of Strindberg*, he would probably wipe his bottom with it, or eat it. And his disciples all yelping and spitting and backslapping, as though it is midnight in some bierkeller in the Weimar Republic, not ten in the morning in Bayswater. The sawdust is filthy, and as a boy brings a little tray for her, she points out to him discreetly that the steps need to be mopped – over there, leading down to the lavatories. And there are *fingerprints* on the *bread*. What a common establishment, really. Mr Ballantine does his best but his wife hails from Peckham. Still, wiser to say nothing when politeness is offered. A certain class can take offence where none is intended.

> *All drawn up, Britannia's sons*
> *Faced the Russian tyrant's guns,*
> *And bravely dared his shells and bombs*
> *On the bonny heights of Alma.*

Oh, a fresh day now. Does a body good to venture out. Blow away the cobwebs, begin again. Too long in that room, girl. Pulled-in. An old turtle. Little wonder there would be sadnesses and night-thoughts and regrets and butterflies of recollection flitting about half the day and the scuttle of the past out of cupboards. Sure if you went to sleep sane in a room such as that, you would wake up mad as a monk. Must eat decorously, not too fast, because people might be watching, and while it is hard to remember propriety while hungry in the extreme, one can make oneself ill if one wolfs like a docker, and it is unladylike to weep even for gratitude. Slow, take your time, it is a beautiful day, a morning that never before dawned on the planet, and the hunger will pass, and there is kindness and fellowship, and frost on the leaves and no cyanide pellets bursting and a script to be performed and old songs to be remembered and a Scotsman to be teased for getting married. The world is not an abattoir. No. It is not. It can turn upside down if you allow it.

She sees herself entering the panelled recording studio in the basement at the BBC, the younger actors half turning and collegially smiling, a pretty secretary distributing annotations. The microphone like a little maypole around which they will gather in a circle, four minutes before transmission commences. Tongue-twisters quickly whispered to loosen the mouth. Red lorry yellow lorry red lorry yellow lorry. The bootblack bought the black boot back. Oh the exhilaration, the thrilling anxiety of those evaporating seconds. Mr Hartnett will be in his booth; the arc light will be dimmed, someone will whisper a compliment on her appearance. *What a lovely blouse, Molly. Is it a Worth? Ah, I thought so. It is so wonderful to see you again.* Mr Hartnett will shush the studio and remind the newcomers, the ingénues, of the importance of regarding every microphone as live.

They will cluster towards it. Two minutes. The test-tone will be sounded. India is listening now. Australia. New Zealand. Places where it is night-time or sweltering noon. Storm-beaten islands. Ships. And some will never have heard a play in the whole of their lives. Houseboys in Rhodesia, sweating farmhands in the outback, shopkeepers in frazzled Shanghai. And if millions will turn the dial, uninterested, seeking elsewhere, through the crackling susurration and interplanetary shrillings, perhaps somewhere a child will not. Awesome, the power. You could not afford to think of it. She will touch a colleague's wrist as the countdown to the five pips commences. 'Be calm,' will say her smile. 'Trust your lines. That is all.' *This is the BBC World Service broadcasting from London. Greenwich Mean Time is eighteen hundred hours. Welcome to the Monday Play.* And someone will start to speak. And another. And another. And the words will come out of the air.

Beamed by Hilversum, Lille, Luxembourg, Allouis, Athlone, Droitwich, Warsaw, Moscow. And perhaps there is an otherworld only radio waves can attain, where the dead are listening quietly together. Her son, her two husbands, the man in the photograph on the mantelshelf, her brothers, her mother, Yeats, her sister. The brave, broken boys who died in the war. The murdered of Auschwitz-Birkenau. Memory is their oxygen, megahertz their rain. Their country has no currency or flag. The aurora borealis is their national anthem, for they are able to hear colours, touch sounds. Their flicker-lit eyes see no blitzes, no firestorms.

Their language needs no word for torture. A foolish idea, maybe; but perhaps it is true. We believe in *Wuthering Heights* despite knowing it is fictional. Heathcliff and Lazarus and Ophelia and the Snow Queen feature equally in whatever scripture she holds precious. And if some play only a bit-part, they also serve. To all things, a season. Nobody is nothing. And maybe some of those fuckers back in Dublin will be listening too. That's right, failed fuckers, I am on the BBC. I'm not gone yet. You envious creeping huers. My name is Molly Allgood. Kiss my Mary Street arse. You rosary-spouting, two-faced, bishop-licking, bullet-mouthed, piss-in-the-bed excuses for hypocrites.

'Mr Ballantine, do you know, I am a silly old scatterbrain. I have not yet baked my Christmas cake and I had intended doing an extra one this year, for a sale of work the British Legion are getting up.'

'Very patriotic I'm sure. Is that allowed?'

'Come again?'

'Well, a fierce Irish rebel such as yourself, my treacle?' He is ribbing her now, his broken-veined face wrinkling into a sad man's smile.

'An artist has no country, Mr Ballantine,' she counters. 'One blooms where one is planted, or attempts to.'

'Now that's a lovely way of putting things. That is handsome, that is. Stone me if there ain't times I reckon I should be writing down your sayings, Miss O'Neill. You're as good as a philosopher and that's the God's truth. The gift of the gab, eh? Your profession, of course. Me, I've always liked an Irishman. Never no bother. Find him easy old companionship if that's the right phrase. Once he learns to hold his beer, mind. And it ain't all of them as can. Mean to say, there's a rotten apple or two wherever you look in the world. And in my own line of work, can't say I ain't never picked one. Probably the very same in your own profession, is it? But give your Pat half a chance and he won't never change you short. He's a different way of seeing things — but he's entitled, he's entitled. Just steer him wide of hard liquor and get him married if you can. He don't make a happy bachelor. Wants a nice little Eileen. That's what Ted Ballantine's always found. And another lovely thing about your Irishman generally . . .'

Dearest hand of Jesus, but he does go on. He'll be running up the tricolour in a minute. Oh then don't be so mean, Molly. He is so good-natured, keep smiling. Conversation, for Mr Ballantine, is a sort of perpetual-motion roundabout, an occupational hazard for all persons who earn a living where alcohol is dispensed, and the next time it revolves in the direction of the Christmas cake it will be important for you to jump on and hold firm.

'I will need a gill of inexpensive brandy in which to soak the fruit, Mr Ballantine. Do you think you might possibly assist me?'

'Thing is.' He sucks his moustache and releases a small sigh, as though what he is about to say is hard for him. 'There's a little owed on the slate, pet. I don't mean to mention it. Only it's four pound ten. Been owing a little while. There's questions been asked in Parliament, if you take my meaning. The missus has been giving me earfuls.'

'I am expecting a considerable cheque from the BBC presently. They are most dreadfully tardy. One often thinks they're all Communists. Or millionaires. The very moment I receive it, we shall settle up without delay. I give you my private word of honour, Mr Ballantine.'

'I shouldn't, my pigeon. Really and truly.'

'A week. At the absolute latest.'

'Not a word to the Contessa then? She'll have my guts for garters.'

'I quite understand. Careless talk costs lives.'

'Blummin castrations, more like.'

He returns behind the bar, wraps the bottle in a fold of newspaper and hurriedly pushes it into her pocket.

'Just a tick,' he adds quietly, disappearing into the kitchen. She stands amid the laughter and the howls about dart scores and by the time he comes back, bearing a brown paper bag, one of her headaches is starting to bloom. Easing the bag into her hands, he accompanies her towards the door, whistling a tune she recognises vaguely but whose name will not come.

'Good day to you, Mr Ballantine.'

'God bless, love. Mind how you go.'

She wants to say more. But she is not certain what it is. His wife is peering at her strangely; tight-lipped; hard. Mrs Danvers in curlers and housecoat. Their son, Miss O'Neill supposes. One must be understanding; forgiving. It is not easy for a mother who has lost a child to war. Mr Ballantine clasps her elbow lightly and opens the door to the traffic.

'Wrap up against the cold, won't you? There's my darling girl.'

In the bag is a pair of socks and a packet of cigarettes. But it is the bottle of milk that makes her weep. At last.

3

KINGSTOWN, A PROSPEROUS SUBURB
OF DUBLIN
1908

There is a part of the garden, by the cluster of sycamores, near the bend in the drive where the gravel is wearing thin. If he stands there, quietly, on a still Sunday morning, when none of the servants is around to annoy him, and when Mother is up in her room at her scriptures, he can hear the distant approach of the train from Dublin: the windborne shush-and-chug that means she might be coming to him again. He is thirty-six now, already very ill. Painful years have passed since he stopped believing he could be loved. The power of what is happening terrifies him.

He leaves his mother's garden, makes hurriedly for Glenageary station: up the willow-lined avenue, towards St Paul's, Church of Ireland. Past the entrance to the quarry lanes known locally as 'The Metals', through which the granites were hefted long ago for the stanchions of Kingstown Pier. There are days when he feels hammered; his breathing sometimes knifes him. But punctuality is important, a sign of respect.

The walk from his mother's house takes about seven minutes. Often, he arrives as the locomotive is chuntering to its screechy standstill and belching grimy spumes of cinders and mizzle. He skulks in the station portico, not daring to hope, lowering his eyes quickly if a neighbour happens past. It would not do to be seen: not yet, not here. There is the age difference between them, but that is not all. There are the differences that cannot be noticed in an instant.

And then – where can she be? – she materialises through the

smoke. There she is, beckoning circumspectly from a second-class window. It is like a small moment out of Tolstoy, perhaps, one of those seemingly simple but reverberating images he values in the novels of Russia. He pictures her stepping down through the vapour, the soot, then hurrying along the platform to him, parasol in hand. She comes to him through the filth, her face hopeful and kind, the steam moistening a strand of hair to her forehead. But this cannot happen. People might see. There would be talk around Glenageary.

Instead he boards the train, takes the bench opposite her in the carriage. They are like a couple of collaborators plotting an act of treason. Outside, the conductor is slamming the doors. A whistle is blown. A green flag is flourished. As the engine gives a shriek and they judder away from Glenageary, he begins to feel something like relief.

From the pocket of her raincoat is protruding a playscript. She uses the journey from the city to learn her lines. Nobody could say she is beautiful, exactly, but she is an actress: she is able to decide whether to be beautiful or plain. Like a 'changeling', he tells her; his preferred endearment: like many sweet nothings, an ambiguity.

The train clatters into the tunnel at Killiney. He is alone with her in darkness. He feels her hand steal into his. This thrills him, charges him. *No one can see.* The moment passes quickly, there is a dazzle of light, and the panorama of the bay is magnificent: Italian. Along the clifftop at Shanganagh. A cormorant hangs in the air. It will not be too long before they come coasting into Bray, where nobody knows him. Bray is safe.

Passers-by might think them a father and daughter, as they exit Bray station and she links him at the elbow, and they go walking down the promenade in the direction of the Head, through a swirl of dirty gulls and old newspapers. He looks older than his years; she looks younger than hers. He has achieved some recognition in the field of play-writing – translations of two of his works have been performed in Prague and Berlin, he is co-director of the Irish National Theatre Society — but few in this frumpy Little Brighton would know he was a writer, and fewer, if they knew, would care. His companion has appeared in three of his plays: bit parts at first, but she was soon elevated to leads.

Cold, grey wavelets breaking on the stones. The suck in the runnels of strand.

When she came in with her sister, he was standing near the book-case in the downstairs rehearsal room, wearing a burgundy velvet smoking-jacket that looked as though it had once belonged to someone larger. A peasant-man's neckerchief draped loosely about the collar, a tuft of withering heather in the lapel. His eyes ranged everywhere except upon the assembled actors, whose presence seemed to embarrass him, as though a fuss were being made. Lady Gregory had introduced him: John Synge, our friend. A coming giant of the drama, a veritable Shakespeare. It appeared that each commendation was another nail through his heart. He flushed to the maroon of his jacket.

His hair was black and glossy, pomaded a little too heavily, and yet it was untidy too, like a ploughboy's. The strangeness and the beauty of his mode of speech. He made even plummy Yeats seem down to earth. His accent was of the Protestant Dublin suburbs, modulated, deaconish, replete with correcti-tude, but complicated by an Irishry that felt very slightly overemphasised, as one note that wanted damping in a gorgeous chord. The soft Dublin 't' in the way he pronounced *theatre*. The long Etonian vowels in *drama*. He addressed the gathering for ten minutes, checking the allotted time on his fob watch, rarely meeting anyone's stare. Similes, self-contradictions, allu-sions to Gaelic fairy tales, quotations from French novels and dusty Greek myths: he took it for granted that everyone knew what he meant. The actors were a little afraid of him, and he of them. He never met your eyes unless he wished to.

She walked the longer way home that evening, across Sackville Street, down the quays, past the junkshop above which she had been born, past the bookstalls and the boarding houses, for already she had come to a point where the ghetto life of Mary Street could only be endured by postponing it. A squabble was stewing in the house, about money, the rent. A black pot in the kitchen seemed to bubble with rage, its lid clicking furiously on the rim. She had gone immediately to the little bedroom she shared with her sisters and grandmother, looked for a long time over the scutch-yard at the rear of the tenement. Boys had found an abandoned piebald and tethered it near the ash-pits, where it was feeding from a rusted bathtub. The tolling of the quarter-to-eight bell from Mary's Abbey coaxed the slaughterers from the market, their grey overalls reddened, in silent twos and threes to the pub. And the sky reddening, too, and the steeples slowly blackening, and the siren from the gasworks through the rain.

Sara had not come home by suppertime; there was a Francis Street boy she liked and she was bankrupting the poor fellow, a junior clerk in Crosbie & Alleyne, by making him take her to dine at Burton's. The nightly rosary came and went. It grew dark in the bedroom. Shadows lengthened and disappeared. She dreamed she was in the junkshop on a Saturday afternoon, assisting her mother with the customers, endlessly opening drawers in old sideboards, the faded green felt of their linings. A woman who might have been Lady Gregory had passed on the quay – but it was hard to be certain through the rain-spattered window. When she awoke, it was dark. Sara was asleep beside her, the little ones curled in the foot of the bed. She could hear the repeated triple-toned bark of a dog. Her mother's only coat had been placed over her.

Next morning as she was walking to rehearsal she saw him near the General Post Office in Sackville Street, as still as a lamp-post and staring up at a rooftop, his battered tweed tam and drover's muddy boots giving him the appearance of a countryman lost. His scarf looked as though it had once been employed to mop up a stable after a flood. Was it a bird he was looking at? A steeplejack working? Lord Nelson on his pillar, perhaps? A nun passed him quizzically, herself glancing up at the sky before continuing her progress towards the river. He raised a hand to shade his gaze. He looked frail; older than yesterday. Perhaps the nervousness of having to address them had rushed blood to his face. Now it was the colour of ashes.

'Mr Synge, sir,' she had said apprehensively. 'Are you all right? Is that yourself?'

The fragility and gentleness of his mien as he turned to her. 'Forgive me, Miss. Do I know you?' His eyes moving fitfully as though he had been listening to strange music in the halls of his mind and it had altered its tempo or stopped.

'Miss O'Neill, sir. Molly O'Neill. I work at the theatre.'

'At a theatre you say? Well, that is a nice pancake.'

'At the Abbey, sir, yes. I am one of the apprentice players. You were in with us yesterday. Are you quite all right?'

'Oh, entirely. I was just daydreaming. I was thinking about Germany. Were you ever in Germany at all?'

'I was never out of Dublin, sir. Have you been there yourself?'

'Interesting sort of place. The music and so on. Would you like to have a plum? I bought some in Moore Street.' Patting his overcoat pockets and searching inside his jacket. 'Oh, Moses. Seem to have mislaid them somehow.'

'Are you going to the theatre, sir?'

'Yes I am. May I walk with you?'

'Of course, sir. I have to hurry along but.'

'There was an enormous storm cloud — it has passed now — which reminded me of Cologne Cathedral. Exact silhouette. Quite remarkable. They say the devil appeared there once. Do you believe in the devil?'

'My mother does be saying it isn't that gentleman but the living we'd be wise to fear, sir.'

'I dare say that's right. What did you say you are called? I'm so sorry, didn't catch it. I was away with the faeries.'

'Molly Allgood is my given name, sir. I go by Maire O'Neill.'

'Ah yes. I have you now. You are Sally's sister, I think?'

'I am, sir.'

'I believe she will be a very great artist, likely far too good for Ireland. Tell me: do you and your family call her Sally or Sara?'

'Sally, sir. Though she's been called worse now and again in the house.'

'I'm sorry?'

'I was – making a joke, sir. About Sally.'

'Ah. Quite. I have you now. Please forgive me.'

'For what, sir?'

'Well, for being such a silly muff and not recognising you and whatnot. I am not at all good with faces. But I remember your voice. It is beautiful. Most musical. I was thinking about it yesterday evening. You have a voice of some potential. Have you ever considered singing lessons?'

'Lessons? I haven't, sir, no.'

'If you'll take my advice, you will do. It would be a string to your bow.'

'Thank you, sir. I will. I like singing.'

'Lovely, that little verse of Yeats you were speaking in the break. Quite brought it to life for me. Hadn't truly got it before. Good on the stars and so on, old Yeats, isn't he?'

'He is, sir.'

'Yes, old Yeats does the stars. I do everything else.' He smiled shyly. 'Little joke of my own.'

It had been difficult to concentrate that morning at rehearsal, for progress was maddeningly slow. The leading man was absent, his understudy was unhappy, kept forgetting his lines; asking for prompts, simplifications. Yeats and Lady Gregory had been tense, exchanging inscrutable looks, like Easter Island statues contemplating adultery or murder. But he would change nothing at all. Not a speech, not a syllable. He had that curious conviction of those privately lacking confidence and an unusual amiability in its deployment. Also, he had money, or had once had it anyway, and the bearing of wealth never fully departs, even as the stock markets plummet. What haunted the rehearsal room was the uneasy certainty that if he didn't receive complete obedience he would leave. And he would do so in a way that would not give affront or cause a scene. He would simply gather his note-books and numerous pencils, probably apologising on his way out the door. He was invested elsewhere. He didn't take his coat off. He could say things without having to say them, appearing puzzled by simple questions. Even his aura of eccentric inepti-tude came to seem a means of getting his way.

'Begging your pardon, Mr Synge. But that is not how the country people do be talking here in Ireland, sir. I mean no offence to you. But it's a little bit music-hall, sir. A touch on the flowery side, if you get me.'

'Really? Do you tell me so, Mr Grennan? We certainly don't want to gild the lily.'

'It's lovely and melodious, sir. God you'd nearly sing it so you would.' Some of the other actors emitted affirmative sounds, for Grennan had a Dubliner's ability to express disapproval by the giving of compliments, a useful facility in his profession and in many others. 'It trips like a ballad. The poetical aspect. I don't doubt that it's fine literature, sir. It's the true Ally-Daly. It's only it'd nearly want to be more – what is the word?'

'Are you – asking me a question, Mr Grennan?'

'More . . . natural. If you get me, sir. Lord, what is the phrase? *Truer to life* I suppose is my meaning, sir. Like the country people themselves. Down to earth. Not too fancy. The audience do get a great kick out of a thing being true to life.'

'Do they?'

'Oh they do, sir. You can tell. And you up on the stage playing. There's a silence does come over them, or a certain class of laughter, and you'd nearly hear them nudging one another and saying *That's you* or *That's the mother*. Do you get what I'm driving at, sir? It's a lovely thing when it happens. There's a nice sort of an innocence in the room like.'

'Might I use your Christian name, Mr Grennan? One finds surnames so formal.'

Yeats glanced about himself suspiciously, as though suspecting a practical joke of some sort. Lady Gregory appeared vaguely in need of the smelling salts. She now seated herself wordlessly, as though a performance were about to commence, and when Lady Gregory sat down, especially when she did so wordlessly, it was almost as worrying as when she stood up.

'God of course, sir,' murmured the understudy, himself a little discomfited. 'Blaze away. Sure we're all on the same ticket here.'

'I was born in Ireland, Willie. I have walked a good deal in Ireland. Have a decent enough smattering of the old Gaelic too. Know a bit of it yourself, I expect?'

'Not really, sir, no . . . Not as such like.'

'Ah. Pity. That may well be the difficulty. Anyhow I must re-assure you and set your mind at ease, there is not a line in the piece that I myself have not heard spoken, in Aran or Wicklow or the proper Irish places where an artificially imported way of talking has not taken root among the peasantry. Perhaps you need to clear out your ears, my good Willie Grennan. Perhaps Dublin has polluted you. Eh? But I will consider most carefully your point of view on the question and I am supernally grateful for your admirable frankness.'

The smiles from the players were watery, uncertain. He had clapped the understudy on the back in an overly familiar way, as a master might buck up a recalcitrant manservant whose request for a holiday is impossible. And then he had slunk back to the bookshelf in the corner, leaning against it lightly, his eyes closed fast; his ring-covered fingers propping his chin like the Thinker's as he waited for the rehearsal to resume. It was itself a perform-ance and she apprehended this. She sensed he was frightened behind the front.

Later that evening, as she made her way homeward through the city, she stopped before the windows of a musical instru-ment shop on Capel Street. Dusk reddened the panes. A slum child was calling for alms. It was ludicrous, utter folly, the differences between them – his age, his class, his accent, his crippling wistfulness, his way of eying the walls when he spoke to her, or about her. It could never happen. She wouldn't want it to happen. Probably he wouldn't either. This wasn't a play.

Their affair is a year old. He has been hurt in love previously, has long been introspective, harrowed by depressions. Social life in Dublin he finds a crucifixion. He loathes the vulgarity, the backslappery and falseness: 'the cheap commonplace merriment' of it all. He tells her she should be 'steadily polite' to her fellow actors but must always wear a mask, must never trust outsiders. By 'outsiders' he means everyone except himself. Above all, their engagement is to remain a secret. There could be whisperings in the theatre. People would have views. Yeats and Lady Gregory do not think it quite correct for a co-director and a mere actress to be so familiar. There is also the problem of Mother, of course. The news will have to be broken very gradually to Mother.

They slog around Bray, back to Loughlinstown, or Shankill, trudging weedy rutted laneways, puddled boreens, like a schoolboy and his first sweetheart on a glum little tryst with no money to go in someplace out of the rain. The things he finds fascinating, she can't understand them. Rocks. Bushes. Moths. Deserted nests. A squirrel – look! – falling out of a tree! ('Holy Moses,' yelps the playwright: his favourite profanity.) This dreamer is a man who gazes into a hedgerow like a debutante contemplating a jeweller's window.

She does not like all this walking, becomes tired very quickly. Unlike her Old Tramp – this is how he styles himself – she has to work ceaselessly hard, no matter how she feels. There are no housemaids, no servants in the place she calls home. Her wages are thirty shillings a week. She rehearses all day, is on the stage most nights. She has not yet fully learned the breathing techniques of an actor, that acting is about the body as much as the instincts, and the director, Mr Fay, is pushing her hard. Her accent is too common, too Dublin, not artistic. *You must not say 'draymin'. The word is 'dreaming', Miss O'Neill. You are playing a druidical princess, not a fishwife.* The work is exhausting. She has to help the seamstresses. The wigs are louse-infested and heavy. So she sees walking as primarily a means of getting to some destination, whereas her storyteller appears to regard it as an end in itself. Occasionally she suspects he feels the same way about courtship. An agreeable hobby, leading to nothing but literature.

The embarrassing son, the pretender to beggary, the tramp in Savile Row boots inherited from his father, whom he does not remember and does not resemble and whose feet were a larger size. But his mother never discarded them, and anyway they were his father's, and if every man must walk in his father's boots, one may as well do so literally, he smiles.

And he walks and he walks in the chafing old boots, and she walks alongside him, through the heat and the rain. They are so often beside one another, hardly ever face-to-face, and their footprints on a strand form graciously pleasing parallels that only occasionally merge.

He feels strongly that she should learn, should improve her mind. It is time for her to stop reading 'dressmaker's trash'. He gives her novels he has selected, volumes of verse. Soon she will be 'the best-educated actress in Europe', he says. The phrase strikes her as odd. It would look queer on a poster. He wants her to take pride in what he insists on terming her progress. She is to keep notebooks of her reading, as he does of his own, listing works for which she cares and the reasons why. He has 'wheelbarrow-loads' of such jotters at home in Glenageary. He has been keeping them since his schooldays. She should acquire this practice. There is a touch of Pygmalion and the Statue in what is happening between them, but there are times when she wonders which of them is which.

'Come down and learn to love and be alive.' In the version by

William Morris, whose work he admires, such is the plea of unhappy Pygmalion to the cold marble effigy he so agonisingly loves. She wonders if her playwright, her lover of stones, has ever given thought to this supplication, how he would respond if he found himself its recipient.

He drifts, this tweedy tramp, dusty gentleman of the roads. Kilmacanogue. Enniskerry. The dolmens of Ballybrack. The backwoods and cart tracks of the Dublin–Wicklow borderlands. He has no map, no compass, no plan except to keep walking. Over the crest of the next hummock there will always be another. Around lakes. Into grottoes. Through forests. Across streams. Jesus, can he walk. He must be the healthiest invalid in Ireland. No holy well or hermitage is allowed to remain unpoked-at. They traipse up and down the Sugarloaf until she can tell all the sheep apart. A pity love is not measured in worn-out soles; if it were, she would be a married woman by now.

The subject of setting a date drifts into the conversation. Always he finds a reason to talk about something else. As a student, a capable violinist, he gave up the ambition of professional musicianship because the petrifaction of stage fright was too much for him to face. He is still frozen in the wings, she sometimes thinks, afraid to step out into the scene that is begging for him.

Probably some of this is Mother's doing. His childhood was one of 'well-meant but extraordinary cruelty'. She gruelled him on the Bible, on the castigations of Hell. He has been slowly roasted on the flames of her widowhood. He could never be a father, he resolved while still a child; parents bequeath us only their susceptibilities. 'I will never create beings to suffer as I am suffering.' She has an image of a terrified newborn, croup-racked, asthmatic, flailing at the banshees that swoop at his cot.

He doesn't belong. Doesn't want to belong. Wanting not to belong is exhausting. 'I am always a kind of outsider,' he claims, yet he never stops fretting about what people will think. Life is unendingly dreary in the bourgeois suburbs: 'Kingstown, the heat, and the frowsy women.' But it is to here he returns at the close of the day, when the rambles are over and the house lights fade up. His changeling is left to rehearse unspoken lines on a train to a room in the city.

When they see one another at rehearsal in the theatre during the week, he does not like them to converse privately. People might be eavesdropping. 'You must not mind,' he writes to her, 'if I seem a little distant. We can have our talk on green hills that are better than all the greenrooms in the world.' Her sister and the priest in Confession advise great caution: when a man is not willing to be seen in public with a girl, there is something deeply the matter, or his word is not true. And never to have a child? How could any woman agree? It's a diversion he's after, an escapade with a wild native colleen, before marrying a filly of his own inbred sort, some Henrietta with her eyes just a tad too close together, webbed toes and a dowry of diamond mines. But she won't be counselled: they don't understand. She is not yet nineteen; she knows this is love. What matter if he's a little odd? Writers often are.

There are weeks when he disappears, journeying alone into Wicklow, where he roams the hills and glens like a hermit. Few know where he lodges, when he plans to return, how his mountain days are filled, if they are permitted to be empty. If she has a rival, it is Wicklow, the motherland of his solitudes; he vanishes when she calls to him, roves her byways, craves her emptiness – yet avoids her in the everyday and unimportant conversations, as a husband deflecting attention from an infidelity. There will always be Wicklow. It must be accepted in silence. Some men bring a lost love, no matter where.

In the ladies' lavatories at the theatre, one rainy Friday morning, as she approaches the sink to bathe her face after a nosebleed, she sees words traced in the condensation that has fogged the splintered mirror. JMS HAS SIFILIS.

'Mister John, you are welcome home, sir,' the elderly housekeeper says quietly. 'Will I help you off with your coat and the haversack?'

'Thank you, Alice. I am bushed. Supper almost ready?'

'It is, sir. I'll tell the girls. You had good walking down beyond?'

'What? Oh yes. All shipshape here? Holy Moses, look at the muck on these boots.'

'Your mother is . . . not in the best, sir. She's been out of sorts while you were gone. Above in the room half the day and barely the pick itself of food. I thought I should tell you, sir. I hope I amn't speaking out of turn.'

'No no. Thank you, Alice. Been particularly bad, has it?'

'Dr Haughton was up to us the Tuesday, and again yesterday morning. She swore me not to tell you, sir, I don't rightly know why. But I felt, in all conscience . . .'

'Quite. You acted correctly. You appear worried, Alice. Not yourself.'

With dread, he now sees that the housekeeper is weeping. The woman turns away briefly, the back of her neck reddening. 'Mister John,' she begins, but then pauses, dabbing her eyes with her apron, and when she speaks again her voice is controlled. 'I don't know, Mister John, if she'll be with us long more. That's the God's living truth, sir. Thank God you're come home. There's a light after going out of her, sir, I seen it happen before, when your father Lord have mercy on him was taken.'

'Alice – oh my dear Alice – I'm so sorry you have been distressed. Please won't you sit down a moment? Would you take a small sherry with me, perhaps?'

'I'd rather not do that, sir; I've the girls in the kitchen to think about.'

'If we stepped into the library a moment, I don't think anarchy would result.'

'All the same, sir, I'd prefer not. But will you go and talk to her, Mister John? We're all frighted half to death. She's been so good to us down the years. If there's anything we can do, sir.

Anything at all. I've the girls offering the rosary for her this night.'

'She's a game old bird, Alice. She'll see us all down. Come on now, there's the good scout, buck up.'

'You don't understand me, sir — begging your pardon, sir — but what it is I'm trying to tell you . . .'

'Dear, kind Alice . . . Oh no . . . Please don't cry.'

'Lawyer Morgan is after being here, sir. He was sent to Dublin for, yesterday. He was in with her an hour and another man along. Bridget was asked for paper, sir, and a bottle of ink. When the tea was brought in beyond, they were talking of your mother's Will, sir. It's my opinion it's come to that, sir . . . I don't know what to do . . .'

'I see. Well, don't be upset. The girls need your example. And we mustn't put the worst complexion on matters we don't understand.'

'Don't be letting on to herself that I told you, sir. Sure you won't?'

'Of course not. Thank you, Alice. Your discretion does you credit. We are so fortunate to have you. You are not to worry about anything. Now, tell Bridget I'll be ready presently. And assist my mother to the dining table if you would.'

He washes in his bedroom, looking out at the trees, the walls of the neighbours' gardens, the conservatories. To be away from people now. In some quaking, black bog. To raise one's face to a rainstorm.

'Good evening, Mother. Have you been well?'

She does not reply. The dining room is cold as a November orchard.

'I am sorry my return was delayed. I was down in Wicklow, walking. The weather was that charming I took a room at the inn in Rathnew. I asked a local type to send a telegram for me but I gather from Alice it didn't arrive.'

'Do you wish to kill me, John? Has this family not suffered enough?'

'I beg your pardon?'

'Have I not been wounded and cut at sufficiently to placate the wicked selfishness you appear to regard as a devoted parent's due?'

'I can see that you have upset yourself, Mother. Now what is the matter?'

'Teasy Ryan was able to tell me that you had been seen at Greystones. Swimming.'

'What of it?'

'With some female. Is this allegation true?'

'Is it an offence against the by-laws to bathe on a hot day? I shall take care not to commit it again if so.'

'With a female? Can you be serious? Is this disingenuousness or stupidity? Have you the scantest regard for propriety? You are not in Paris now!'

'She is a friend. It was sunny. We went bathing at the public strand. She is a colleague at the theatre. Afterwards we had ices. Now you have the entire penny-dreadful.'

'I knew it. Your so-called theatre. Some little typist who sells tickets. I imagine she must be good and proud of herself to have ensnared you quite so readily. One need not speculate as to how.'

'She is not a typist, Mother. You may as well know she is an actress.'

Her frightened, beautiful face seems to lose all its colour, and a quiver briefly distends her mouth. 'So it is true, then. The worst is true. Do you hate me so much? The woman who gave you life?'

'Mother –'

'What have I done to you?' Tears come staining her cheeks. 'Have I not loved you enough? Protected you? Supported you? It is commanded of us that we honour our father and mother and yet this beautiful injunction, on which all decent society is predicated, is to be trampled with its nine companions. To imagine that you would invite an individual of that sort to an *inn*, as you call it. You are aware, I think, that we are known throughout Wicklow? Have the words "shame" and "scandal" been expunged from your vocabulary? That is to say nothing of the girl's reputation, if she has one.'

'She is a person of faultless integrity and she quite obviously did not stay with me at the inn, which is incidentally a perfectly respectable establishment. She came down on the train one morning and returned to Dublin in the evening. We had a day outing; that is all. I stayed there alone. I felt one of my fevers coming on and thought the mountain air would do me good.'

'A Roman Catholic, one assumes?'

'For pity's sake, Mother –'

'Where are your loyalties? Is allegiance so unknown to you?'

'My friend – she is called Miss Allgood – is of a mixed marriage, as it happens. Her late father, if it matters, was a Presbyterian, I am told. And you are being – if I may say so – well, I would rather not use the word.'

'I am reliably informed she was born in a rag-and-bone shop. Is this so?'

'I think you will find, when you meet Miss Allgood –'

'When I *what*, sir?'

'I had hoped, in the fullness of time, to have the honour of introducing her. She is a person of the most warm-hearted and gentle, courageous kindness.'

'Never! Do you understand me? *Never, John*. Do not ask it. Should you be deluded enough to assume that I shall legitimise whatever infantile flouting this represents, you will find that you are gravely mistaken.'

'Very well, I shall not ask. But I shall live by my own lights. If that inflames your petty bigotries, for that is what they are, I wash my hands entirely of blame and wish you happiness.'

'May I remind you, sir –'

'Do not call me "sir", Mother. It is demeaning in the extreme.'

'May I remind you, *sir*, that every farthing in your idle pocket is supplied by myself through the providence of your late father? No natural respect or affection you have for his widow – this I know too well – again and *again* you have made it quite clear – but one would have imagined you might have some regard for what people say.'

'They may say what they wish. I do not give two damns what they *say*.'

'Do not blaspheme in my presence, John, I warn you — *I warn you*.'

'Teasy Ryan, a woman who enters this house to collect laundry once a week, is now to be public arbiter and informant as to morality?'

'She has been loyal to this family always. How dare you presume to speak of her in that manner?'

'Is one to care about the prattle of tinkers and peasants?'

'You seem fond enough of tinkers, from what I am informed of the female.'

'Withdraw that remark.'

'I shan't.'

'*Withdraw it, Mother. Immediately. Or I shall leave this table without delay.*'

'*You must do as you will.* My response shall be the same: *Thou shalt not make unto thee any graven image —*'

'I have heard it before — *I have heard it all my life* . . .'

'*Or any likeness of any thing that is in heaven above, or that is in the earth beneath, or that is in the water under the earth.* The theatre is the liar's house. It is *itself* a lie. And any woman who would solicit remuneration by exhibiting herself publicly merits a word I shall not utter but you know.'

'Say the word, Mother. You are burning to do so.'

'Listen to how you are speaking to me. *Listen* to the hatred in your voice. The woman who *bore* you. The widow of your father. *I am broken with their whorish heart, which hath departed from me, and with their eyes, which go a whoring after their idols.*'

'Is this your Christian charity? Do they comfort, such sanctities?'

'I shall speak my conscience freely at the table I supply. *You will obey my orders, John. And that is an end to it.* While you reside beneath my roof, you will comport yourself in a manner I deem to be appropriate. Your standards shall be *mine*, not those of the supposedly aesthetic louts with whom you have chosen to surround yourself.'

'I am thirty-seven, Mother.'

'*And you would do well to reflect on it.*'

'I am to be a prisoner, then? Is that what you wish?'

'The door of this house opens. You may use it at any time. It also closes. And it locks. And the prison you inhabit, if inhabit one you do, is guarded by the magistrate in your heart. He will *always* be there, John. You will face him at the close. You shall stand before the Mercy Seat one terrible day. "He shall come to be glorified in His saints".'

'Mother —'

'Only know that when you leave, you shall never be welcomed again. You shall sail under your own steam, I shall make plain certain of that. I should have done it long ago but of course I was weak. You shall earn your own bread, sir, as the good God intended for a man. If that is indeed what you are.'

'Then I shall leave as soon as is practicable. I shall find a boarding-house room in the city. Since that is quite evidently what you would prefer.'

'In some alley of the slums, no doubt. Good and close to your whore.'

'Correct, Mother, yes. I shall live among whores.'

'Yes, run. *Run.* Like the faithless coward you always were. *You make me sick that ever I saw you.*'

The maidservant enters with the soup. The conversation is extinguished.

'You're welcome back to us, Mister John,' murmurs the serving girl apprehensively. 'You had good walking down beyond, I hope.'

'Thank you, Bridget, yes . . . But it is agreeable to be home . . . Ah . . . Mulligatawny . . . My favourite.'

Soup spoons observe him. Portraits scrutinise him. Everything in the house has eyes.

4

RETURNING TO MISS O'NEILL IN LONDON ON THE DAY WE FIRST MET HER

THE NATIONAL PORTRAIT GALLERY
11.32 a.m.

Heavens to Betsy, what an ugly old trout. Face like a bag of rusted spanners. Imagine, someone paid good money for that glower to be painted. More beauty in the door of a jakes, that's the God's honest truth. My Jesus Almighty, but there's hope for us all, Molls. 'The Duchess of Blandford.' Looks like Mussolini in a wig. *Il Duce* with udders. God help us.

But it is good for the soul, being exposed to art. Just can take a little while to feel the benefit. Like dumb-bells. Or going to seances. Or voting Conservative. And what harm, when you think of it, ever came from a picture? Isn't it only little stains on a scrap of old canvas? Nobody was ever murdered by a painting.

And maybe she *was* a beauty, the Duchess of Blandford, before marriage to the Duke and the rest of the Blandfords and having to produce the heir and spares. Perhaps he had a mistress and it broke her frettish heart. Because you know what it's like with the aristocracy, Molly. Up and down with their drawers like a funicular railway and they rutting like rabbits, every half chance they get. And I know they don't *look* like that when you see them in portraits. But then again, neither do rabbits.

Poor ghastly face. But you're no beauty yourself any more. Be honest – the years aren't kind. And you feel that you have submerged into fretfulness with age, hear yourself murmuring of your anxieties with the troubled watchfulness of a child in an unfathomable world. And your old woman's *voice* – how did that happen? Your wheezing, brittle croakiness, distracted, muted, and you gossiping to the teacups for company. There was a day many years ago, in Connemara or Kerry, when you happened upon an old rowboat that had been dumped in a bog. Cross-bench crushed and buckled, rotting tiller wrenched askew, it had sunk to its oarlocks in the oozing, black peat. Often, of late, when you become aware of your voice, the image has appeared in your thoughts.

And getting up earlier. Another symptom, that. What young person ever got up at dawn out of choice? And talking to the wireless. And talking to the rain. And talking to dogs and to flowers in people's gardens. And talking to clothes that don't fit you any more and to dishes that need washing but haven't been washed, and to Sean the moan O'*Casey*, who you never truly liked, though the imaginary version at least doesn't answer. And to Shakespeare and the Prime Minister and the Leader of the Opposition, and whoever invented brassieres, and Mozart, and Stalin, and the Beverley Sisters, and Franco, and the Holy Child of Prague, and the Boogie-Woogie Bugle Boy of Company 'B', and whoever put the zips in the *back* of women's dresses, a presumption, if ever there was one, that every woman is married, and whole *conversations* with your*self*.

—*They must have family still over beyond in Jamaica. Wouldn't you think they'd miss them, Molly?*

—*Oh, you would.*

—*A wife maybe. Or little ones. And they without a father in life. It's sad when you think of it. God love them all the same.*

—*They're terribly nice people, I've found.*

—*I mean plenty of our own had to go, I'm not saying they didn't. In the Famine times and later. Jesus help them, they'd no choice. Wicklow was hit terrible. Whole townlands died in Wicklow. Little weanlings left to starve on the side of the road. And that bitch Queen Victoria giving five pounds to the relief fund. Same as you'd give a dogs' home. Imagine.*

—*Is that true?*

—Even in my own day. I was all for going myself. I was often sorry I didn't. Boston I'd have liked. They've great lives for themselves altogether over in Boston, I believe. But himself never wanted to. And he wouldn't be contradicted. So I suppose we can't be giving out and the boot on the other foot.

—Oh, no.

—That's right. The world does be turning. That's all.

Ah, the better day now. When we're out, we're out. And it's soothing in here, like a church. And the gas thing about brandy, it isn't like gin. Brandy's a nice wooziness, like you're warm and in Jersey, and the heat grinning up through the soles of your sandals, but gin is a rancidness that will always taste of London, doesn't matter a damn where in the world you're drinking it. Took Pegeen to Jersey one time. Twelve she was, maybe. Most beautiful child at the carnival that day, and the blue calico frock and the ribbons on the bonnet, and the carousels turning behind her.

And Christmas will bring trials, for your son-in-law is not only teetotal but branch secretary of the East Aberdeen Labour Party. Oh, a fiend for the red flag and what's mine is yours, comrade, but not a thimbleful of port, nor a swallow of amontillado, nor a flame's worth of whiskey for the pudding. Treasurer of the Working Men's Temperance Society. Sherry trifle for the afters – without the sherry. Still, the twins, lovely monkeys, and Pegeen in her apron, and all of us together in the flat. And it's his roof you'll be under, so it's himself makes the rules, and don't you go stirring up trouble again, Molls. It isn't fair to ask a woman to side against her husband. And he can't be all bad, when he's father to those children. Their wild laughter when he lofts them in his arms.

Now look at that man and he gawping at me sternish, like the seam of his bollocks is hand-stitched. Well, shame be damned, you old bull without a pizzle. And haven't I the *right* to be here, just the same as yourself? Put your eyeballs back in your head, pet. Give your face a little holiday. Was it cold in the ground this morning?

Smouldering Hell to the lot of them. Devil the bit of harm I'm doing. I've a son gave his life for this country, my buck, and if I can't look at its pictures same as any other covey in the kingdom, then my name isn't Molly Allgood, it's Sam. So turn the other cheek if you don't like the look of me, and kiss my arse like it owes you the rent.

'Good morning, Reverend.'

'Good morning, madam.'

'I hope it keeps fine for you.' Give a smile. It confuses them. And fuck them all bar Nelson. But why not Nelson too? Because Nelson's fucked already, Molly. That's why.

You roam the quiet rooms, moving deeper into the building, past the faces of the famous and forgotten. A schoolteacher is trying to quieten a restless flock of girls who have no more interest in what the guide is telling them about the techniques of impasto than a monkey would have in a bicycle. You pass beneath a skylight and the hailstones surge so sharply that everyone looks up at the glass. The attendant, who is Polish, gives you a complaisant smile, as though the weather is a charmingly naughty child who must be endured. A soldier and his girl are canoodling in an alcove. God love them. So hard for the young. Hope the porters let them alone and not be moving them along. Won't we all be a long time dead?

Sepulchral, the silence of the long, empty halls. In your mind arise the place names of rural north Wicklow, as snowflakes blowing about a hiker. *Knocksink. Carrickgollogan. Crone Wood. Deep Dargle.* Your mother's voice pronouncing them. And then Sean O'Casey's. And a voice you haven't heard in a long time but have often remembered: Edwardian, proper, mellifluously Anglo-Irish, shy, precise, slightly afraid. The intonation of a man who died many years ago. It pronounces your love-place *Wickleau.*

And if you were to hold on to his letter until the woman from America comes? Perhaps she might be willing to pay more? But maybe she'll never come. Plans can change, after all. Anyhow, giving it to some stranger simply wouldn't feel right – not like giving it to nice Mr Duglacz. She will have to be content, if you agree to see her at all, with whatever scraps of stories you can unearth. But you don't have many of those, only pictures, torn fragments. How you envy those many of your profession who are able to deploy anecdotes like spivs passing out stolen stockings.

But now — sit down, Molly, take a rest on the bench — close your eyes for a moment. No one minds. A quarter-moon behind the obelisk on the summit of Killiney Hill and the jingle of the buckles on the jarvey's undercarriage. The driver clicking his tongue to chirk along the horse and the road begins a winding descent. A few miles in the distance must be the mountains of Wicklow but it is too dark to see them now. You imagine being on the Sugarloaf — gorse in mist, the smell of goats — and as if to incarnate your thoughts, the gardens of the mansions sprout boulders and crag-heaps, walls of broken undercliff, outcrops and buttes of schist. A great singer lives in that villa; there are often young people by its gates like the famished awaiting scraps in a hymn. Past a ruined Martello tower, an ivy-swathed gate-lodge, a manse, a converted rectory, a retirement home, a castle. The ghosts of the people who lived in them once: their maidservants, stable-grooms, butlers, wrecked sons, scholars turned native, dowagers. The rain summons presences as you nod beneath the skylights.

You are riding a night train through western America. You watch yourself calmly, like some member of an audience watching a story that is only a diversion. And it's a story about actors. It would make a good play. They're bound for New York City, a journey that will take five days. Because the Express is not running, and nobody seems to know why. But Miss O'Neill, yes that's her name, or Miss Allgood, that's another, suspects it's a gallon of hogwash about the Express not running, that the producer wishes to scrimp and is too devious to admit it. He'd dynamite the walls of Jerusalem for two bucks and a beer, piss in the bottle and sell it back to you for champagne. And so the days will be gruelling, wearying; hungry. And the nights, too, will be far from easy, although night travel on a train through the unrolling American unseen is not without its moments of glum awe. Even claustrophobia can give way to a sense of gloomy redemption when it is experienced while on the move. The necessary makings-do and compromised privacies, the little improvisations and overheard rinsings are sanctified by the drumming of tracks in the night and the whoop of a whistle through the blackness. Such treks have been endured by Moody many times — Moody is the dresser, this is her eighth tour attending Madame, who can be a handful when sober and is a vixen when not — but Moody's views on the expedition, as on most other matters, have not been invited or offered. She is a part-time theatrical dresser. She does as she is ordered. It is how she gets to eat now and then.

Once arrived at New York City they will rest for two days. Madame will need to see the doctor and there are some items to be redeemed from the pawnbroker's, and this will all have to be arranged without any of the company knowing, although all of them will know *everything* of course. But knowing and *knowing* are not the same thing, as any good storyteller can tell you. And on Friday they will board the packet boat the *Prince of Denmark* for the seven-day passage back to Cobh.

Let's see now; let's see. Where does the scene *go*? So thirsty, oh my mouth. Is it dawn now or dusk? Well, the train is being drawn through a long, uphill tunnel, and the roll of the carriage raises creaks. The tour is after being difficult, too protracted, too arduous, the hotels of Dickensian shabbiness and the rest breaks too few. The police arrived to the theatre on the opening night in Philadelphia and arrested the whole cast for obscenity. Someone is creaming the takings. The food is filthy muck. The play has seen rioting in many American cities and the programme has been changed, with too little time for rehearsal and the wages are not *at all* what she has been used to. She suspects her husband and her sister are being far better paid, although both of them have denied it, have accused her of troublemaking. Everyone in the company seems to have a protector, but Madame has none any more.

And she has not been well lately, is grown older than her years. So slow in the mornings, too heavy, uneasy, forgetful of matters she wishes she could dredge up and remembering too much that hurts. Her night-thoughts are difficult. She sleeps with a light on. Her drinking could easily become ruinous.

But who in the name of God would want to read any story like that? Depressing auld film it would make. Was it the year after he died? Oh, *open your eyes*, for God's sake. You'd want to catch a hold of yourself. Look again at the art. Because these things are glories, the treasures of Empire. Generals, expeditionists, writers, Prime Ministers. Isn't it lucky you're allowed to lay eyes on them at all, and Africans starving today?

Dr Mercia Vinson. What would you tell her? That many years after his death you would still imagine you saw him? In the street, in a park, in a box at the theatre. At night you had dreams of him. He would come to you silently — watchful as your own reflection in water. You had a sense of being on a stage and of knowing he was in the darkness of the hall, the curious intimation that he was observing you.

You saw him on Second Avenue once, and across Central Park on a Christmas morning, through the windows of a tramcar as it truckled down the Bowery, fleetingly behind you in the browned old mirror of the dressing room in the Empire Theatre, Philadelphia. He would be dressed as he had been on the first evening he took you out. Always he appeared not to have aged. And once, you were certain, you had heard his diffident voice as you waited to go on stage in Washington. You were standing in the darkness, listening intently for the cue, the leather-bound book that was your prop in your hand, when from the scrupulous blackness of the backstage behind, you heard his tentative utterance:

Changeling . . .

You had stumbled, shaken, as you stepped into the light.

The house had been full. America loved you. The audience applauded wildly the moment they saw you — threw flowers — called your name — stood up in their rows — for they loved what they knew of your past, your story, and your long-awaited presence stopped the show. Around you, the other actors gave out their lines bleakly, accustoming to the fact of your bombproof eminence. It is hard to share a scene with someone's muse.

Several years had passed since your greatest performances, but that did not seem to matter to the audience or the actors. And really, it didn't matter to you. You were bowing in a theatre where a president had been shot, but nobody was thinking about the President that night. You knelt to the ovation, touched your breast like a diva. The gallery boys roared, hurled inundations of lilies. 'Milk them just a little,' he had always advised you. 'Then exit while they are begging for more. And once you go, stay gone. Let the gallery riot. *Never* give them everything they want.'

Reporters coming to talk to you. Their sweet, stupid questions. How his ghost seemed to glow with repudiation.

—*He was a great man, Miss O'Neill?*

—*He was a great artist, yes.*

—*And also a great man?*

—*What is that?*

—*Well — how did it feel — being his inspiration? His muse?*

—*I dislike that word. It belongs to mythology. A great artist needs nothing but his own woundedness, I have found. I was merely his servant. If that.*

—*His servant?*

—*In the sense that an actor is the servant of the text. That is my training. Others see it differently. But I have forgotten a great deal about Mr Synge, to be honest. I would prefer to talk about the piece I am playing now.*

You rise and move away, through the stillness of the corridors, past the admirals and the queens and the courtiers and the merchants. But some pictures are harder to move away from.

The day you rowed out to Dalkey Island, a cold, overcast April, dampness in the air, the sky grey as gulls' eggs, an arc of smoky cloud stretching all the way from Howth Head into the mist-wreathed mountains of Wicklow. In the distance the Liverpool steam-packet sat moored in the bay, and a red and white light-ship was breasting its way out towards the Skelligs where a fog bank was beginning to drift in. The grey-green sea rolled slowly on the strand, sucking stones in its wake, fizzing lowly on the grits, and a seal popped its head through one of the slopping breakers like a surfacing merman in a folk tale.

You trudged around for a while, him taking photographs and making notes in a jotter, but a spattering rain commenced before you'd been there an hour and there were no trees under which shelter might be had. You huddled close to the wall of the derelict Martello tower, paper bags on your heads making the rainfall smack thunderously. A quartet of wild goats came wandering over the rocks, the male staring resentfully at the churning sea, shaking his dirty beard at it like King Lear. Across the Sound, a herd of schoolboys appeared in Coliemore Park. Some started waving, gesticulating crazily, but they were too far away for their words to be audible. A hare scutted out from a hole in the tower wall and went lolloping away towards the sandflats.

You shared a sodden cigarette. The needling rain eased resent-fully into mizzle as though driven away by the smoke. Yachts appeared near the pier, their yellow-white sails. The Dublin train clattered by on the clifftop.

It had been clear to you from the start that his way of dealing with uncomfortable subjects was to avoid them or displace them by unsubtle attempts at irony. It had not been a difficulty. If anything, you were glad. But you wondered to yourself, then, as you headed away from the tower and back towards the greasy beach where he had tied up the rowboat, if someone employing these defences could ever love anyone or be approached in such a way that you could know him. It seemed to you that he carried experiences not grieved for or even experienced. He was one of

— 67 —

those people who would make sandwiches at a parent's funeral, being brave, unselfish, deflecting unwelcome questions, sweeping a broom around the coffin in the church. He was good at redirecting. You barely noticed he was doing it until the subject of your conversation had moved on. And by then it would be bad manners to try to go back. He understood how most people work. But such thoughts were about to disappear like snow off a rope. When you returned to the beach, the boat was gone.

'Holy Moses.'

'Where is it, John?'

'I mustn't have tied it properly. Damn.'

You ascended a mound of rocks and saw it fifty yards away in the Sound, bobbing and slowly circling, its oars trailing from the oarlocks, its mooring-guy dragging behind like a tail. A cormorant was perched on the cross-bench, proprietorial somehow, as though having pirated the dory away out of spite. It occurred to you suddenly what the schoolboys had been shouting about.

'Damn,' he said, again. 'This is a very nice pancake.'

'It is all right. Let's not be panicking. Calm down.'

He stripped off his shirt and waded into the water, which must have been achingly cold. And it is odd, because when you remember this, for some reason there is a reversal. It is *you* who are conscious of the pounding of your heart, the hardness of breathing, the sting of the waves, the terror encountered by the unskilled swimmer that the whole world is made of water. Somehow he clambered in, his frantic flailing almost capsizing the dory, and by the time he had sculled a way back through the crosscurrent to the beach, your clothes were soaked rags and you were shaking. It was an incident you would often feel should be funny to remember. But in truth it wasn't funny at all.

The next day you were at the theatre, on your way to a costume-fitting backstage, when you overheard Lady Gregory speaking to someone in her office. Something queer in her tone magnetised you towards the door, which was an inch or two ajar, an unusual enough occurrence, for Lady Gregory insisted on doors being kept closed in the theatre, except when it was absolutely necessary to open them. It was a matter of shutting the heat in, she would insist to the staff. Coal did not grow on the trees.

It seemed to you at first that some strange play was being read. After a while you could see that this was true, in its way, and you wondered if you yourself were in the wings, as it had seemed then, or were actually at centre stage.

'I am told that when the company was on tour you permitted yourself to be seen in a public place, in a certain attitude with our gifted Miss Allgood.'

'I am not sure what you mean, Augusta. An attitude?'

'With your arm about her shoulder. Or something of that nature.'

'The eyes of the world are observant indeed. You may rest assured it was only her shoulder. Nothing else.'

'My dear John, it is not for me to opine on your private friendships, of course. Nor on the terrestrial coordinates of your arm.'

Her Ladyship had this mode of unimpeachable if clipped courtesy, crosshatched with disenchantment, as though everything being said to her was an apology for some failing and she was being magnanimous in not shrieking at the speaker. Your lover was the only one of her writers who knew how to deal with it, perhaps because he was fluent in it too.

'I value your wisdom greatly under all aspects, Augusta.'

'Dash it all, this is a little difficult. One does not wish to be a Carmelite. But there are younger and impressionable people among the company, as you know.'

'Impressionable?'

'Yeats feels the same way. He feels he cannot speak to you. Perhaps it is because you are both men.'

The passageway was dusty; a dirty sunbeam slanted in through a skylight. You could see the seagulls wheeling or hanging in the airstreams as though in observation of something worth scavenging.

For no reason it occurred to you that the river was close by, and beyond it the cold expanse of Dublin Bay. Beyond that, the freedom of Liverpool or Manchester or Leeds, some room in a town of smokestacks, where nobody knew either of you. You had sensed that the coke-black sternness of England's northern cities was a lie, a camouflage of the liberty that might be found there.

'Strong fences make good neighbours, John. If you follow my line. Fraternisation with the players can cause confusion, a certain restlessness. Especially when it takes place under a public gaze. And there are differences between you and Miss Allgood, of course.'

'Indeed.' He laughed quietly. 'I had noticed.'

'I do not think it entirely a matter for mordant amusement, if you will permit me the licence of fond friendship. I have to tell you that there has been talk of a kind that is not helpful to our work. Among the younger members of the company especially. I feel you know this, of course. You are a listener of immense skilfulness and subtlety.'

'These little backstage snobberies are surely inconsequential.'

'You say snobbery – but it is more a question of fellow feeling for you, John. And for Miss Allgood too. Importantly.'

'Forgive me, dear Augusta, I am not sure I follow.'

'Let me put it to you in the general. As a woman. As your friend. It would be a great violence to any girl to be given baseless expectations or to be allowed to form such expectations unenlightened. Particularly if she were very much younger and less educated than the man who might permit silly hopes. And not – well, you know what I mean.'

'Not what?'

'You are intent on ribbing me by making me use terminologies I do not find it agreeable to employ.'

'You may speak candidly, Augusta, if that is your wish.'

'I never trust people who do that. They are irremediably vulgar. Candour is the last resort of the tasteless.'

'If you mean that Miss Allgood is of a differing social order –'

'Those are your words, John.'

'What are yours?'

'Your inheritances – put it like that – are in few evident ways comparable.'

'Which means?'

'In effect, it means that some of us are bequeathed our furniture. Whereas others buy and sell it as a living.'

'I have not noticed too many debutantes or duchesses on our stage.'

'Your point being?'

'I think you know my point. I need not paint a picture. We have devoted ourselves to that class of people who have inherited nothing but their courage. It is they who are given flesh on our stage every night. But in life, one is to hold one's nose to them?'

'You are speaking to me like a socialist vicar. And you are being a little disingenuous.'

'Augusta –'

'I have had a letter from the girl's grandmother. A redoubtable person. I am informed that there have been anxieties among Miss Allgood's family, John. There is no father, as you know. The girl is very young. Not young in years only but in development, in sensibility. Plainly the feeling exists that there are certain vulnerabilities. I cannot help but feel this, too. On both sides.'

'There are no *sides* to the case.'

'Between a man and a woman? I think there will always be sides. Could we but limit them to two we should be doing the work of wizards.'

'It is essentially a matter of the wholly private sphere, which with great respect is not the proper concern of any other person.'

'Were complexities down the road to conclude your understanding with Miss Allgood, I would ask you to consider the fact that she would face the continuation of her career, which is still in its infancy, in a shadow that might not be pleasant. Some would advise that it were better for the friendship to conclude itself now. Before harm of a serious nature is done.'

'To her career?'

'To that, too.'

'My friendship with Miss Allgood will not be concluding. It is an attachment I have come to value very deeply.'

'Evidently. Well, there it is. Perhaps you will reflect, at any rate.'

'I hope that I will never fail to reflect on the counsel of a well-wisher.'

'Yes. That is always wise. When it happens.'

'May we now return to our work? There is a text needing editing.'

'I would hate the day to arrive when I had to let her go. She may well have a talent. Not that of her sister, of course. Your Miss Allgood lacks the vein of hollowness every actor of the highest order must have. Her excess of personality means that she will never achieve anything great. But she has a gift all the same. I like her voice.'

'I share the hope that the day you envisage does not arrive, Augusta. Because if it did, you would be letting go of me, too.'

'But come, my dear friend. Are you threatening your deepest admirer?'

'I could never threaten the staunchest ally my writing has known. I merely aver that any theatre having no place for Miss Allgood needs other talents than mine.'

'I rarely think it at all shrewd to offer a hostage to fortune, John.'

'Quite. Neither do I. Be assured.'

You halt before a portrait of a kindly looking magistrate in the wig of a Pepysian character. He is red-faced, gouty, but his eyes shine with mildness, and his ruff is as yellow as a cornerboy's teeth, which gives him the faintest little touch of the disreputable rogue, a thing you have always liked in a man. Sir Richard Persse-Leigh. How are *you*, sir? Quite well? You are looking fierce handsome; quite the mickey dazzler. May I remain with you a moment? I will not detain you long. The truth is, I am a little unsteady on my feet this cold morning. The spirituous liquors, alas. But if you will permit me a tiny minute in the balm of your company the steadiness I seek will return. I have been thinking, you see, of events in the past, and they cannot be changed so are better forgotten — but this morning, for some reason, they are at me like dogs, so I need a gallant friend like yourself, sir.

Does it frighten you at night, sir, the quietness of this place? Can you hear the infernal motor cars as they cross Trafalgar Square? In the war, used you awaken to the drone of the bombers? I did, myself. Did you weep? Do you natter to one another when the gallery is empty? Are you courting the Duchess of Blandford, perhaps? Are there great chivalrous dances when you slip from your frames, and gavottes in the halls when the night porter sleeps? I'd say you know what's what when it comes to a woman. You have the look of a right pleasure-man, I'm thinking. Oh now, oh now, don't deny it, you old scallywag. *He's the boogie-woogie bugle boy / Sir Richard Persse-Leigh.*

Would you take me to the Four Hundred or the Milroy some time? Those are nightclubs, sir. I used to go when I was younger. After a first night, perhaps. We would wait for the reviews. All the smart, young poets would be arguing in the alcoves, the air thick with rhymes, and tuxedos on the chair-backs, and oh the champagne and oh the flirtations and the elations of exhausted Soho suppers. Lobster Newberg in Croustades, Crown Roast of Lamb, Potatoes with Parsley Butter, Peas with Mint Cream. An admirer once offered twenty guineas for one of my garters. Can you imagine the impertinence? Do you know what I told him? *Free to those who can afford it, expensive to everyone else.* He whispered that if I would permit him to take me to his bed I could decide into which category he should be placed. Well, I went to his rooms, sir, in Handel Street, Bloomsbury, for I was bold once or twice, there's no point in denials, and he soon stopped me chatting, sir, I will give him that for nothing. He was patient, ruthlessly expert, said little. In the morning we talked. He was not long down from Oxford. Did you ever eat a snail, sir? We should go to L'Escargot. My name is Molly O'Neill, sir. I was once in love myself. It was a long time before the nightclubs and the slippers of vermouth. There are portraits of the man I loved. Not here, though.

He comes to you again as you look at the picture. Always so persistent, so jealous. That day not long after Dalkey Island when you were leaving on tour to England. He had some errands to do in Dublin and you arranged to meet him in a café. He was scrawling in his notebook as you entered slightly late and he gestured to you as you approached the table, rolling his eyes in mock impatience, unable to leave off from his work. Slowly twirling a carpenter's pencil in the fingers of his right hand, his gaze on the ceiling as though trying to see an insect, and his gloved left hand held up to you like a policeman's halting traffic, for fear you might speak and break his spell.

'John?'

'Please. Don't say anything at all. Would you mind very terribly? I am losing my train. Don't move.'

Seven minutes you waited, by the clock on the wall.

'Sorry about that, old thing. Just a scene. How are you?'

'Grand. I am looking forward to the tour.'

'You'll be missed,' he said quietly.

''Tis fierce romantic you are, altogether.'

'I mean it,' he said, perhaps more abruptly than he meant to. Lately his habitual brusqueness had been perplexing you slightly more. You had come to wonder if it was not in fact, like all habitual modes, the result of careful manufacture over time.

You regarded him. 'Come with me, so.'

His laugh by then was harsh, something probably not his fault; an effect of repeated surgery on the glands of his throat, but the guttural hack of his amusement was a difficult thing to hear. He hated hearing it himself, you knew.

'I can't go with you to London, my silly little monkey.' His long musician's fingers now engaged in the making of a cigarette, butterfly paper, cheap, coarse-cut tobacco, like a workingman's, tucking and rolling with the efficiency of long habit but no fluency.

'Why not?'

'You will be busy. You will be working. I don't want to be in your way.'

'Oh yes. My way. Who'd want to be in that?'

'What time is the sailing?'

'In three hours. We'd have to hurry.'

'I can't. I have unbreakable appointments at the theatre.'

'A woman of my charms is practically throwing herself at him for a flit across the water and he can't. Dear God, ladies and gentlemen. What's the world coming to at all?'

'I said I can't, Molly. Now let the matter rest if you would.'

Again it came assertively and you felt the mirth in your expression melt. The waiter brought your orders, placed the plates and water glasses.

'You are very hard sometimes, John.'

'I am sorry. I am tired.'

'You would give a girl the feeling that you are ashamed of her company.'

'I could never be ashamed of my changeling. And you are correct to scold me, Molly. It's this pig of a beastly play. It is sending your ungrateful wretch daft. We shall have a nice little outing the very day you come home. And I shall write to you every night you are gone. You'll see. I shall dream of sitting in the box and cheering you along. And of cursing the rest of the company for clodhoppers.'

He flourished a smile and you returned it. But something between you had curdled. In some ways, it was easier to be together now the feeling was less intimate; your talk came freely, of things that didn't matter, and if he began to look wearier you put it down to the oppressive heat of the café, the noise of nearby conversations, the comings and goings. As in all eating establishments in Dublin, the tables were too close together. You could smell your neighbour's food.

'Then I had better be going, John. There can be crowds at the weekend.'

He paid and you went out to Sackville Street but there were no hackneys on the stand. He waited with you, and you wanted to kiss him but were afraid to do so in public. He slipped his hand into yours without meeting your eyes. The air was sharp and cold, cleansed by the rain. You imagined being with him in London, the crowded noisy streets, an image of the two of you walking across Trafalgar Square towards the gallery, through the beggars and the mournful balladeers. Or simply being on the ship with him, in a windowless cabin, low-raftered, with a lamp, and the creaking of the boards. The sharing of conspiratorial laughter, like disobedient schoolchildren putting a spontaneous mischief into action. The cabin would be warm, so narrow that the bunk would touch two of the walls. You'd eat hungrily, often chuckling as you glanced at one another. The sailing would be atrocious; navvies would be drunk. A small, bright adventure to share.

He gave the jarvey-man five shillings and told him you were in a hurry. You remember it all. Every detail of that day. But the young woman from America would never want to know such a thing. She would think it all irrelevant. Understandably.

5

A REHEARSAL AT THE
ABBEY THEATRE, DUBLIN

'Miss O'Neill, the manner in which you spoke the line is not quite correct.'

'Mr Synge, I am after speaking it the way it is written.'

'An entirely understandable mistake. Please do not admonish yourself too severely. One's intention was for it to be spoken as though your character did not quite fully mean it.'

'There is no direction saying that, so I read it the way it appears.'

'Again, Miss O'Neill, your error is almost entirely forgivable. I would only contend that you will see, if you give consideration to the previous five lines, and indeed to the general tenor and thrust of the scene, and to the numerous previous conversations we have had in the rehearsal room on the question, that undoubtedly she does not mean what she is saying. We have gone over the ground a hundred times. It must surely be clear.'

'That is not clear to me at all.'

'Then perhaps, Miss O'Neill, you should read the soliloquy again.'

'And perhaps, Mr Synge, you should have written it different.'

Yeats looked up slowly from his place in the stalls, as though awoken by a mysterious bell. He took from his waistcoat pocket and wiped thoughtfully on his lapel an object that proved to be a monocle. He was not smiling, exactly, at his colleague, the playwright, but his mouth was perhaps curling, perhaps amiably.

He breathed delicately on the monocle and held it up to the light like a jeweller examining a nugget of lapis lazuli.

'Perhaps indeed,' Synge said, 'but I did not write it different. Or "differently", as I think you must mean. And when I require a lesson in dramaturgy I shall fly to you, Miss O'Neill, for we all value the treasures of wisdom you contribute so ceaselessly on the subject. In the meantime, perhaps you would condescend to speak the actual text as it appears on the page rather than the superior one which appears to exist in your head.'

'If it doesn't exist in my head, Mr Synge, then it doesn't exist at all.'

'I see we have a philosopher as well as a playwright.'

'And I see you'd prefer a parrot.'

'Miss O'Neill, I have appealed to you and now I give you fair warning. You are a professional who is remunerated on the basis of compliance —'

'If you think, Mr Synge, that you are going to lord it over me in that manner, then let me tell you — *You have your porridge.*'

'Miss O'Neill, would you take a grip of yourself —'

'You have your porridge, my buckshee!'

'The girl is only giving an opinion, sir,' intervened an electrician named Dossie Wright who was occasionally put in a loincloth and told he was a warrior when a crowd scene needed bulking out. He was a skirt-chaser who would risk dismissal and consequent beggary if he thought a grope might be attainable as reward. It was said admiringly among the scene-painters that he would ride a scabby duck and once or twice there had been backstage incidents involving angry fathers or husbands, for Mr Wright had played Mr Right to many. 'It's not that any of us would want to be acting the maggot,' he continued, in his slow-witted-but-well-meaning-prison-officer's voice. 'But it's ourselves has to do the playing. And that's a different sausage from the writing. And if Miss O'Neill wants the thing explained, I think it poor order it wouldn't be. That's Dossie Wright's point of view on the matter.' He blazed on her a look of almost violent affability as he fumbled with the yard of cable he was holding.

'If one may be of assistance,' began Yeats, with priestly quietness. 'What Mr Synge has in mind –'

'What one has in *mind* is an actress passably capable of committing to memory the text one has written, and then speaking it without the emission of saliva over the front stalls. Is this asking too much? Or merely too much of your good self, Miss O'Neill? Might you do me the enormous and doubtless undeserved courtesy of looking at me when I address you, do you think?'

'Perhaps, Mr Shakespeare, you would illustrate your meaning.'

'I am sorry? Are you now *smoking*? Would you extinguish that cigarette, please?'

'I will extinguish it when I am good and ready, my little man cut short. And since you are the world's blessed expert on my never-ending faults, you would be doing me a great obligement entirely to mosey up here onto the stage and give us out the line in the way that suits you best for I am sure all of us in the company would get a chuckle out of it anyhow. Wouldn't we, ladies and gentlemen?'

'No no, Miss O'Neill, I have a better idea. Why don't *you* come down here and I shall give you a pen and you can rewrite the entire piece to your liking.'

'You know where you can stick your pen.'

'I shall fetch Lady Gregory,' he warned.

'I was talking, Your Majesty, about your inkwell.'

Yeats arose slowly and splayed his fingers on the seat-back before him, like a senator about to commence a funeral oration. His sharp Roman features were sternly arranged and he wore his sense of the moment like a mantle. The monocle had been set in the place that ophthalmology intended. It was going to be a difficult few minutes.

'If one may, Synge?' he murmured.

The playwright nodded back morosely.

'That will be enough out of you, Miss O'Neill,' said the poet.

'I'm only saying,' she said, 'and I amn't being listened to. And playwrights screeching away at me like a zoo full of chimps.'

'*That will do you now, Miss,*' Yeats snapped.

He waited for utter silence to descend on the gathering, like a man expecting a train he knows for certain is coming but might take a little time to arrive. One glove he unbuttoned and unhurriedly removed. Then, blinking like a cow, he regarded her. She was interested to see exactly how he would rise to the occasion, for by now she had noticed a sort of poignancy about Yeats: that there was in him, as in most men, no matter their class, a small, bright unease about relative position, that his envy of Synge's inheritance, the air of tattered lordliness, the fluency in old languages, the savoir-faire, the rumoured trust-fund, had taken a form she would often see again, that of wanting to be the nobleman's cornerboy. It was a kind of love, perhaps, but it was other things too. She ground out her cigarette in a goblet.

'We appear to be experiencing a difficulty,' he said reedily. 'A difficulty of recognition. A difficulty of blindness. Well, no matter. It is to be expected. This can occur when our instincts are underdeveloped. We become mired in capriciousness, the false belief that we have earned importance. This man' – he pointed the monocle at Synge – 'is a genius. Do you understand me?'

'Yes, Mr Yeats,' mumbled two of the actors.

'What is he? All of you!'

'*A genius, Mr Yeats.*'

'Yes. That is correct. He is our Aeschylus. Our Ibsen. He is one of the very magi, belittling himself in our stable. We are the swine, the *kine*, the cud-chewers at the apotheosis. We are the excrement in the straw. *What are we?*'

'Excrement, Mr Yeats,' replied one of the walk-ons obediently. Nobody turned to look at him.

'Yes. We are ordure. We are expellable. *Vileness.* And when you, and you – and especially *you* – are deservedly long forgotten and part of the dust, the works of this Homer shall be glorified. He shall

ride our wingèd horse into the sunbursts of Olympus whilst your . . .
bicycles rust in the pawnshop. We are none of us worthy — *I say none
of us, mind* — to fasten the very lacing of his brogue. And when you
are old and full of weariness, the best any of you will have to recol-
lect of your miserable, *futile* huckstering existences is that once you
were in the presence of a Titan. You will fetch down the very script
you now besmirch by your egregious dribblings, from the shelf
upon which it will have rested for years — perhaps decades — and
the ancient hearth of our muse shall scald you for shame that you
did not kneel when you had the opportunity of genuflection.'

'I say Yeats, old man, I think you're being a little too —'

'Be quiet, Synge!'

He turned again to the actors, a sneer of derision making him
appear taller, and pushed a hand through the flop of his hair.
'You pitiable, counter-jumping ingrates,' he continued grimly.
'You boils on the thigh of a peasant.'

'Ah, here,' said Dossie Wright.

'You are an irrelevance, Wright. A vacuum. A *hole*. You are all
of you *a surplus population*. Whoreson zeds. Unnecessary letters.
Sans the work of this genius you are . . . umlauts!' He said the
last word lavishly, pretending not to enjoy it. There were mysti-
fied glances. Someone released an unfortunately audible belch.

It was only at this point that Yeats vacated his place, striding
heavily, sombrely, towards the lip of the stage, and slowing even
more markedly the closer he got to it, like a battleship approaching
a mutinous colony. The tone he was aiming at was more-sorrowful-
than-angry but it came out as disdain mixed with rage suppressed,
which was so remarkably similar to his customary mode, for everything from reciting a lyric to ordering a mop-lady where to mop,
that it was difficult to know if he was being completely serious
or was giving a comically deprecating imitation of himself in an
effort to explode the tension. It was only when the cape was flung
desultorily over the stiffened left shoulder in the manner of a
toreador about to pose for a portraitist that it became clear he
wasn't playing for laughs.

'God's Wounds,' he said quietly, seeming to peer at his hands. A stupid onlooker might have formed the notion he was talking to his fingers. In fact, it was his way of letting you know that you weren't worth the exertion of looking at. 'Can you face yourselves? Truly? Have you the audacity to exist? Is there no crevice, no nook, for you to slither into and expire? You bits of *sucked sugar-stick*. You abattoir's *effluvia*. You would make of the Holy Grail *a spittoon*.' Here he raised his furious eyes, his ancient, glittering eyes, and they had nothing in the way of gaiety. 'You wastrels of the precious. You squanderers. You *bawds*. You stains left on a pew. You vague . . . *dampnesses*. I weep when I think on the riches you have wasted. Alone, in my rooms, I weep. You will enunciate these pearls of our art as Mr Synge intended or you may streel yourselves back to the . . . *cabbage-patches* you belong in. Do I render myself comprehensible to you?'

'Yes, Mr Yeats.'

'Good. That is good. I shall now resume my seat. And you shall recommence from scene three. And you shall speak the lines accurately. And if there is another solitary *twitter* of insurgency out of yourself, Miss O'Neill, I shall personally take a stick to you before flinging myself upon the mercy of the court. The tuppence-ha'penny fine I should receive for doing what your mother should have done would be a farthing too severe, in my view.'

'You have your porridge, Mr Yeats, if you think you're talking to Molly O'Neill like that . . .'

'No! You have *your* porridge! Now eat it!'

———

Sunday is their day; she takes the quarter-to-eleven from the city. It is a standing arrangement, but he reminds her of it by letter. They roam the furzy slopes of Killiney Hill or lie among its alpines looking down at the bay. The setting has the dual advantage of being Wordsworthian and discreet. Here they can be alone, almost certain of privacy. They feed one another the wild berries that grow near the obelisk: *fraughans* in the vernacular, but she calls them 'purple grapes'. It becomes one of their euphemisms, a love phrase charged with intimate meaning. The fairy-woman and the vagabond, their transgressive liaison. It is like a scene from a folk tale, the seed of one of his plays. But who is emancipating whom?

Sometimes he recites the lyrics he has written for her: his gifts. 'I wrote another poem on you last night,' he confides, as though he had somehow imprinted it on her flesh. But these verses are rarely sensual, are often oblique. Only seldom does he tell her, shyly, like a boy, how much he likes to see her 'in light summer clothes'. At such moments, strangely, she has a powerful sense of his brokenness, of how difficult he finds it just being alive. There are days when he looks at an oak and sees only the makings of a coffin. He has no memory of his father, who died when he was a baby.

She pictures the cancer that is in him as a militia of tiny lights moving slowly around his innards, leaving no corner unscarred. She sees herself extinguishing a single one of them every time she does him a kindness. It has something to do with a sermon she once heard as a girl in the great vaulted bastion of St Nicholas of Myra church. The priest had said grace was a gathering of candles waiting to be lit by the sinner. It has stayed with her always, this evocative depiction, even as her faith gives inevitable ground to the editings and adjustments that come with adult life. God, providence, the balm in Gilead – they need to be met halfway.

If he coughs in her presence, she blesses him silently. If he gasps, she sends him a prayer. As though observing a vast city at the approach of dawn, she sees the lights of his cancer flicker out one by one. She envisages his lungs – radiant with pain – and the snuffer of her benignity sets to its work. If she could only touch them – physically touch them – the air in them would sweeten and cleanse and renew and the flames that always scorch them would puff into nothingness like wicks pinched out by her fingers.

She encourages him to eat, to drink if he wishes to; he was raised with a puritan's views on alcohol. He has gone into public houses while on his rambles around Wicklow, where he talks with the tinkers and trampers and poachers, but has never truly escaped from the notion of his rearing, that drink is the devil's doorway. Porter is healthy, a tonic, she tells him. Her mother has given birth to eight children in her time and often says a nightly glass of porter was the only reason she had been able to do it. It was also, remarks her grandmother, in a meaningful way, the only reason half of them had been conceived.

He gains a little weight in their first months together. He abandons his talk of Switzerland. There is a clinic in the Alps for people with his condition, where they feed you up with strudel, stuff you like an archduke, and force you out to walk in the cold mountain air and to listen to yokels with alpenhorns. He laughs as he tells these stories but she can see he is afraid. He is often wild with gaiety when frightened.

He can be jealous, furiously so, if he senses a rival in the picture. She is not to talk to other men, never to take one by the arm. Dossie Wright, especially, is to be shunned, he insists. And there are others against whom he advises unceasing caution. Musicians are untrustworthy. Many have unspeakable diseases. Medical students are debauchers who 'dangle out of actresses' and brag of their seductions, of innocents ruined. He is not himself a dangler, a stage-door Johnnie. No gentleman would inveigle a girl by holding out false hopes.

He is not conventionally handsome; that goatee makes him appear shifty. A face like a blacking brush, as Sara sometimes puts it. He looks faintly like a typical Irishman in an old *Punch* cartoon: beetle-browed, mercurial, recently down from the trees. But he is not a typical Irishman: he loves to listen. His few true confidantes have all been women. ('People like Yeats who sneer at old-fashioned goodness and steadiness in women seem to want to rob the world of what is most sacred in it.') She talks to him about her clothes, about hats and gowns, her difficult sister, problems with money, arguments at rehearsal, ghastly 'digs' she has stayed in, grim tours around the provinces, her painful menstruation. He arranges for her to attend an eminent gynaecologist in Dublin; cannot bear the thought that she would be in needless pain. As a child she had been sent to an orphanage following the death of her father, for her mother so suddenly widowed had been unable to cope. She tells him stories of the beadles, the bible-study, the gruel, how she escaped and ran back to Mary Street, begged her mother to allow her remain. Her later life as a shop-girl in Switzers drapery: she tells him about that, and he listens as though entranced. She smokes like a soldier. He nags at her to stop.

She finds him so queer. He is 'highly-strung', he informs her. Every writer is. This is the price of art. She knows the price of art, has been paying it for some time. Some of the love poems she has inspired seem like howls of grief.

He talks to her about Paris, about Germany and the Aran Islands, where the people are serious and allow you to be alone. He longs to show her Brittany, Normandy, Inishmaan. Everything will be better when they marry, he promises, though his mother has often wondered aloud, as he himself has wondered in silence, how he and any wife could manage on a writer's pittance. This appears to be Mother's way of making it clear that the family silver will not be subsidising love in a garret. He hungers for the success that can give them independence. To escape from Glenageary, to make his own way: the need comes to fume in him like a lust.

He is working on a strange piece, set in a hamlet in Mayo, about a storyteller who bludgeons his father and somehow becomes a hero when he makes a boasting song of the crime. The play is sending him mad; he is afraid to follow whatever instincts he has about its shape and its poetry and its savagery. He has been trying to conceal his uncertainty with what he calls 'strong writing', but is beginning to discern that this is a cheat, that form and content must be inextricably wedded. It must be what it must. It is not a pantomime or a parable. And if people do not like it, it still must be itself. He comes to feel there is a great role in it for his changeling girl. His 'Pigeen', as he has taken to calling her.

They discuss this role. He listens while she talks. She is adaptable, amenable. Which changeling is not? She thinks he is a genius. He tells her that *she* is. She loves his dedication, his monkish graveness. Beside him, even severe old Augusta Gregory can seem a high-kicker auditioning for a cabaret. He talks about his characters as though they were real. 'I wrestle with that playboy,' he jokes bleakly, but he means it. It is as though these voluble buckos and fiery-tongued beauties were to be encountered any evening on a stroll through Mother's garden.

One warm Sunday evening on Killiney Hill, he reads her a few soliloquies of the play set in Mayo. A bachelor is a ridiculous figure, he recites, 'like an old braying jackass strayed upon the rocks'. He looks up at her hopefully. Is that the right tone? Is it true? Is it funny? Will they laugh?

He claims to his changeling that he writes out of the desire for consolation, that something in story-making eases him, assuages his demons. But it also exhausts him. He has to be careful. ('A man cannot work with the cream of his brain for more than six hours at a sitting.') Late at night he goes to his study in the stilled, dark house and looks at what he has written that day. A quarter-measure of watered whiskey, and he reads over his pages, and the crippled old Labrador snores on the camp-bed that is set beneath a tapestry of hunters. She can picture the room, the green shade on the lamp, the leather-mounted blotter on the sea-captain's desk, a Waterford vase of buttercups from the railway embankment wilting on the bedside table. The dim mullioned window, the soft scratch of his nib, his shirt-sleeves unbuttoned like a gambler's at a table where the game is running on long. Sometimes he looks out at Dalkey Quarry in the moonlit distance, or he listens to the servants moving quietly about the house. Where are they going so late? What are their stories? Why do they pause by my door? The rasp of the match and the small globe of flame as he lights a last bowl of tobacco.

He knows there is only one thing that separates us from the beasts: it is that everyone carries an Eden, an inner realm of silence, and this is what some call the soul, having no other name for it. The point is to allow people to reach it, be blessed by it, even briefly, to save them from the filthy undermurmur of living.

And at some point he realises he has twenty strong pages. Then what becomes important is bravery. To go on might yield nothing – everything can die. Anyone can make a beginning; to embark on a second act takes the courage. It is like building a house, he says. The smallest error is fatal. Every course of brick-work must be angled correctly or the whole will collapse in the end. By fifty pages, sixty, he knows if the impossible is happening. The people summoned into being by the old power of words might begin to unfurl, to walk about and love, to say things he himself would never dream of uttering, in voices not his but theirs. It is like watching the muzzle-flash of a gun through fog yet wanting the bullets to hit you, he says. Essential to hold your nerve, not to let the excitement of the alchemy throw you into crowd-pleasing stupidities or grandiosities. Who can say where they come from, these people who never lived? But he is one of the intermediaries they come to. He seems to think of himself in the third person, as perhaps all do from time to time. Is it possible he sees himself as a character?

It is whispered among the costume girls that his people are landlords down the country, that they evicted tenants in the bad times, burned their cabins. Many's the penniless tramp created by a Synge, someone says, and relatively few of them fictional. She refuses to believe it, turns her ears from the rumours. She gathers that he has quarrelled with Mother about political matters, but Mother pointed out, evidently with scriptural vehemence, that the tenants down the country were paying for his freedom to write, so he was hardly in a position to be adopting revolutionary poses. Mother and her sister grew up on the neighbouring estate to the Parnells', often rocked the Chief's little cradle when he was a baby. In later years, Aunt Jane grew fond of remarking what a pity it was that they hadn't strangled him.

Months turn to seasons. Rehearsals turn to shows. His eyes are darkening; the weather she sees in them is sullen. He seems half in love with death, like Keats watching nightingales. Operations come and go, and he coughs like a broken train, and still the old lady refuses to die. He is nearly always sick now: the growth on his neck makes him quake. There are fears he might be tubercular. He may need aggressive surgery. Often, he takes to his bed for days. He becomes convinced that the effort of writing brings fever.

And there is trouble at the theatre; there are faction fights, rows. What is it in theatre people that they must always squabble? He is not a committee man like Yeats, or a battler like Her Ladyship, though he is conscientious about management, thinks it important to be a peacemaker. But he'd rather be in Wicklow, roaming his rocks, 'away from all good commonplace people', he says. He starts to advise his changeling to become a playwright herself. She is already a sort of playwright; it is only that she doesn't know it, hasn't realised he is making notes of her phrasings and coinages. Loving her is becoming the same for him as loving his work. 'My mirror, my air,' he calls her.

They write to each other daily, sometimes twice in the space of a morning. Often, while he is headlocking the playboy in Glenageary, or bicycling the dappled avenues, which he likes to do at dusk, when everything is quiet and he can breathe a little easier, she drifts on to the stage of his mind. He loves her so fiercely; he won't let anyone hurt her, ever. 'Not even yourself,' he can't help but add. His true nature is so kind, so scrupulously gentle; but always he feels the need to cloak it in ironies. He is the saddest kind of man, the sort who seems embarrassed by his own decency. 'An afflicted poor devil,' as he sometimes says.

She feels that if they courted more openly and often there would be less of a need for letters, and that this would be a relief, like the windows of an old mansion being thrown open. He rarely stops chiding her for not writing to him more. She doesn't say what she means, she writes too briefly, she forgets about his illnesses, she breaks all her promises, she wants too much from him, she doesn't want enough, she looked at him coldly, she winked at some spear-carrier. *'You are rolling the stone off my grave.'* A Kingstown postmark makes her feel trepidation; the way his mother would feel if she glanced up from Leviticus and saw a tricolour flapping from the conservatory roof. If only they could spend time actually having their feelings, rather than thinking up new ways of putting them into words. But he seems to think nothing is real unless it is written down. The heroine of his Mayo play will be first encountered writing a letter.

She has noticed that 'lonesome' is the adjective he most uses about himself. He is nearly always lonesome in his missives to his changeling. Another word he likes to deploy is 'disappointed'. It is sprinkled over his letters like a tartish cologne. She disappoints him so often, so deeply and unforgivably, that there are times when she can't help but wonder what he is doing with her at all.

He often repeats a story she has always found curious, emblematic of him in some way neither of them quite understands: about a particular sojourn he once made in Wicklow, when the room in which he was quartered was directly above a kitchen, so that if he knelt down on the floorboards and put his ear to the chinks, he could eavesdrop on the serving girls talking below him. An admirer of Shakespeare, perhaps he thought of Pyramus and Thisbe, those lovers doomed to commune through a fissure in a wall. Maybe – is it possible? – he sees her as a conduit, a way of negotiating away that separation? It is easier for a camel to go through the eye of a needle than for a Kingstowner to navigate that eye in the floor. She is the only woman not of his class with whom he has ever been truly intimate. Unless some gurleen over in Aran? – but no. He'd be afraid. Is her role to be conductress, to allow him *admission* to something? 'Be careful not to get greasepaint in your eyes,' he once told her. Be careful yourself, she wants to reply. The twilight is not real; it is only limelight burning low. So much in the theatre is smoke and mirrors.

She sees him in the lobby of the Abbey, surrounded by admirers. Would he consent to inscribe a programme, would he shake the hand of an enthusiast? *Monsieur Synge, cher maître*, I bring you salutations from France. She watches from the half-curtained vantage of the dressing-room door, Dossie Wright and the other actors behind her, laughing, drinking. Yeats and the old lady leading him by the cuffs across the foyer, their latest exhibit, like something dug out of a bog. She wants to scream at them: *Leave him alone, you are breaking him; can you not see it? You smash the very thing you want from him.* He turns and meets her glance but offers no other acknowledgement. He vanishes in a snowstorm of compliments.

They are kissing in a printer's doorway, hands in one another's coats. He turns from her, throwing glances over his shoulder at the street. The last tram to Kingstown is about to depart. Its wet, dark windows. The people inside, wrapped up.

—*Might I see you home at least, Molly?*

—*The neighbours might notice.*

—*I wish I had the courage to ask what I want.*

—*There will be other nights again. I love you.*

The tram jolts down Sackville Street. She is alone with his ghost. Home to his mother in Kingstown.

Like many self-doubting people, he sometimes has the arrogance of a Pharaoh. She has received love letters before, but never like his. Who in the name of the suffering saints does this thread-arsed playmaker think he is? The proper mode of such correspondence, when written by men, is to pronounce oneself unworthy of the fairy-one's favours, to do a little begging and gasping about your sleeplessness, and make a few suggestive comparisons to mytho-logical hip-swingers. It doesn't matter that you don't mean it: Christ, it's only good form. But the playboy doesn't play. These are not billets-doux.

He tells her, approvingly, that she is 'pretty and quiet and nice'. Is that really what he burns for in a lover, she wonders, and is this sandwich of stone-like, deadly words the best way a poet would have of presenting it? Why does he never say exactly what he wants? If beauties were before me, stepping out of their clothes, it would be you that I'd beg for; it could only be you. Why can he never write her anything like that?

Mostly, his tone is sardonic, schoolmasterly; so brusque he seems to want to push her away. 'I will not wait for you in Bray, so don't miss your train.' 'I'm afraid I'm spoiling you by writing to you every day.' 'When I have anything I don't approve of, I'll let you know fast enough.' 'Why are you so changeable when you know how much it harms me?' He is an example of the man many women have known: the suitor who craves you but secretly wants to be dismissed.

Their quarrels are Vesuvian tirades of invective. 'You are ludicrous!' she accuses him, reefing her handkerchief into two with rage. 'You may stop your letters if you like. I don't care if I never hear from you again, so there!' She is faithless, he is 'self-pitiful', she is spiteful, he is 'an old stick in the mud'. She is making him ill. He is wearing her out. She will leave off acting and 'get a shop' if he keeps this up, or be a dancing-girl in some low pantomime, and how will he like that? One of her outbursts is countered by Glenageary's ultimate denunciation: 'You have finally *ruined* my holiday.'

They beg him at the theatre to make changes to the Mayo play. It is going to cause trouble. The patriots won't like it. You cannot portray an Irishman who *boasts* of being a murderer – a thug who has slaughtered his father! It is folly. And for the heroine to be *aroused* by his claimed brutality is tantamount to inviting the burning of the theatre. Rehearsals are uneasy. The reviewers will destroy it. The authorities will close the place down. The scene in which the peasants are seen to torture a man by fire – it is too much; it is grotesque and obscene. He will not change a word. It must be what it must. This is the role that will make her a legend, he promises. Is that what she wishes to be?

The Sunday before *The Playboy of the Western World* receives its premiere, they take a cold, rain-soaked walk from Carrickmines to Glencullen, through a boulder-strewn valley with a distant view of the Sugarloaf. That night she dreams of him in a wild garden, rhododendrons gone to seed, a hawk perched on his boot, feathers bloodstained.

He does not attend the first night: too ill, short of breath. She imagines his presence, sees him slipping in late, seated by himself in the consoling darkness of the balcony, watching her move about in the scorch of the light: the poise with which she holds herself, her strength as she speaks his lines. The fact of her speaking them, a lovemaking.

She moves across the footlights, knowing he is watching – in the black-dark windows of his fevered room in Kingstown he can see the reflections, the rage. Up here, she is the artist, he the apprentice. He is out beyond the point where anything matters. Not riots. Not hypocrisies. Not batons. Not policemen. The hatred of the crowd means nothing. Their spittle and her sweat will all be washed away, and the show will be played to the close. '*That is not the West*' a man in the audience cries out, as though he were in the play, which, in a way, he is; he will always be in it now, no matter where or in what circumstances it is ever performed again. To America, Australia, places she never thought she would see, the memory of him will follow, his denunciations ringing. And she feels for this man. She understands his grief. All those years he was told his West was a land of apes. He wants it to be a land of angels, is upset and frightened that it isn't. His grandparents starved to death in the land they were born in, a country where the idle took everything but the stones. His people died in the workhouses, on the ships, in the prisons, they were not worth the price of a grave. He cannot bear the shame and the cruelty he has inherited, spat into his face by this story. But she clings to the lines. People are screaming. As the cries grow more wounded, the insults more brutal, she pictures her lover silently mouthing his lines along with her, alone in a rainstorm on Kingstown Pier, the spray in his beard, on his clothes. She feels like weeping, but that will not happen. She breathes and speaks, she speaks and breathes, and the words he wrote in silence are pushed into the air. Acting is *breathing*: the body gives life. Some reason, a small one, but it isn't nothing, to go on existing in this vicious world, where hurts abound, and the body fails, and the crushed hopes of childhood are never far away. It is an act of mercy, the thing she does every night. She breathes for him; allows him to die temporarily. Most nights, he stays at home.

The neighbours in Mary Street give long, cold glares. The whole town is speaking of that filthy, vile play. A disgrace to Irish womanhood. A libel on the peasantry. A cur who savages his father; the Jezebel who lusts for him — imagine such a crawling horror on *the stage of a Christian city*. The traitress who would demean herself by appearing in this affront to a people's innocence — could she ever be forgiven such a betrayal?

A LETTER TO *THE TIMES*

November 1952

Sir –

Something will have to be done about the number of indigent persons roaming London. Recently, whilst on a visit to our capital city, I happened to cross Trafalgar Square at approximately half-past twelve on a weekday, accompanied by my wife and our daughter. We were assailed by the sight of a woman of not inconsiderably advanced years who was asleep at the base of Nelson's Column. A bottle was visible in this female's hand. She was in a condition of quite revolting disarray. As a taxpayer, and as one who served his kingdom proudly in time of war, I was affronted and not inconsiderably angered that I should have to subsidise the indolence of a person such as this, who should know that impressionable younger people might be going about their business, not to mention the effect on visitors to the city. The female, on being approached by a member of the constabulary, proved herself a native of a neighbouring island – I might add, a Republic – that has been notably far from friendly to Her Majesty's subjects, whilst continuing to export multitudes of her own. It really is 'a bit Irish', if I might coin a popular phrase.

Yours, etcetera,
Concerned rates-payer from Berkshire.

INTERMISSION AT GLENCREE

Two people are walking the rutted, tussocked cart track that leads northward out of the village of Annamoe, in County Wicklow, through country of tweedy purples and rain-bleached umbers and hip-high ripening barley. Past stone-filled, hilly, irregularly shaped fields that are bordered by low walls of lichen-yellowed boulders. At the edges of the meadows, masses of wet bluebells under low-grown, crooked willows. The stillness so pleasing; the damp Irish emptiness and the faint smell of rained-on goats.

It has rained the night before, it has rained all night; but as the sun rises higher, slow as molasses, the morning warms and mellows, and a coconut aroma arises from the gorse-covered outcrops. A ewe emerges cautiously from a tumbled thatchless cottage that has bog cotton growing in its rafters. Seeing the man and the bicycle and the girl go past, it stares as though rooted by an apparition. The strange bloom of the red bracken in the early morning sun is like the sheen, remarks the man, from a pregnant woman's skin.

'Like the what?' she laughs.

'Is that not right?'

'It's away with the faeries you are.'

Tufts of sheep-fleece on the jags of rusting barbed wire. Rainwater pooling in the lowland meadows.

Nine miles they walk until the track becomes little more than a footpath, overgrown here and there by nettles and black-berry copses grown madwoman crazy from neglect. The curlew.

The gannet. Do you remember those, too? He was telling you their Latin names.

They climb the cliff track slowly; it is stony and loose. He sweats as he wheels the old bicycle. The girl is suffering in the heat, but the man, being a man, is permitted to unfasten his shirt. Oh the air lividly murmurous with bees and wasps. Armies of water midges in the puddled, narrow laneways that are formed by the high, wild hedgerows. The girl, a city-dweller, beats at the air around her. 'They'd have you demented,' she says.

Crushed butterwort and heather and the odour of mountain chives. Sheep-shit, honeysuckle, bog myrtle and rose-root; the sweetness of wet wild strawberries. In the distance, breasting the coast, the southbound train from Dublin leaves an after-thought of smoke in its wake. The trundling of its engine is borne faintly to them on a breeze that smells of the peat and the dulse. A shrieked, mournful hoot as it chugs into a tunnel gouged years ago through the groin of Eagle Mountain. The cry summons a neighbour's boy, a cellar-digger by trade, who emigrated to Brooklyn and died in an explosion there. Beyond the tracks, the sea is an impossible colour – the iridescent blue of the Virgin's sash in a Renaissance Italian altar-panel the man once showed her in the gallery. And they can see the little pleasure-boats that ply out of Greystones and the fishermen's smacks trailing petticoats of netting, but an immensity of gnarled granite arises through the breakers, lending strangeness, an anxiety, to the scene. Around the island bob black coracles, from which navvies hurry with grapples, and with slates and jemmies and spikes and coils of chain, for they are constructing a beacon on that wave-beaten rock – the old lighthouse has been decommissioned.

The girl and her companion take turns with his telescope. The task will be gruelling, the man mutters. She watches a soldier on the crag driving in iron stakes with a mallet; his high, hard, rhythmic swings. Like any living creature observed through a tele-scope, he looks mysterious, otherworldly as an angel. A sergeant is bawling at him but she cannot hear his commands. The soldier strikes harder with the hammer.

They walk on. The bicycle creaks. The map he has is old, has been folded so many times that its creases are frayed quite through. Someone has inked contour lines here and there on its quadrants, as though the declivities they reference have somehow not been noticed by the cartographer. A bookplate has been pasted on to its cover near the cartouche, reading *Ex Libris Trinity College Dublin*. Below it, in elegant copperplate, a hand not the man's has inscribed a curious rhyme.

> *If this chart — thou steal'st away,*
> *What shalt thou say*
> *— On Judgment Day?*
> *Yet if this map be — wrongly drawn*
> *Trav'ller — mercy — from thy scorn.*

She reads the final couplet aloud. He chuckles at her pronunciation. In his accent, it rhymes. In hers, it does not. For less have millions starved.

It was stormy last night; an angry wind roared up the mouth of the Liffey. Soldiers from the barracks were mustered to Phoenix Park; a stand of ancient elms had been toppled in the Lord-Lieutenant's demesne, threatening the stable-blocks and guest quarters and the ice-house. It had seemed to the girl that the holiday plotted so carefully and long might have to be postponed a little longer. Each of them had told lies so as to allow it to happen. The hurricane was troubling, its so-sudden coming-on an intimation of exposure, punishment. The bilious roar of thunder. She could not face the bed she shared with her sisters. It was summertime in Ireland again.

The gaslight in the kitchen was warm, consoling. Her brother came in from his work. His dress suit was soaked — his work was waiting tables — and she helped him out of the waterlogged jacket. The restaurant had been busy. A party from the Castle. 'West Brits and the turncoats who lick them.' No more give you a tip than the steam off their piss. Like many who make a living being fleetingly pleasant to strangers, his belligerence at home was almost constant. But his vehemence could be softened when his favourite sister was present, becoming merely a role he seemed to feel he had to play for her: the long-suffering drudge, the put-upon mule, the man forced to live amongst women.

'There's a night. Where's Mother?' His eyes were glimmering.

'She went out to the sodality. She'll be home in a while.'

'Mother of Jesus, were we running. *Your* friend was there. That character Yeats. I'd say he says more than his prayers.'

'Sit in to the table, Georgie, till I heat up your supper.'

'That's a covey I'd no more trust than I could spit a bloody rat. Says I: You know my sister, sir, she's below in your play-house. Know what he says to me?'

'We've no bread in the house, Georgie. Will you take a mug of porter?'

'*She has a most refained speaking voice.* Staring up at me so he was, the dirty long drink of water. And his butties all chuckling into the soup like lords and they shaking the oyster sauce off their dewlaps. D'make you heave up your supper at the sight so it would. And the talk out of them – Jesus almighty. Some play-maker was with them and he spouting more drivel than you'd hear in a leap year's travel. Manners of a carthorse, the whole plain crew. They'd nearly shite trotting if they were let.'

The whomp of her heart like a breaker striking a ship.

'Don't be cursing in the house, Georgie. Do you want the porter?'

'Ah, go and boil the back of my arse.'

'If you want it, it's there. I've washing to see to.'

'You're gone fierce secretive lately. There's nothing the matter?'

'No, Georgie. I'm fine. Eat your supper.'

A go-between came at midnight, saying the appointment still held, she was to be at Westland Row station at dawn, was to sit in the fourteenth carriage. The man would board the train when it pulled into Glenageary. She was not to acknowledge or greet him.

'Who was that article,' demanded her mother, 'and he calling at this hour?'

'Only a boy from the theatre saying the tour isn't cancelled.'

'I'll theatre him now. And yourself along with him. And you streeling to the door of a Christian house in the black-dark night in your pelt. *Close up your buttons for the sanctified Jesus.* Is it a wet-nurse I'm after raring? Or worse?'

At the summit of Henry's Hill they come to the triangulation point that was placed there, he tells her, by Queen Victoria's sappers. The last of the haze is burning away; the day, they know now, will be violently hot, as a drover in Annamoe predicted when they approached him for directions. Below them, in the glen, is an L-shaped whitewashed cabin surrounded by the remains of a tillage field. No road leads down to the homestead but there is a trail worn through the sedge-grass, and as they pick their way along it they see head-high bulrushes, hear the mournful croaking of frogs.

The cottage is unlocked, its door on the latch, its foot-long key inside on a hook. Cauldrons hanging from the rafters and in the cinder-filled hearth. A cracked daguerreotype of Daniel O'Connell over the inglenook. The room smells of linseed and musty old linen that wasn't allowed to dry properly after laundering. On the mantelshelf is a black candle that has no wick, and he looks at it curiously and hefts it in his hand. She has to tell him it is a cake of furniture polish.

The room contains a bed in a rusting iron frame that someone has long ago distempered black but the paint is flaking badly.

'What is that you're after taking out of your haversack, John?'

'A hammock, you owl. I shall naturally sleep outside.'

'That it may keep fine for you,' she says, nonplussed.

———————————

The nearest shop is at a distance of eleven miles. In the mornings, very early, he bicycles to Annamoe for bread, fresh eggs, yesterday's London *Times*. ('Should anything of consequence be occurring in Ireland, it will be reported in the London *Times*.') If the huckster's is open he buys butter, tobacco. He likes to converse with the postmaster and his three dirty children who are 'surly as Satan', he says. Sometimes he makes photographs of the villagers or their houses. He can be gone three hours or more.

While he is away, she sweeps the cabin, goes down to the streamlet for water, launders their clothes; reads quietly in the ruined yard. She finds the thought exciting that her mother does not know where she is. She has lied to her mother for the sake of a man. It has the makings of a novel or a certain sort of play. She wonders who the leading character is.

What is her mother doing now? Probably opening the shop, or sitting among the tallboys and wardrobes in the window, fingering her beads and waiting. She is a small, jolly, disenchanted woman, who, if you lick her hand playfully, as her younger children sometimes do, tastes faintly of disappointment. She was once haughtily beautiful, so the neighbours attest, cruel-tongued and dark and Spanish-looking. Every boy in the Liberties was destroyed by her in his time; her choice of husband disappointed her parents. *They were right*, she says. *I hadn't a pick of sense*. She has a tiny back kitchen 'for the steam and the smells'. Marriage smells of cabbage and twice-boiled mutton and towards the end of the week, of dripping. 'A man's body is the map of Ireland. Keep your hand away from Limerick. And if any of youse shame this house by coming home with a surprise in your belly, do you know what will happen before you've the door on the latch? I'll put your grandmother out on the street – not you.'

Difficult to read in the flat dead heat. The sunshine on the yellowed old pages. She attempts to make use of his hammock but the midges are so numerous beneath the twin bent yews that it is impossible to lie still for long. What is the history of this field, this cabin? Were children ever born here? Where are they now? And that rusted double bed with its creaking quoits – but it is better not to imagine such scenes. She finds a crumpled dollar bill that has been glued beneath the dresser, the words *'do not tell him'* inked across Abraham Lincoln's face. On St James's Eve — she is wildly over-imaginative, he has often teased her — she turns in the yard, her blood shocked to riot, convinced she has heard an infant mewling from the midden-heap. But it is only a cat in heat.

They hike to the abandoned lighthouse. The claustrophically narrow spiral staircase, its heavy blockwork leading up to the beacon room. The putty around the shattered panes flaking to powder in her fingertips. In the distance, to the south, several miles down the coast, is the jagged island from which the arising beacon will glitter in two years. He will be dead by then. But neither of them knows it. They look out at the spray and the seabirds. In the bole of an oak she finds an eyeless rag doll, arms and legs gnawed to flitters.

One morning she bathes naked in Aurora Lake, the water fierily cold, lacings of moss on its surface. The echo of the corncrakes on the scree-terraced cliffs. She sees him silhouetted on the hill-side as he returns from the village, pedalling hard, his cape trailing behind him. She calls out but some trick of the water means that he cannot hear her. Wild swans in the sky. An eagle.

There is a script of Lady Gregory's she has to learn: her role is difficult, complex. He reads the other parts for her, offers insights. He is a laughably dreadful actor, hamming lines, waving his arms, stomping around the cabin soliloquising to the rafters. His attempt at a Connemara accent would cause a turnip to cringe, but he knows he is no good so it doesn't matter. He batters the love lines by saying them too loud, eviscerates the hate lines by speaking them too quietly, misses cues, waits too long, stutters, interrupts, and lisps when he means to be menacing. His oath-swearing warriors are gibbering clowns and his warlocks are effete English head-masters. One night he insists on donning a bedspread as the mystical robe of Cuchulainn. He raves in it, eyes bulging, his trouser-legs rolled up, his finger pointing vengeance on the fireplace.

After a few days he comes to look like a countryman: sunburnt, dishevelled, his hair and beard bleaching, red earth on his clothes. His bleak, grey eyes seem filled with reflections. His stockings are holed. She darns them.

'There is a wasp in your beard, John. Sit you easy till I get a cloth for to flurry it.'

'It will not sting me, don't worry.'

'How do you know?'

'They smell the sickness in my blood. It repels them.'

'Don't be daft.'

'Or perhaps they are afraid of Protestants.'

He has heard it said there is a Wicklow mushroom that has hallucinogenic properties. One sees visions and phantoms if one eats it. ('Old Yeats tried some once. Sent him out of his mind. Course, he didn't have far to go.') She loves when he mimics Yeats; it is remorselessly accurate – the gestures, the accent, the studied floridness of expression. It is as though they are naughty schoolchildren lampooning a master who might materialise through the floorboards at any moment.

'You're an awful cur to go making a jeer of Mr Yeats. And I thinking youse the greatest friends ever heard of.'

'*You*, my little dunce. I shall put you across my knee. "Ewes" is the plural of mature female sheep.'

'Oh is it, Professor? I'll wax your moustache for you in a minute.'

'Poor, trying old Yeats. I adore him, of course. He is so slow and fierce and sleek and subtle. Like a great silverback gorilla in a cummerbund. His valet strips him down and shaves his back of a morning, did you know?'

'He goes down like a dinner with Her Ladyship anyhow.'

'Darling old Augusta. You know she breast-feeds him, don't you? Every night during the second interval.'

'That is enough blah out of you now. Let me alone to read, you scruff-hound.'

'Actually I tell a lie. You do realise Augusta is a man?'

'Would you quit your playacting this minute and give me some peace!'

'Willie Fay told me he dandered into the jakes at the Abbey one morning and here's Augusta, saving your presence, making Adam's ale standing. Says Augusta: *Me bould hack, that's the soft day now*. Says Fay: *Deed and it is, Ma'am, thank God*. And the two of them a-widdle like water-clocks in a fountain. Told me she pissed like a buffalo.'

'There's talk out of you now. Merciful hour but you're lovely.'

He finds a sickle in the thatch of the cottage and takes it into the forest, returning with an armful of nettles he asks her to boil, but the slick, green juice is too bitter. Vital to exercise caution in the countryside of Ireland, for certain of the flora can kill you. The berries of a yew, so lusciously scarlet, have poisoned whole legions of the ignorant.

———

One morning she is wandering the laneways while he is away to Annamoe for bread, when a young policeman approaches on a bicycle. He is handsome, like a boxer, and he salutes as he dismounts. He is the girl's own age, perhaps.

Walking up the boreen with the constable at her side, she makes small talk about the weather, the birds. The constable is a Mayoman, 'a blow-in' as he puts it, and the phrase seems to hang in the air between them. It is clear he knows she is one of the people staying at the cottage. He is a policeman: omniscience is his trade. A boy returning from haymaking with a scythe over his shoulder glances back at the curious combination as they continue along the lane. The gorse in the fields smells richly sweet. You could hang a hat on the constable's cheekbones.

'I'm told himself is a writer, Miss.'

'He is. Well, he tries.'

'Sure, that's all any of us can do in the end.'

'It is.'

'My father now, God be good to him. That was the man could tell a story if you like, Miss. When the neighbours came in of a winter's night. They do talk of him yet in the townland down at home – though he's gone this fourteen year. He'd have you in transports with a story so he would.'

'Would he?'

'Of the hard days, you know, Miss, when the Famine was in it. The people and they going to America. He'd a queer enough story of how the big house got burnt one time and himself and the brother tried to save the landlord's family. But the flames was gone too high on him so he couldn't do aught for it. He was harrowed by it. You know, Miss. The not being able to do nothing. For there was childer in the house, a little fellow there was. Never done a harm to no one, a little puppy, no more. The mother said he was never the same after.'

'They were terrible times. When you think of the suffering.'

'Indeed and they were. It's better off out of them we are. The people set against one another and murder walking the country. God send we'll never see the likes again.'

'Well, we're coming to the cabin. Would you take a cup of tea?'

'Faith, I would if it's no trouble, Miss. It's gracious of you now.'

He walks around the ruined garden, looking silently at the ground, before approaching a little shed and examining its lock. He tries the bolt once or twice. She makes him his tea. He removes his beautiful cap and places it carefully on a boulder.

'We can't change the past, Miss. In't that the way it is?'

'That's what my mother does be saying.'

'And himself is away to Annamoe. Is it long he's going to be?'

'Two or three hours. Sometimes more.'

'More, I'd be thinking. Annamoe's the road will sort them.'

Wind moves the branches and a filigree of sunlight surrounds him. He toes speculatively at the earth as though the action might uncover something. Bending, he picks up a fist-sized, mossy stone, which he throws into a distant field.

'The auld aim is gone on me,' he says with a laugh. 'One time I'd have hit a crow from forty yards.'

'You've a strong throw,' she says. 'I've a brother plays handball.'

'Used to play it the odd time myself. Down in Mayo, I mean. There wouldn't be the call for it in Wicklow.'

She watches as he throws, the *huff* as he releases, pictures him naked in a river, his tough body sunburnt as he bends to wash his shining black hair. Or inside in the cabin. Slowly barring the door. Watching as you unbutton your dress. God forgive you but it would be wonderful to be bedded a lazy hour by someone so hard and young. No love, no words, no past, no future, just his sweat dripping on your face and your back and your breasts. Christ, a bull he'd be like; you'd be destroyed with the pleasure. It would be worth a thousand years of Purgatory. Do men have such thoughts? Do other women, too? Does your Tramp? Does the young policeman?

'You'll be busy today, so? Or just going the roads?'

'I've to take myself up to Enniskerry with the sergeant later on. There was a house robbed the other night. A bad business.'

'Aren't you brave? I wouldn't envy you. Will you catch them that did it?'

'I don't know about that now. I'd say they're flown, the same heroes. I was up with the squire yester-morning. He's a decent auld sort. Says I: "You'd want to keep a weather eye on any girleen in the house, sir. A housemaid or that. You're a man of the world, sir. Only some of the girls that's going now do keep queer enough company. They say more than their prayers, the same young-ones."'

'Aren't you an awful man now, to go blaming everything on the girls.'

'God keep your innocence, Miss. That it might always be your blessing. But a young-one today, her head can be turned. These flyboys do be clever as Satan in brogues. They do hang about the dance halls and they sly as you want, with an eye for the decent girl in service. Or above on the esplanade in Bray when the girls do be walking. It's allanah macree and the old sweet song and they talking the rain out of wetting them. The same fox will inveigle his cunning way. I needn't tell you how, Miss. Some girls has no sense. Next thing we know it's when does your mistress be out? Would there be e'er a bob of money left about in the house? Is there silver you do be polishing? Aren't you the great lassie now. We've seen many such cases in recent times. And the girleen ruined, to boot.'

'It's well they've yourself to protect their honour all the same.'

'The sergeant does say there's more harm done in Ireland by dance halls and courting than all the dynamite ever come from America.'

'What a terrible auld misery. And have you no sweetheart yourself?'

'There was one I was great with. But she went to Massachusetts on me in the end. Two year we were courting – near enough to two year. I thought we'd be married. But didn't she change her mind for Boston. Last Martinmas a year ago she went.'

'And you've not been with another? Not in all that time?'

Everything in the garden is silent for a moment. A blackbird arises from a cluster of rhododendrons. It settles on the roof of the pigsty near the kitchen beds and seems to cock its wise face at the sky. The constable's eyes are steady as he meets the girl's gaze.

'If they all looked like yourself, Miss, the world would be sweet.'

She feels herself flare. The stillness of the heather. No one would ever know. Only the blackbird and the midges.

'I'd better let you go on,' she says, very quietly.

'If you're certain, so, Miss . . . God keep you.'

Sometimes in the evenings he sings melancholy songs in Gaelic, the knowledge of which he is trying to improve in her. He sings with his eyes closed like a whiskied balladeer, rocking himself gently, his arms folded tight, or his hands reaching out to some spectral invisibility summoned or driven away by language. His voice is not strong; his breathing is so pained, and at night it becomes frailer, a wheeze that often makes him tremble, but he knows about timing and drama in a song. He allows the mournful couplets to fall on you like leaves – the pleadings, the entreaties, the dark imprecations.

> *You have taken the east from me.*
> *You have taken the west from me.*
> *And my fear is great*
> *You have taken great God from me.*

'Come sit on my lap, Molly.'

'We know where that leads.'

'Don't you like where it leads, my little innocent wildcat?'

'Very sharp now, Mister, and mind you don't cut yourself.'

He grows stronger, gains weight, hiking ten miles every day, over stony rough country, fording rivers, climbing cliffs. He finds a long-forgotten track that leads through Crone Wood to Powerscourt waterfall. ('I name it Molly's Path! Hallelujah.') He becomes convinced of the existence of a holy well in the valley, goes scouting for it with the aid of his ancient map. But it is his changeling who finds it, pulling back the thorn bush. The water is oily black.

'Throw a leaf in it for luck, Molly.'

'More likely I'll do something else in it.'

'Holy Moses, but you have the mouth of a harlot.'

'You like my mouth sometimes. Or so you do be telling me.'

'Mary O'Neill. I despair of you.'

He comes to her one evening while they are walking in the pinewood, asking with his hands and his eyes. Unfasten your dress, love. Think it no sin. A stag bounds from a copse, its hair-trigger hearing startled by her whispers as she comes.

She washes her hair in the sandy waters of Considine's Lake.

The dirt of the city seems to sweat itself out. It is as though a layer of her skin has been removed.

He reads Racine, Pierre Loti, translates Shakespeare's 130th sonnet into Irish – or tries to, abandoning the attempt after a day. 'No good writer can ever be translated,' he says, and she teases him for making excuses. He quaffs the sweet country milk a quart at a time, sometimes with a capful of whiskey 'for luck', as the fishermen on Aranmore taught him. The taste of Wicklow buttermilk has him moaning with pleasure. 'Oh, you simply must try it, Molly. They drank it on Olympus.' It trickles through his beard and he laps at himself like a dog, laughing all the while, or sighing. He eats hungrily, with great relish, often without speaking, mopping at his plate with his bread.

There comes a day of golden sumptuousness, the shifting breezes scented with wild rosemary. Every blade of snipegrass can be heard as it grows or is mown into sweet-smelling death. Larks and blue linnets arise from the furrows as she walks to the streamlet in the morning. Within, she feels the pulse and run of her blood, the calendar of the body, its flow.

There is a fish among the osiers, a small silver trout, and she knows she could grasp it if that was her desire and kiss its lipless mouth before releasing it. If you do such a thing, the fish will speak a blessing, telling the name of your true-love and the name of your husband. If it utters only one name you will be the happy girl indeed.

He glances up, dazed with reading; gives a drowsy, abashed smile.

'Would there be e'er a drain o' tay itself for a Christian tongue?'

'Wusha, Misther, but there would, and I wettin it now in a minute.'

'May the shadow of you never grow shorter.'

It has become part of their love talk, this mockery of his lines. They speak to one another like characters in one of his plays. His smile is like the sparkling of sun on dark water. Something in being mocked by her delights him.

She rises earlier, in the quarter-light, at the first reddening of the mountain, so as to make the days last longer. To walk the wet fields through the wakening birdsong is to feel the marriage of joy and sadness, the black miracles of the trees. A tinker comes daily with buttermilk and apples. Breakfast often lasts an hour.

To stir in sleep beside him. To know he is there. The warm male aroma and the rhythm of his breathing, and the moon making shadows of the oak boughs. But close to dawn one morning he flails awake from a nightmare.

'I dreamed I had lost you. My father was there.'

'Your father?'

'I think so. Sweet Christ.'

One day, having lain together, they laze on in the heather-beds looking up at the corncrakes they have frightened off with their cries. The scent of bog myrtle and lavender and willowherb. There is sweet sleepiness in him at such moments; he is like a tender boy. He tells her his imaginings of New York.

'We shall go there when I recover. They would adore you in America. You would conquer whole cities. They live very freely. They are like every people who have rid themselves of aristo-cracies: obsessed by the differences between the classes. They love beauty and bravery. I do not understand them. They are the most magnificent people in the world.'

He cuts his hand while shortening firewood; she bathes it, dresses it. He covers her pillowslip with wild asphodels from the heath. He carves her name in an alder.

There comes a rainy afternoon when he kisses her breasts for what feels a whole hour, until she begs him, with profane murmurs, to go further. Then her hands gripping hard to the rungs of the bedstead; she had never imagined a man's mouth could be so gentle. Afterwards she does not want to look at him, feels opened, revealed. There is a quietness after the storm.

He reaches and takes from her hair a length of broken wheatgrass.

'A penny for your thoughts, my brown-eyes.'

'Have you been with many girls, John?'

'Not many. A few in France.'

'Did you love them?'

'I thought so. There was one I thought I loved.'

She pushes him and he laughs again, running the blade of wheat across her wet nipples, then kissing her hair and face.

'You smell of strawberry leaves,' he whispers. 'I adore you. My little succulence.'

'I'll strawberry *you* in a minute. Tell me about her, so. My rival.'

'Oh it was all very long ago. There were differences of religion.'

'She was Catholic?'

'No. She was a Plymouth Brethren. She was a neighbour of ours in Kingstown.'

'Did she break your poor heart?'

He pauses a long time before replying. 'I was younger. I suppose I thought so. I was a very different person then. But none of it matters any more. My little elf.'

Atkinson's Gazetteer to Great Britain
including Ireland
For Amblers, Ramblers & Cavers

At nights, while he is working, she reads in his guidebook, the spine of which is cracked and the mouldering pages loose. He has underscored many lines – whole passages sometimes. She ponders them for what they might reveal of him.

The bosom of Wicklow affords the inner man a plethora of delights, her natives being amenably charming to the visitor, possessing the pleasing, happy countenances of those of Her Majesty's contented subjects encountered in the Empire's sunnier climes.

He begins writing a novel set in a hospital, sorting notes, shaping scenes. She hears him mumbling to his characters the way he sometimes speaks to her: nagging, cajoling, begging them to come to him. '*Whore's bastard, come out!*' he bawls so hard that the rooks go clattering from the thatch. As though the words are midges around him and his task is to grasp a particular one of them. She pictures him in a swarm of language.

He reads her a drafted chapter as she soaks in the old beaten-copper bathtub, the water reeking deliciously of turf. She tells him it isn't good. He knows, he says. That night they watch a gorse fire spreading across Lugnaquilla, red and golden flames, jags of purple sparks, tiny black figures hurrying through the glow with pitchforks, billhooks and scythes.

'Oh, I shall be gone for the afternoon. You shall have a little peace. I said I would lunch with Yeats. He is visiting at Powerscourt. It will be tedious but it has to be faced.'

'You didn't tell me before.'

'It slipped my mind, I am sorry.'

'Should I come with you? Would you mind? It would be nice to have an outing.'

'Yeats . . .' he pauses, 'does not know quite the extent of our friendship. As I think you are aware. I had been meaning to apprise him. He is rather old-fashioned sometimes. Curiously so.'

'Couldn't we say it was a coincidence? You met me in Annamoe. I was visiting a friend who was sick.'

'Oh, the conversation would bore you. You know how Yeats drones on. Rather too much for the white man to bear. I shall escape by five at the latest.'

'But it's only gone nine in the morning. What am I to do the whole day?'

'I shall be back before dark. Unless you wish me not to go.'

'Of course you must go if you gave your word to Mr Yeats.'

'Your tone of voice surprises me. I have upset you, I think.'

By midnight he has not returned. The night is full of sounds. The last candle in the cabin burns low. A wind buffets up, and the haw near the window begins a bleak insistent tap on the glass. The bedding reeks of his soap, of the unguent for his chest. The candle gutters out with a last jig of shadows. The smell of molten wax haunts the room.

In the small hours she arises, suddenly maddened by thirst, and goes dazedly to the ewer by the window. The tiny yellow globe of a storm lantern in the distance.

'John?' she calls out. The light stops moving. And somehow she knows it isn't his.

She slams and bars the door. Realises she is shaking. Watches as the lantern-light approaches through the blue gloom, hears the trudge of heavy footsteps, the low male voices. Three — maybe four — it is hard to be certain. Boots on the gravel. Coughs.

'I was frightened half to death. Why wouldn't I and the heart put across me! And you sitting up at Powerscourt on your sweet Fanny Brown.'

'They were probably only poachers. Or gamekeepers, perhaps.' He gives his soft, eluding laugh and peers away towards the lake. 'They are often the same thing, of course. Especially in Wicklow. I am sorry you were alarmed. My little sparrow.'

It is only later, at the back of the cabin, that they see the freshly whitewashed words.

EVICTORS GET OUT OR BE GOT

'So they have come,' he says quietly. 'We were too happy.'

'But — what do they mean, John? What call had they to go writing that?'

He regards the distant Sugarloaf, the bitterns wheeling and hooting. For what seems a long time he offers no response, and when finally he speaks it is as though something new has happened to him or a discomfiting light has been shone into his eyes by someone he can't quite see. 'There were incidents in the past. On my family's estate. I wish to say no more about the matter.'

'But not evictions, surely?'

He seems to be ageing as you watch him.

'John? Not evictions? Why can't you look at me?'

'They refused to pay their arrears. What could we do for it? There were agitators among them of the very worst sort. Revolutionaries, seditionists, call them what you will. My brother – he is the land agent – attempted to find common ground. He is a good man, my brother. He sought the common ground. But they acted like stubborn children, refusing all compromise. It was a wretched bloody business and I am very thoroughly sick of it.'

'How many?'

'Can that matter?'

She looks at him closely.

'I think seven.'

'Seven people?'

'Seven families. Or eight.'

'But John – that could be forty people. You put them out on the road?'

'*I* put them nowhere. *I* put them nowhere! I was living in Paris, I knew nothing of the matter and neither was I asked an opinion.'

'And had you been?'

'They refused to assist themselves, to take the slightest *responsibility* –'

She continues, riding over him. '*Had you been?*'

'Some of them had paid no rent in fifteen years. Why do you look at me like that? I was living in Paris. What is it in these people that must always crave trouble? One despairs of whatever it is that must always *inflame* in this godforsaken sewer of a country.'

'If by *these people* you mean the poor –'

'That is not what I meant.'

'Are their families to starve?'

'*Is mine?*'

'You are ridiculous. Do you know that? Why play the village idiot?'

'Is my mother to go hungry? That income is all she has. Will you help me fetch some water, Molly? I will wash that filth away.'

'John —'

'I did not make the world, Molly. Neither did you. I am going to the lake. For water.'

An old peasant woman appears in the lane with a ram on a string and a creel of black turf on her shoulder. She looks like the Comanche chieftain on the cover of his almanac. She begs a smoke of his pipe. She has a son in Illinois.

He tries to speak to her in Gaelic, of local legend, folkways, the place names of rural north Wicklow. Has she memories of the Famine? Has she people in England? She does not understand what he is saying. When he explains that he is speaking Irish, she regards him amiably enough, as one might smile on an arch child who has asked an inconvenient question. There was a professor from Germany here in the Glen last summer, and scarves of the blessed Gaelic flowing out of his mouth (God be good to Your Honour but you never heard the likes) with a notebook the size of the Protestant Bible and a huntsman's feather cawpeen on his head. And he traipsing up the bogs with the book in his oxter and he asking th'aul bogmen for legends. And they scratching themselves in their waterboots beyond in the river and your man shouting down to them about Vikings. Tormented he'd have you. Had you stories of saints? Had you ever shtuck a pig? Were you Christian at all, like? Faith, but he would fairly ask you what you do be having for breakfast in the morning, things a *peeler* wouldn't ask you this ploughboy would ask, and the hunger and th'emigration and all th'auld sorrows and he wishing to be writing them in his book. And saving your presence, only who would be reading that? If a body *could* read. Which wasn't likely here in the Glen. And devil the hunger nor a soul ever knew that a book of this world could sate, sir. In't there misery enough now, don't you think, in the world, without adding to it by writing it down, sir? We must laugh at the devil, sir, in't that the only way? Laugh, and the devil does be frit. But this German professor or whatever else he was, God keep him alive, sir, and no disrespect to His Honour, but he'd nearly be disappointed no one belonging to you never got drownded nor got the belly kicked off him be a redcoat. Away with him to Germany and little to show. Nobody around here could remember nothing.

'Silly-headed old wagon.'

'Droleen, please.'

'It's in the Bedlam asylum should be the likes of herself. I don't know why you go talking to them at all.'

'They interest me. The people. They are like the ancient Greeks.'

'They are like my sanctified arse.'

'I wish you would not speak in that uncouth manner.'

'Did you see the maggoty beard on her? She was worse than the ram. Like a sow staring into a swill barrel.'

'I said I wish you would not speak in that uncouth manner, Molly.'

'Oh do you, My Lord? Well I'm awfully worried.'

'Nevertheless. Why do you conduct yourself like that when you know it hurts me? The poor woman has done you no harm. Your attitude unnerved her.'

He is whittling a lump of oak he found in the bog.

'There is something troubling you, I think.'

'No, John. I am tired.'

'What is it?'

'Well, since you ask – Could we not be married?'

He thumbs at a nodule of candle grease on the tabletop, takes a long, slow breath, like a tenor about to commence an aria. 'I am impatient too. But there are various impediments, as you know. We shall have to show forbearance a while more.'

'How much of a while more? Till we are old and grey, is it? Is it swither and dither till we've not a tooth left between us?'

'My health is fragile since the surgery. You know this very well.'

'That fragile it couldn't stand a blessing and a sprinkle of confetti?'

'I have not the means to support a wife. Surely you can see this.'

'I am worn out telling you it need not matter.'

'It would obviously matter to me, though. As a man, it would matter. And what would people say if it were seen that I could not maintain my wife? The gossips would have a carnival. As you know.'

She rises quickly from the bench and busies herself at the old dresser where the plates and tableware are kept.

'In any case, what is marriage but the final admission that one's parents were right? It is the dreariest way imaginable for society to regulate the natural impulse.'

'The natural impulse?'

'Well, what would you call it?'

'I have heard it called many things. One of them is love, John.'

'Ah yes – love. The dressmaker's friend.'

She looks at him and drops a heavy stack of delft on the flag-stones, where some pieces smash and others roll about, and a platter cracks cleanly into three. The jags are blue and white, like broken bits of the sky. Something in the chimney gives a scuttle.

'What in the name of Holy Moses are you doing?'

'You huer's melt and cur. You may leave me well alone from this out. You may sleep in your blasted *hammock*, my buck.'

'Is the hysteria to continue, do you know, at all?' His words are measured carefully but she can see that he is frightened. It interests her to glimpse his helplessness before a woman's anger and she wonders about the source of that fear. He blurs in her eyes as she commences to weep. He takes the broom from its hook, his boots scrunching quietly on the debris.

'If you open the door, I shall help you clear up, Molly. These little accidents happen.'

She begins to pack her clothes into the ancient carpetbag she always brings on tour.

'So you will leave when I need you? How do you intend returning to Dublin?'

'On my feet if I must. I am damn well able to walk. It's the only useful thing knowing yourself ever taught me.'

'You are ridiculous, of course. You will jeopardise everything.'

'Do I take it that you will refuse me a shilling for a train fare?'

'For the love of Christ, woman, need you act in this manner?'

'Call it payment if you like. *Call it payment!* Do you mind me? I want never to see your liar's face again.'

A tour in northern England. Then Wales. Then Scotland. His telegrams and letters you ignored. But speaking his lines every night brought him to you anyway. A ferociousness to his words, full of deliberate discords in their arrangement, that would make you draw in your breath and mutter and turn to your neighbour and feel strange things were being named in the room.

What had happened between you became a thing that would have to be let go. You sensed the messages from him were either a duty he felt he had to keep faith with or a sort of weaning-off he needed too. You were unmooring one another. Perhaps nobody would be hurt. One evening after a performance in Manchester, you went walking with your sister and told her a little of your feelings, of the promises not kept. She pointed out that you were speaking of him in the past tense now, advised you to allow him a last chance. What was holding you back? You owed it to yourself to try. The worst that could happen was a final rejection, but could you continue in the lie that you did not care for him any more, a fiction you must surely be able to recognise?

You dreamed of Wicklow: hidden lakes, the ruins of old mines, bog meadows, Ravens' Glen, the waterfall at Powerscourt. You had been a reason to visit again the places of his childhood summers — that was all you had been: a diversion. A reason to speak the place names he found soothing to say, the words sounding beautiful in his Kingstown accent: Djouce Mountain, Tonduff, Carrickgollogan. Knocksink. Aughavanna, Glenmalure, Annamoe, Lough Nahanagan. The graves in the Protestant churchyard at Enniskerry, not far from Lover's Leap rock. You had asked him to show you his favourite view of all; he'd brought you hiking up a switchback path above the forest at Kilmolin. On the eastern horizon you could make out the peaks of Snowdonia, the bald drumlin of Holy Island at the entrance to Holyhead. You dreamed of that vista and awoke in a boarding house in Liverpool. There was a letter from him waiting. You burned it.

Manchester, Oxford. The Medway towns. York. Carlisle. Great Yarmouth. You dreamed of being with him at Brittas Bay, grim sandwiches in the dunes, and of the ruins of a fairy ring near a maltings at Arklow, still transmitting its menace a thousand years after it was made, according to the children hunting wrens nearby. A farmer had tried to fell it; his hammer had burst into flames the moment he entered the rath — he was dead before it hit the ground. 'That's as true as Jesus, Mister, I seen it myself.'

'Way to God, you gowl,' scoffed another lad, whispering lowly to his girl. But the first boy insisted on the veracity of the story. 'I'd no more cross that circle than pish on a grave. They'd come after you, so they would. They're evil, so they are. An oul tinker used to live up the way told me ma the fairies took his wife. An you seen him yourself you'd believe it.'

———————

You played London for a week in August. He was rumoured to be coming. A note arrived from him to the effect that he was grateful for your first-night performance but unfortunately had had to leave early, due to illness. The costume girl read it to you. You made no response. Someone brought champagne. You drank it.

He had written that he missed you, had wanted to meet you off the train at King's Cross, had set out from his club before realising it was too insistent a gesture, something you might not want. He had walked the streets around the station in the rain and the wind, sat in a café trying to sort his thoughts. He watched the trains coming in. You would be on one of them, he knew. To approach you across the platform, to embrace you, take your bag? Would you be happy to see him there or find his presence unnerving? In the end he had sat so long that you must have arrived by then, were probably in the cab to the hotel, or the theatre. Doubtless, you did not wish to see him anyway.

You dreamed of him that night, you were walking Russell Square in London, and there was such freedom and lightness in whatever he was saying that to wake in the dark of morning was hard. You began what soon became a love letter; it was honest, too lengthy. You wrote that you had come to think of him as the source of whatever happiness and courage you knew; that the thought of a future without him was unbearable. You considered a long time before writing the word 'unbearable', sensing declarations of such heatedness would frighten or anger him; they would certainly have this effect on you. And then you simply let go, writing anything you felt, for you knew you would never send it, lacked the mettle to be revealed. Foolish phrases came crowding. It didn't matter now. Quotations from love poems, from songs that had come to mean something. As you watched the letter burn, you felt the strange, bright hope that its destruction would somehow anatomise the realities it had tried to describe. You wondered why you had spent so long writing it.

———————

A thunderstorm in Leeds. His chest against your back. From outside on the street you heard the young people shrieking. You had missed a cue earlier. The house had been poor. At the hotel, you'd had too much to drink.

First time it ever happened. Dr Leverett's Tonic Wine. 'For feminine maladies and general regularity.' The room was very cold, the blankets too heavy. You heard him singing quietly into the nest of your matted hair.

Last year, at Lady Mary's Fair . . . and I being in Dundee . . .
I met a boy I'd parted from . . . and he being on a spree.
His company I did accept, and with him I did go,
But to my sad misfortune, it proved my overthrow . . .

'I'm warning you, if you want any sleep, you better stop,' you whispered.

He stopped. And he started again.

And you know it was only a dream but it didn't matter at the time. In Leeds, one night in a storm.

———————

After you broke with him, it became your habit to walk in the evenings. Stephen's Green was a sort of destination but often you would circle back, to the bookshops on Nassau Street, through the quadrangles of Trinity College, along the north quays of the Liffey, through the bleak expanse of Phoenix Park. Autumn was coming. Darkness descended earlier. Schoolchildren would come into the park to fell chestnuts.

It had always been the season when you saw most beauty in the city. One afternoon you walked to the old library to see an exhibition of rare volumes but found the sight of the guillemots whirling in the sky over Kildare Street more touching than what could be written in verses. It was one of those Dublin summer evenings that smells of fresh linen; pale golden light was spilling into the streets and it made even the shop windows seem magical.

You had paused to look at the stacks outside an antiquarian bookshop when you felt a presence behind you on Duke Street.

'Molly?'

You turned.

His expression was a mingling of hope and defensiveness. A cautious, half-fearful anticipatory look, as one testing the edge of a blade or a word.

'Molly. Dear God. How are you?'

'Quite well.'

'What a surprise. I was literally only thinking of you this minute, as a matter of fact. Thought I saw you from the tram. How rum.'

Your impulse was to hurry away. You felt doors opening inside you, and you didn't want to go through any of them again.

'What has you in town, John? Were you going to the theatre?'

'Thinking of it. Vaguely. But there's nothing much playing. Just gypsying about, to tell the truth.'

The crowd moved around you. A fire-juggler began performing.

'You look healthy, Molly.'

'I don't.' You glanced at your watch. 'I'm after putting on the few pounds. That's what comes of going on tour, of course. They think when you're Irish all you eat is the potatoes. Half the company's gone the size of a balloon.'

'You'd barely notice. It suits you. Your face has filled out.'

'Dossie Wright says a troop of actors always weighs the same amount. There's some do go up and some do go down but all together it comes to the same. Like a family.'

'What an interesting theory. How is Sally keeping these days?'

'She's mighty. I think. Course, I wouldn't be told if she wasn't. That's our Sally, as you know. Keeps it close to the chest.'

'Molly —'

'Maybe she's the wise girl to do so.'

'Could we perhaps take a cup of tea together? You've probably no time, have you?'

'I have an appointment presently.'

'An appointment?'

'Yes.'

'Ten minutes, then? Or fifteen? Are you terribly pushed?'

'I think it would be better not to. My friend would be offended. And there is nothing I want to say to you anyhow.'

'I quite understand. Only spare me five minutes? For old times' sake, if it must be?'

You didn't want to go with him and yet found it impossible to decline. You passed through the street and to the Imperial Café, but there were no available tables at first. You stood together on the stairway that led to the mezzanine. He was hot, shocked, fumbling his sentences; he had never been good at being in a café. You could smell the musk of his shaving soap, the pomade in his hair. You wondered if there was some way to leave without making a scene you'd no heart for. You didn't want to give it to him to say. All the time you waited for a table, you kept up your side of the platitudinous conversation while desperately wishing you could smoke.

A silence descended. It was as though some uninvited bore had sat down between you. You could see that he, too, was regretting having invited you. Shouts and catcalls arose suddenly from the street below, where policemen were chasing a slum child.

'I think about you often, Molly. Every moment of the day. There is so much that I have wanted to say to you. About our quarrel, our misunderstanding.'

You hadn't a reply. He looked younger than you'd remembered. Strangely distancing to hear him speak your name. He had combed his hair differently, was wearing a cravat with a triple-spiral pin and expensive-looking clothes you wondered how he could afford. It was too hot in the café; his spectacles were misting. A church bell was tolling in the alley nearby. People made the sign of the cross.

'And your friend?' he asked quietly. 'May I enquire if I know him?'

'I do not see that that is a question you are entitled to put, John.'

'Is it Wright?'

'I hardly think it is any of your business.'

'No. Just so. There it is.'

'And your mother is well, I hope?'

'I believe so. Of course, she is never *terribly* well. But she sort of soldiers on. It's rather admirable and stoic in its way.'

'I must go to meet my friend. I am meeting him at the bridge.'

'May I walk with you?'

'All right. I must hurry.'

Your heartbeat was that intense you could feel it in your gums as you went together through the crowded streets. Silently you linked his arm as you crossed College Green. In front of Trinity gate, young people were waiting for their sweethearts, and a woman with a baby in a blanket drifted between them holding out a cup. It was after six o'clock and the offices were closing. You were walking through the city for the last time together. He was talking about a piece he was writing, the tour to Scotland and Wales; all the things that did not matter at all. A balladeer bawled a chorus and shook his fist at the sky, raising mockeries from a party of passing schoolgirls. Too quickly you were standing by the steps to the Ha'penny Bridge. Wind blew dead ivy-leaves slowly along the quay and one of them clung flappingly to his lapel.

'Could we start again, Molly?'

When you looked at him he was weeping, his head bowed low, his shoulders shaking fiercely. Like a man who is ashamed to weep.

'John – for pity's sake – people are staring.'

'I am sorry. Truly sorry. For the hurt I have done you. I beg your forgiveness, Molly. It's a wretched fool I've been.'

'What is done is done, John. I do not make you happy. There is some other girl who will. We must be courageous now.'

'There is no other girl, Molly. There never shall be again.'

'You mustn't say such things. You are a very fine man.'

'No, you don't understand. They have told me I am dying. Not in those words. But I know. I know.'

The crowds pushed past you. In the river there were cloudscapes. You took him by the hand and watched them.

You are walking up Bray Head with him, as you often do on Sundays, and the sea below the cliff path is a rolling grey-green. There were evenings in the past, you would have gone as far as Greystones. Lately it's too far for him. He leans heavily on your arm. People are nudging. They know him now. The Kingstown little tinker who wrote that filthy play. The dirty Protestant smut-monger. His turncoat slut. Making us out to be savages and murderers and drunks, our women nothing but whores in homespun. Oh they laugh at us in England. And why wouldn't they laugh? Judases like Synge and his tart of the tenements will always sell their country to the conqueror. Sometimes for money, other times for power: this time for the spittle on the overlord's lips as he wipes his cackling maw in a playhouse. Synge, the bitch's traitor, puppeteer of stage-Irishmen, contriver of the seductively garrulous killer, part Frankenstein's monster, part clown. He does not seem put out, nor even surprised. 'We are an event,' he tells you, and you carry on with the climb. Pushing together, into the slab of the gradient. It is as though he is trying to persuade himself that none of it matters. ('It makes me rage when I think of the people who go on as if art and literature and writing were the first thing in the world.') He is so disingenuous sometimes. A protection.

Soon he will alter his term of address. 'My child,' he will call you, instead of 'my changeling'. He is ageing with every step, is often in crippling pain. 'I am so proud of you,' he says. 'I am so fond of you. I love you.'

He is in Germany recuperating from failed surgery when his mother dies of cancer, so old that he doesn't remember her age. His loyalty to her ghost is unqualified, fervent. It is as though she is still in the house, watching over his shoulder, still waiting for him to atone for all the disappointments. 'I cannot tell you how unspeakably sacred her memory seems to me,' he will write. 'There is nothing in the world better than a single-hearted wife and mother. I wish you had known her better. I hope you'll be as good to me as she was.' How hard it must have been to write such words. But harder to have had to read them.

He will stay on in the big house at Glenageary for a time, but will find it difficult to be alone in the old empty rooms, with only 'that little donkey of a servant' for company. He will inherit some money, not very much, but enough to live quietly in some suburb like Dundrum. That is all he wants now: his child and Dundrum. A home without memories. A few quiet years together. He is becoming like Lear, as the play nears its end: begging for the consolations he refused in Act One. Being killed by the gods for their sport.

He will talk to you again about marriage, the future. 'If only my health holds we will be able to get on now.' But the cues have all been missed; he did not recognise them when they came, and the long rehearsals are not to be realised. He is brought to a nursing home in the city, where the orderlies wheel him to a window so he can see his beloved Wicklow Mountains in the distance. He withers, drugged by ether, gaze fixing on lost Wicklows. You soak your handkerchief, touch it to his lips, his eyelids. There comes a night when he manages to murmur for a sip of champagne. Five painful months after the death of his mother, he himself will die, aged thirty-seven, following a hopeless operation for Hodgkin's disease. Distraught, you will beseech a priest to say a requiem mass, but will be told that the request is difficult to grant. He was not one of us. He was of the other persuasion. There have to be limits, after all.

Probably he would have understood, would not have wanted any fuss. All his life he had to attune to subtle transmissions of his unacceptability. He knew what it is to find yourself walled out, separated by boundaries you did not yourself make; to have to gaze through whatever chink may be found at the people whose acknowledgement you burn for. At the time of his death, no member of his immediate family has ever seen one of his plays.

'My dearest Love,' begins his farewell letter. 'This is a mere line for you, my poor child, to bid you good-bye and ask you to be brave and good and not to forget the good times we've had and the beautiful things we've seen together.'

It is signed 'Your old Friend'. He is no longer the tramp. There is no need to be in character any more.

Her daughter will be called 'Pegeen' after her mother's greatest role: the heroine in *The Playboy of the Western World*, a woman who loves a storyteller, but loses him too soon, when the past lurches out from the dark backstage in the shape of his wounded parent.

'All art is a collaboration,' wrote the father of the play.

'To me, he was everything,' said the mother.

8

THE THEATRE DISTRICT, LONDON

1.10 p.m.

Eros on his plinth; his arrowless bow. Around the fountain's filth-strewn basin, clustered youths are looking murderous as they eye the passing street-girls and policemen. Through Jermyn Street and Haymarket, and the feathers of snow. If the Lyons Corner House were open, you would have a little plunge: perhaps a cup of beef tea, some of those pretty iced cakes. It would be wise to take a coffee now; you have had a little too much of the brandy, and drunkenness in daylight is not a pleasant sensation, especially when the daylight is grey. But the café is closed. How strange. And it coming up to lunchtime. You stare at the doors, as though staring could unlock them. It is the curse of modern England: people don't want to work. Idleness has corrupted the kingdom.

Not like in your day. By Jesus, no. Your growing had exhausted you; perpetual faintness in the month of your fourteenth birthday, a swimmy-headedness you both feared and found queerly exhilarating, but out to work every Saturday morning come rain, sleet or hurricane, and devil the malingering accepted. The doctor at the public dispensary had recommended a patented iron tonic, with a nightly glass of Guinness – it would help. And your grandmother mocking such prescriptions and those who availed of them. *It's well off are the young women and never a minute's peace out of them. In my own time we'd no excuses for idleness.*

The summer you left school, exultant never to have to talk to another nun. You apprenticed in Manny Scheindlin's, stitching hems, tracing patterns, accompanying your employer's sons to the market for the silks and the bobbins of English chenille. Those teasing, handsome lunks — what's this was their names? The particular way sunlight shone through the high old windows of the market; the hagglings, back-and-forthings, banterings among the merchants, the apples and ices you and the boys would sometimes buy as you wended a way back to Little Jerusalem. The elder lad so lazy; his brother so conscientious. You were happy as a threaded needle.

A length of American cotton draped across your wrists one afternoon, like a banner of dignified surrender.

Rudolf, was it? Jacob? Or was that someone else? Oh so maddening, how memory works, or doesn't work, when you are old. Every square in a counterpane you owned when you were five, you remember the sequence, the colours. But then people so important to you, and now even their names are melted away. Molly, you old fool, you're drifting.

And when that younger boy would sing, oh dear Jesus, was it beautiful. Unearthly, the grace of him, and the grief in that voice; it would make a glass eye weep. 'The Last Rose of Summer' or 'Che gelida manina' or 'The Ballad of Brave Michael Dwyer'.

The soldiers searched the Wicklow vales, and toward the dawn of
*   day*
Discovered where the outlaws bold, the dauntless rebels lay.
Around the little cottage poor, they formed into a ring
And called: 'United Irishmen! Surrender to the king!'

Then burst forth war's red lightning, then poured the leaden rain;
And Wicklow's hills did echo with the thunder peals again,
Brave Dwyer and his comrades bold, they fought and fell with pride,
And the skies of Wicklow wept that morn, when Michael Dwyer
*   died.*

Their father ancient and placid, handsome as a prophet, and his accent a waterfall of vowels. ('Dressing vell it is a talent, a way of surviving, little Molly. We do not need money for to do it, no, no. You will remember three things, yes, every woman need to know? Keep your clothes clean and mended, and rest them when you can. And buy one *wery* good skirt. It will last.') For a man who worked with his hands he was clumsy in his movements, and yet his stitching was flawless, better than any seamstress's in Dublin. Oh from Kingstown they'd come, and Killiney, and Drumcondra, and the wilds of Chapelizod and the jungles of the Coombe, for his nearly invisible fixings. ('Only two things in life cannot be mended, little Molly. The heart and a buckled wheel.') And then sometimes him and his wife speaking the Hungarian to one another – little endearments or scoldings and, for some reason, measurements – they would never use the English words 'yard' or 'inch' – it was as though it were a private superstition between them. On their Sabbath they went to the synagogue where Mr Scheindlin was a cantor, leaving you alone in the sewing room with the spools and the tweeds and the shears and the skeins of yarn. Once – you had ensured you were alone – you found yourself touching the breast of one of the mannequins. The day was swelteringly hot. Something fierce had stirred in you. You found it hard to look at the boys when they returned.

Another time, while bowed over at work, you heard him singing the sacred music upstairs – his sons pulling smirks and muttering quips in their language – and the mournfully beautiful music had welled your tired eyes. It was the day your periods began – the shocking redness of that blood. You had been stitching a child's shift, had pricked your finger like Sleeping Beauty, and for many years afterwards, in the middle of the month, you would remember the moment when that entreating music had entered you, would relate the music to your womanhood, your woman-hood to the music, and both to a half-forgotten afternoon.

And it wasn't long afterwards you first attended a play, in the Printers' Union lecture hall at the back end of Kevin Street. Oh the glamour of it all. *L'élégance!* Your sister was one of the bit-players. It was appallingly done. Twenty rows of desks and the half of them empty and Ophelia like a Prussia Street scrub-woman. Dismal weather – oh Molls, do you remember the sound? For the smack of the sleet on the corrugated roof was nearly the only applause. But then, after the performance, when the players were gathering up their props, didn't a little clerk approach the platform and he handing Sally a flower. A bedraggled auld lily – but an offering all the same. And he asking her for an appoint-ment, turning his cap in his hands, and if Sally had declined, she had nevertheless been asked. And that, my little Molly, was that, so it was. Then burst forth war's red lightning.

Hurrying home through the rain aware that your life had been altered and could never again be as it was. No, it wasn't joy you felt, not a falling-in-love. For you knew what had happened to you would bring many sorrows; that you'd always be poor, that you'd never inherit the shop, that your mother would disapprove, that your father's ghost would rage, but that one night someone unexpected would materialise out of the darkness with a bundle of Easter lilies in his hands. God be with the youth of you. Such little you wanted. Well, it is as it is. You chose it.

Roaming the countryside, crossroads towns, sleepy villages. You'd arrive at the hall in the early afternoon to make ready for the one-night stand. Elsinore would be improvised from whatever junk was available: chairs, tea chests, there might be a yellow-toothed piano for the fanfares; an old door would do duty as a battlement. The manager passing out handbills announcing the show. *The Greatest Hibernian Artistes.*

Farmers, tinkers, barefooted tenants. There are nights they still come to you in dreams. Some of them never saw a play before, didn't know why they should bother seeing one now, but were drawn by the promise of escape. And they applauding the love scenes or nattering to one another during a death scene, remarking that the corpse was still breathing. *Puck him agin, Mister! Another poke and he's gone!* Taking bets on the sword fights, *huuahing* their champions, hissing and blaspheming the villains. Or a vicar might come, with his wife and neat children — always greeted respectfully, no nonsense, no nonsense — but never, for some reason, a Catholic priest. Perhaps he would have seen the players as rivals.

The audience eating noisily, or drinking, or conversing, the little ones wandering about, left to roam by their mothers, and a pedlar straggling in and out as though the show were a fairground and he moseying the aisles with his ribbons. And by God, you earned their tolerance. If you didn't, you'd regret it. The audience was *always* a part of the play. That's one thing you learned good and hard.

And the beds in railway station hotels, and the tours in Wales and England. And the cutting up at night, the flirtations, and communal breakfasting. Walking a wintry town the morning after a performance and the cornerboys and spalpeens eying you from the grog-shops and they whistling with false courage in your wake. A goddess, you were. You could have any living one of them. People said you were prettier than Sara.

You were bold once or twice. Oh you were, don't pretend. Poor, dear Dossie Wright. How many years now is he dead? Well, he wasn't dead that night. All there, so he was. God forgive us, but the size of it fairly crossed your eyes so it did, and it stiff as a beefeater outside Buckingham Palace when the Queen is sighted coming down the Mall. What he wanted you to do to it, the dirty little monkey, and the balls of him hefty as fat, juicy oranges and he begging and coaxing and promising. Oh, the beautiful face of him, arch-liar and messer and lascivious whoremonger that he was. But by Jesus, did he know what to do with his hands and all of it nicely forgotten in the morning. Did he ever get married? Poor wife, if he did. He'd need a two-bucket woman to put manners on him.

And what about the other time, with that handsome cad Shannon? Mr J. Seamus Shannon. Fifty was he, maybe? To you, he seemed ancient. Often played druidical chieftains, or the kindlier uncles in Dickens. He was married with eleven children and a house in the suburbs and a wife who did not understand. It occurred to you that she had understood at least eleven times, but perhaps it would be rude to point out the obvious. There was friendship, said Seamus Shannon, and then there was desire, the bliss of the angels, the honey of longing; the ecstasy of the climactic moment. (*'Le petit mort, as they call it. You speak French of course, my child? You do not? Ah — so much to learn.'*) Yes, the pleasure of which he spoke was a glimpse of the Paradise that was awaiting the faithful for all eternity. It was a matter of theology. The body was holy. We must conquer our ignorant fear of it. Heaven was a state of perpetual culmination, in the corporeal as well as the spiritual sense. You had probably not heard these terms? Did you know to what they adverted? It was a catechism that had not been given to you by any of the nuns, and the fact that one or two of them might be experiencing perpetual culmination now was a somewhat uneasy thought. Paradise must be a tiring place and also a noisy one. You'd want to keep your eyes closed as you went about.

Molly, you are bold! There is badness in you, Changeling. Mr J. Seamus Shannon, poor lecherous auld goat. He'd stick his lad in a ham sandwich if he thought there was pleasure in it. Yes, and ate it afterwards. Probably down in Purgatory at this stage of the game, and he convincing the lady devils that to ride him ragged would be a punishment. We should never be ashamed, my dear. We are artists. Rebels. We must scoff at bloodless convention. It is our *duty* not to serve. No artist worthy of the calling could ever be a virgin for he, or she, would be merely half living — *insulting* life, in fact. His, or her, impulses, the *juices*, the *zest*, would be evaporated by the heat of such a denial. The Hindus saw the act of coition as a godly endowment. He was personally a devotee of Brahma.

You were a young woman, he assured you. You had a tremendous future. He had seen many young women come into the profession. Not one of them had ever shown such remarkable possibility, such sweet buds of potentiality, if he might employ a poetical phrase. And then he had uttered the remark that had opened your dress: 'You have a far greater talent than your sister's.'

But a young woman had needs, he assured you repeatedly. The silly old sausage. Why didn't he just ask? A young woman often stirred at night thinking thoughts of raw hunger, felt her body wanting to give itself – it was natural, pagan. ('That is what we *do*, my dear. We *give*. We only give. Never think of it as acting. It is *giving*.') You felt it wiser not to mention the existence of a brat named Jimmy Gunnery, with whom you had often gone walking when your mother thought you were at Mass, in whose hands you had experienced, if not the blisses of Bangalore, the occasional nice revelation.

Evidently what Mr Shannon wanted was a girl-next-door purity; well, that was all right. It was well within your range. Anyone who had ever played an Irishwoman on stage would know how to masquerade innocence. Indeed, it might be somewhat difficult for you to play anything else, since harlots were kept mainly in the wings. No, you told your mentor, you had never heard those words. Yes – you tried to blush – you had sometimes found yourself beset by certain thoughts. Once or twice you had even – no – it would be too shameful to say. You would think so little of me, Mr Shannon, if I confessed the reprehensible sin. Oh I *couldn't*, I really couldn't; you are so kind and good. I had to be given ten Hail Marys by Father Furey in Confession. He told me blindness would be inevitable if I persisted.

Mr Shannon radiated compassion as he crossed his legs. You were not to believe such nonsenses; they were circulated by the lifeless, those who wished upon us only fear and servitude. Little wonder, he added sadly, that the asylums of this poor benighted country were howling with those who had denied themselves. And a bit more of his guff about the intoxicating sap of youthfulness and how they did things on the Continent and the Greeks and William Blake, and you nodding back shyly, doing fascinated-yet-demure, wondering if he would ever get around to the point.

Not only would it be *bourgeois* for pleasure to be denied – in his own case it might be physically dangerous. He gave you his heart – that was how he put it – one torrentially rainy night in Borris-in-Ossory, while in the parlour downstairs a one-legged fiddler played 'The Croppy Boy' to an audience of commercial travellers. He was breathtakingly skilful – Seamus Shannon, not the fiddler – and vigorous for a fat man of his age. He had read passages in many French novels that had been banned throughout the Empire and he seemed to know what they were secretly about. Orotund pronunciation of Shakespearian soliloquy was not the only thing he could do with his gob. But there was an efficiency to his prowess that was somewhat off-putting, in that you felt he was constantly *expecting* something, had mentally advanced to the next scene, like a smiling but impatient waiter who wants to go home, and that whatever bliss you were experiencing, as you gaspingly were, redounded to his credit and existed mainly to be observed. After a while he produced 'a device', rinsed it desultorily in his shaving bowl, and attempted to roll it onto his mickey. A difficult moment ensued as he began losing what interested you most. The poor dunderhead was visibly embarrassed. You wondered if you should give him the attention Jimmy Gunnery was never done requesting but you felt it might be riskily forward. Instead you uttered the phrase: 'Please – I beg you – you won't ever tell anyone you ruined me?' and it stood to attentive readiness like a flagpole. You took it in your hand. He was soon tiptoeing on the spot and spouting extracts from the Song of Solomon.

The following nineteen minutes were never less than interesting. A reviewer would have described them positively. When you opened your eyes in mid-throe only to observe him glancing at his fob watch, his thrusting, white buttocks reflecting palely in the windowpane, it temporarily put you off what he insisted on calling your 'stride' but otherwise you had no complaints. He asked, with sweaty seriousness, if you had ever seen wild horses mating – a relatively uncommon sight in Mary Street and environs – but its imitation proved pleasurable to the fraudulent old booby and, to be fair, had the desired effect on you too. He was generous, attentive and pleasured you practically unconscious before asking your permission to 'bring down the curtain'. As 'The Croppy Boy' reached its heart-rending crescendo, so did J. Seamus Shannon, and you felt he had thoroughly earned it. On returning to Dublin, he had returned to his wife, accompanied, presumably, by his heart. Jimmy Gunnery received a pleasant surprise, indeed something of an education. He would be engaged many times but would never marry.

—*You better not have done on that 'tour' of yours what I think you done.*

—*How do you mean, Mother?*

—*Innocent Annie. Is it simple you think I'm after going? You are not gone so big and bold that I will not redden your arse for you. You are not in your playhouse now.*

—*That is nice talk to your own daughter.*

—*Is it wrong, all the same? Look me in the eye if you dare, and don't be flashing me your impudent face or you'll feel my hand across it. There isn't a decent man in Ireland wants to buy a cracked jug.*

—*I do not get your meaning. You will have to explain.*

—*Oh you were rared a pet, weren't you? It's a nice reputation in store. Do you think I don't be seeing you flaunting yourself to every gurrier on the street, like the first girl in Dublin ever had a rump on her to swing or a couple of handfuls in her blouse?*

—*Am I not allowed speak to a fellow barring I ask your permission?*

—*The brazen lip of you, Miss, and you barely out of school. Let me tell you, they run good and fast when they've taken what they want. Get up to that bed and say a prayer.*

———————————

Giddy Aunt, to be indoors, to get out of this coldness. That cinema on the corner, perhaps? An extravagance. Yes. But we can be too sensible for our own good, and there are no pockets in a shroud after all. And it will be a talking-point, later, at the BBC, when you and the other actors are having coffee and cigarettes, and the sound-effects producer is taking glockenspiels from his suitcase and hitting them with little hammers, looking serious. Yes, I popped into the pictures earlier, I was just in town and felt restless. Do you know, I thoroughly enjoyed it. Quite *marvellously* vulgar. And the young people will chuckle at your mischievous Irish spirit and the effects-man will activate his cuckoo clock.

Giant masks of Comedy and Tragedy by the entrances to the lavatories. But the leer of poor old Comedy is distastefully licentious, and the frenzied glumness of Tragedy looks like a clown's, put on. There is a counter where sweets and orangeade are sold, but nobody is attending it now.

Why no pockets in a shroud? Could that not be arranged? If one specified it, for example, in one's Last Will and Testament? Might it not be a comfort, having some little keepsake in there with you? Or perhaps it would be merely an irritant. Your relatives would be loading you down you with photographs and trinkets, letters they should have sent you, curls they snipped off themselves, probably unpaid bills. No, it doesn't bear thinking about. You'd end up like a pack mule. Better to face eternity pocketless.

You pay your threepence to the girl in the booth and are directed towards the shadowy passageway, along which are hung posters for films you are not certain you have heard of. Musicals, possibly, for the actors appear so happy, the women smiling manically, their lips redder than a jazzman's socks, and the men sculpturally handsome with wide mauve eyes and necks slightly thicker than their heads. The auditorium smells of damp, the picture has already started, but you pick up the story easily for you once saw it as a play. *A Streetcar Named Desire*. You murmur the title to yourself. A beautiful title is half the battle.

As you adjust to the darkness, you realise you are almost alone, that there is nobody except yourself in the row. With what you hope is a restrained and deftly executed half-turn, as someone seeking out a friend with whom an appointment has been agreed, you see that there is only one man in all the rows behind you, a codger in a raincoat, with an umbrella in the seat beside him fully and inappropriately extended. He is sitting with his hat on, which irks you slightly. It is not done for a gentleman to be wearing a hat when indoors. And one would think they would know that, after all this time. Do they not have wives? Is etiquette quite dead? It matters not that he is alone, that is *in no sense* the point, for if we all behaved exactly as we pleased while alone, it would be a very fine pancake indeed. But what is to be done? These days, one can say nothing. London is becoming a slum.

You try to enter the story but the star is too distractingly handsome. You slip the bottle from your carpetbag, a couple of long sips. The boy is not only beautiful; he is an admirable actor, far too luminously skilful for the pictures. He would make a dazzling Hamlet or an American Christy Mahon come home to break the hearts of Mayo. He pouts. He smoulders. He stares. He exudes. He has the eyes of a panther wondering if killing you would be worth the effort. Despite the critics saying he is good, he actually *is* good, in the subtle ways only a fellow professional would notice or understand: in his turns, in his glances, in the conscientiousness of his diction, every plosive sound audible, every vowel made distinct. We must efface ourselves as we play; one can see that he knows this. The words are everything; we serve them. And Hollywood, with its baubles and faked grandiosities, its vulgarisation of everything tautly fine in the drama (something poor deluded Sara could never quite see), its awards for this, its mansions for that, will probably destroy him before long. Because he is a sensitive man; one can discern it in his sullen mien. A man who would rather be away, who was not made for others, but whose gift will condemn him to the public dungeon of admiration. And it's well you know the sufferings of a man who becomes admired when to be hated is all he's been raised for.

Your tears spring hotly. Ridiculous. Ludicrous. *He* was not

out of Crone Forest and see him at a distance. He is standing by the wall of a bent stone bridge, dropping fern fronds into the river like a child. You judder back to the picture house, its shaft of bluish light. Now Molly, do not doze. It is not done to sleep in public. A long yawn makes your ears click; you cover your mouth. You try to settle into the picture but it is difficult, difficult. The brandy is dissolving the threads.

Days and nights pass. Lakes turn a mild blue. A woman is talking about him quietly; you cannot see her through her veil. The words of that silly old letter he wrote after Killiney are bubbling up now, wanting remembrance. They *know* that you know them. They are buried in you, Changeling, and they want to come back from the dead. You make yourself resurface. Certain dreams are stoppable. Your fingertips so cold, as though emitting a colour. On a sudden the picture stops and the house lights fade up; the projectionist is changing the reels. A slide reading INTERVAL appears on the screen. Pearls of sweat on his forehead, smudging his scribble as they dripped on the paper. And one night you awoke, thinking the cottage was on fire, to see the hearth silhouetting him, roaring and hissing, and he shovelling handfuls of his work into the flames.

He went swimming in the mornings or when he suffered from headaches, which were brought on by a surfeit of work. And he hunching over the table five hours without respite, the fingertips of his left hand massaging his temple furiously while his right blackened endless pages. When he exhausted his supply of paper he wrote on anything he could find: in margins, on sugar bags, on the frontispieces of books, on flyleaves, in the corners of newspapers. It was a compulsion, a kind of madness, a country to which none would ever be permitted entry, and its flag was his sweat-soaked handkerchief. One could come up to its borders, was permitted to peer in, but would never be granted citizenship.

The thinness of his wrists. His wren-like appetite; result, so he told you, of his student days in Paris, when money had been so scarce and friends so few that often he had gone to his bed hungry. He had fainted one evening in the rue de l'Université – 'the world swam up at me, the shadows were so beautiful'. Once, for a fortnight, he had eaten only bread. What would that be like? Only bread. The house lights are darkened and the picture resumes. But it is like watching water. You nod again.

A cart trundles down Foley Street, drawn by a shabby quarter horse piebald whose lugubrious clop draws children from the yards. His sticks of ramshackle furniture roped on the back – unwanted lampstands, a wrecked armchair, a hatstand with no pegs – like the cargo of the ragman arriving outside your mother's shop having scavenged the ruins of a mansion. Dusty old paintings recently de-lofted. The coffin of an oaken wardrobe with its backboards missing. A potted geranium like a kidnapped contessa. A single mattress smirched with cloudlike stains.

The horse shakes its halter and looks up at the sky. The children approach it tentatively, silent. There is a boy with him – you assume a servant but actually his sister's child. From a velvet-gloved hand he feeds an apple core to the horse. Its munching teeth, skeletal; the gyration of its jaw.

The carter hefts the bits of lumber down to the pavement with the aid of two men of the slums who have approached the little street drama in search of a sixpence. One of them has only one hand but he is willing to work, his companion says. *He'd do as much as a three-handed man, sir. No word of a lie.* You come forward attempting to help them and the healthy man looks relieved; it is the maimed one who says he resents the pity of a woman. He served with the Dublin Fusiliers, received his wound at Pretoria. He wants none of your assistance, never will.

The narrow, bare staircase smells of mildew and stale piss. The wallpaper over the fireplace is peeling. He is standing in the window embrasure, rubbing at the glass with his glove.

A canework chair. A broken ottoman. Two sundering cardboard suitcases.

Mouse droppings in the empty cupboards; spiderweb in the chamber pot, a pyramid of empty porter bottles in the corner nearest the door. It occurs to you that it must have taken someone much effort to construct and you feel bad as you take it down. A sheaf of brochures and handbills about emigration to America, their pages rotted together by time and sticky mould. An illustration of Abraham Lincoln regards you from a frontispiece. Someone had altered it obscenely.

The boy is jumping on the mattress but it doesn't have much bounce. The carter produces a hammer; his mouth is full of nails. You go about the two rooms hanging the couple of paintings over the burgundy-coloured rectangles left on the wallpaper.

A mangle. His typewriter. A bockety hatstand. A rug his older brother brought back from China, its colours too vivid for their mother to find it acceptable. Another rug, much smaller, rolled and bound like a scroll, tautened by a man's belt and two threadbare Trinity College neckties.

It is already growing dark. He fills and lights a lamp. The beautiful amber glow on his face.

—*Things always look better in lamplight. Don't you find?*

—*Yes, John.*

—*I can offer you nothing to eat. I am sorry.*

From your carpetbag you produce the little packets your mother has prepared: sandwiches, a couple of apples, three bottles of porter.

—*Oh how kind you are, Molly. What a supper of delights. Shall we picnic on the floor like Frenchmen in a picture?*

He lolls lengthwise on the Chinese rug, slipping off his walking boots. There are holes in his stockings and his toenails are long. The night is coming colder. There is nothing to burn. He rummages in a tea chest and finds a sod of black turf he once picked up in Connemara.

He is kissing you tenderly, sometimes whispering your name. He lies back and looks at the ceiling as though regarding a starlit sky. The flames refracted on the overpainted plaster cornucopias; the writhing, happy putti and harps-twined-in-shamrock.

Someone in a room above you is scraping on a fiddle, a slow air of Thomas Moore's, 'Forget Not the Field', but the player is not skilled and so the higher notes come shriekingly. There is a public house on the corner. You hear the dockers on the street, the whistles and shouts, the blasphemous greetings and summonings.

—*We should go out and find you a hackney. Are you ready, Molly? Your hat?*

—*It is late now, John. And very wet.*

—*Nevertheless, it would not be proper for you to stay with me here.*

You try to speak gently. It is hard to find the words.

—*We are engaged, after all. And no one would know.*

—*Word has a way of going around the town.*

—*But when we were in Wicklow – on our holiday – you remember what I mean . . .*

—*It was different in Wicklow, love. I don't know why. Things are always different in Wicklow.*

—*As you wish. Of course. You will be all right on your own?*

—*I have been in worse places on my own. I shall be fine. I shall miss you.*

—*I shall miss you too, John. I shall think of you all night.*

He touches your face, caresses your cheek with his thumb.

—*What joy when we will be married. We shall never be without each other again. It will be a place of our own. No invaders or nuisances.*

—*We can make it pretty and neat. I will ask Mother about a dresser. And curtains.*

—*There is no need to do that.*

—*She would like to help us, John. She would be offended if I didn't ask.*

—*You deserve so much better, my love. What I would give you if I could. A good house, pretty furnishings, some little place with a garden. I often think of it. I picture it. You rehearsing your lines in a garden. Walking a little orchard with a script in your hand. And a table near a rose bush where I could work when it was fine. And yet you tolerate*

your old tramper and he little better than a tinker. How did I ever deserve
my changeling?
—I shall be very content being here with you. There will be no happier
girl in Ireland . . .

You awaken in the picture house, muttering, thirsty. The film
is over – you don't know when it ended. The house lights are
excruciatingly bright and there is no sound at all. It is difficult
to move. For a moment, you wonder if you are dead. After-images
pulsing and fading.

Fuddled, shaken, you sit there a long time. Is the afterlife a
deserted cinema and a bottle in a bag? Is London outside, its
October streets and storefronts, its hurryings and worryings and
appointments to be kept? Or has everything vanished into
whiteout and mist? Is Wicklow outside? Your mother? Your
playboy? A room in lower Foley Street you used to imagine, that
you never once saw, except in your fantasies? A strange morning
indeed. Another sip of the brandy. And the queerest sensation
of the many besetting you now is that someone else is composing
the day and everything in it. A faraway sentiency has been shaping
and sifting, trying somehow to atone and to put matters right.
For you. For itself. To edit away its failures. Does everyone feel
this sometimes, an opening into space? As a character in a life
whose author is invisible but nevertheless laying out our fate.

You stand painfully, unsteadily, and gather closed your coat.
Your mouth is viciously hot and tastes sour. To lie down a long
while in some dark, deep room. To hear women singing quietly.
To feel nothing. But if God feeds the birds, Moll, they have to
dig the worms. And eternity does not begin today.

'Quiet morning for you now,' you remark to the ticket girl in
the foyer.

'Beg pardon, Miss?' she smiles amiably, glancing up from her
True Romance.

'I say myself and that man, dear. Your only two customers. A
wonder your employer can keep going. But it is a marvellous
picture. I enjoyed it very much. Many thanks.'

'There wasn't any gentleman, Miss. You were the only ticket I sold.'

'But – I distinctly saw a gentleman behind me. He was carrying an umbrella.'

'No, Miss. There was only yourself.'

9

SCENE FROM A HALF-IMAGINED
STAGE PLAY

*Curtain-up on a humble room in a tenement house in Mary Street,
Dublin, 1908. Shabby furniture and fittings, probably leftover stock
from the junkshop. In a corner near a sideboard is a day-bed covered
in rags. A dog at its foot, a shabby, bedraggled wolfhound. A ruined
middle-aged woman uneasily arranging a table; her son in his twenties,
in British Army uniform, drinking porter and playing cards with his
shadow.*

MOLLY [*entering, nervous*]: Mother . . . Georgie . . . This is my
friend, Mr Synge.

> [*He follows her into the room in a miasma of painful optimism,
> right hand outstretched, hat crushed beneath his elbow, in his left
> hand a bouquet of wildflowers in a fold of old newspaper, in his
> right hand a bottle of wine. Her mother comes away from fussing
> at the table and smiles at him fretfully, accepting the offerings; her
> eyes lividly wild with the particular anxiety of those being visited
> by perceived superiors.*]

MOTHER: You shouldn't have bothered yourself, Misther Synge.
Those are lovely. You shouldn't have.

> [*The lilies might wilt in the wither of her blush.*]

SYNGE [*extremely apprehensive*]: I am pleased to meet you, Mrs Allgood. Thank you for inviting me to your home.

MOTHER [*equally on edge*]: I'm sure you're welcome, Misther Synge. Will you not stand in to the fire there? There's a terrible catchin' cold goin' the town so I believe. Georgie, quit your gawkin' and take Misther Synge's coat. That's a beautiful coat, Misther Synge.

[*Her brother, with kiss-curl and dirty smirk, accepts the hat and heavy cloak of the interloper while never looking away from his eyes.*]

MOTHER: There we are now. There we are now. That bit of sunshine the last few weeks was the making of us, wasn't it, Misther Synge? Shure we didn't know where we were at all.

SYNGE: Most agreeable, yes.

MOTHER: And had you a good travel itself out from Kingstown?

SYNGE: Yes, thank you. I bicycled. The evening is pleasant.

MOTHER: But you're not after layvin' it unlocked? Your bicycle? Outside?

SYNGE: I . . . ?

MOTHER: You wouldn't leave anythin' unlocked in this quarter, Misther Synge. They'd rob the spit of an orphan's mouth and sell it back to him.

MOLLY [*mortified*]: Mother, for the love of God – it's in the hall below.

MOTHER: I'm only sayin', with the gougers and gutties does be goin' the street —

MOLLY: Jesus, Mary and Joseph, Mister Synge doesn't want to *know* about that!

[*Mother is duly admonished. Things settle painfully. We're all in our Sunday best.*]

MOTHER: Kingstown is lovely.

SYNGE: Indeed. So it is.

MOTHER: Yes, Kingstown is only lovely. Daddy and myself had our honeymoon out beyond at Kingstown.

SYNGE: I see.

MOTHER: That was neither today not yesterday, the dear knows. Lord, I haven't set eyes on Kingstown this donkey's years now. Not since Adam was a boy. God be with the days. Of course it's healthful to have the sea. I always think that. Even and it raining, what matter?

SYNGE: Quite.

MOTHER: Yes, even and it raining . . . what matter?

SYNGE: Indeed.

[*Silence settles like a dust. The fire crackles quietly. From offstage, the muffled ruction of a couple having an argument in a neighbouring flat.*]

MOTHER [*to mask the din*]: I say 'Kingstown' but really I mean Glasthule. At Muggivan's Boarding House. Do you mind where I mean, Misther Synge? On the sea-front near the bandstand, oh a beautiful place now. Two shillings, it was, and the breakfast a farthing. And you'd want to see the breakfast; you wouldn't eat for a fortnight again you'd be finished. We were there three days. It was a good clean place. Mrs Muggivan and her husband was Protestants from Moate.

SYNGE: From?

MOTHER: Moate. The town. In the County Westmeath?

SYNGE [*is this leading somewhere?*]: Ah.

MOTHER: She'd a son in America, I mind her saying now. In Red Hook, Brooklyn. And he married with a German. What's this was his name?

SYNGE: . . . I . . . ?

MOTHER: Bartley, I think. And he married with a German. Imagine being married with a German. And yourself from Glasthule. Did you ever hear of anything queerer in your natural life, Misther Synge? You'd wonder how they knock it out at all.

MOLLY [*interrupting forcefully*]: Where is Sally after going, Mother, and the supper nearly cold?

MOTHER: I told her seven, child of God, but your sister won't be said. You know my Sally, Misther Synge. She speaks terrible highly of you so she does.

SYNGE: I saw her this morning at the theatre. She will join us later, perhaps?

GEORGIE: She's away to the bazaar at Beggars Bush with some fellow.

MOTHER: You'd want to be up early in the morning for the same girl, Misther Synge. God be with the youth of us but she'd have you near demented so she would, and she courting half the town. Isn't it desperate?

MOLLY: Well we can't be twiddling thumbs on Her Royal Majesty all night. Is Grannie above in the bed or where?

[*As though on cue, the rags on the day-bed suddenly disturb themselves. An astonishingly elderly woman awakens beneath them. We watch as she rises and expectorates copiously in a spittoon; shuffles painfully towards the table, takes a generous snort of snuff.*]

MOTHER: Mammy . . . Er, Mammy . . . This now is Molly's . . . Misther Synge.

GRANNIE [*dismissive*]: Delirious, I'm sure. Is there e'er a bite to be had in a Christian house? I'd ate the leg o' the Lamb of God.

MOTHER: I suppose we might do worse than sit in. Don't be standing on ceremony there, Misther Synge. [*They promptly do as ordered. A pig's head and trimmings are unlidded.*] God above, where is that Sally? Who will say grace?

MOLLY: Mother . . . Mr Synge is of the other persuasion.

GRANNIE [*sternly*]: There'll be the grace of the Catholic Church said in this house every night I'm alive, no matter there's a black Jewman in it.

[*Georgie leads the prayer in a quiet, strained voice, the old hatchet enunciating every word with grim intentness, her face like a plateful of mortal sins.*]

MOTHER: Grannie, do you mind where's the corkscrew? Misther Synge is after bringin' us a bottle of cherry wine.

GRANNIE: It isn't wanted here. Far from wine you were rared.

MOTHER: But the visitor, surely — so as not to show coolness . . .

GRANNIE: *Be damn but I'll be taken as I'm found in my own nest, Miss!*

[*We begin to eat. The silence is unbearable. A few beats, and the intruder makes an effort.*]

SYNGE: May I ask what do you think of the political situation at present, Mrs Harold?

GRANNIE [*bleakly*]: I don't.

SYNGE: Yes. Well, indeed. Well, that is quite understandable. What with the numerous crises besetting us at present. One can only wonder as to the future. So much emigration and so on. I myself attend meetings of a society that has an outlook of socialism —

GEORGE: What's this is that now again? I do hear the boys talk of it.

SYNGE: There are . . . various interpretations, George. It is a sort of nexus of beliefs, but the *crux rei* of the matter is simple enough. It is —

GRANNIE [*interrupting*]: Speak plain for the love of God or don't be speakin' at all. A shut mouth catches no flies.

MOLLY: It means he's up for the working man, Georgie.

GRANNIE: Hup hurrah. Pass us a sup of that tripe. I'd ate a scabby child.

MOTHER: I was only after sayin' to Misther Synge, Mammy, that Daddy and I had our honeymoon beyond at Kingstown. Thirty good years ago if it was a day, Misther Synge. But he was taken and we only married ten.

GRANNIE: And a merciful release. Youd'a served less for murder.

[*Georgie chuckles into his dinner. A tennis game of glances ensues around the table.*]

MOTHER: And Molly is after tellin' us a griddle about you, Misther Synge. Molly and Sally, the both.

SYNGE: . . . A griddle?

MOLLY: It means 'a great deal', John. It's a Dublin way of talking.

SYNGE: But how quaint. Do you mind if I make a note of it, Mrs Allgood?

GEORGIE [*laughing*]: You'll be put in a play, Muddy. You'll be famous entirely.

GRANNIE [*coolly*]: And these *plays* of yours, Gentleman. What do they be about?

SYNGE: Oh, I . . . It is hard to explain, Mrs Harold. Scenes from life, I expect.

GRANNIE: Who in the name of the Immaculate Jesus would want to see that in a playhouse?

SYNGE: . . . ?

GRANNIE: In a playhouse who would want to see life? Don't we not get enough of it? Bad enough havin' to endure it without payin' for to see it.

GEORGIE: Would there be a laugh in them, Misther Synge? I do like a laugh in a play.

SYNGE: One hopes so, yes, George. It rather depends on one's audience. It is often a somewhat underestimated factor: the power of the audience, I mean. They can decide, in a way, if the drama is amusing.

GEORGIE: Is it yourself does be getting the money from the tickets and that?

SYNGE [*attempting levity*]: Not quite enough of it, I am sorry to say. But one is motivated by other, as it were, considerations.

GEORGIE [*genuinely curious*]: Like what?

SYNGE: I suppose the love of beauty. Beauty for its own sake. And then some of us are of the view that beauty can be a servant. To the Irish people, I mean. Their conception of themselves. One feels they need a higher vision in these difficult times.

GRANNIE: Do you know what it is they need? The fine Irish people. A good kick in a place wouldn't blind them.

MOLLY: Grannie, for the love of Jesus . . .

GRANNIE: A root up their holes for them and God send they get another. *Ah me dear dark Erin and the bould Fenian men.* I'd rain bombs on every cur and bitch of them for a pack of huer's melts. Prognosticatin', craw-thumpin' scruff-hounds.

GEORGIE [*laughing*]: Me soul on you, Grannie, but you never lost it so you didn't.

GRANNIE [*coldly*]: And *you* never had it to lose, you idle half-thick. It's a civil wonder to Christ you're able to find your own arse.

[*Strained silence as the meal is continued. Now Mother tries again.*]

MOTHER: And our Molly's a holy terror for the books, Misther Synge. She's that many o' them read, I don't know where to look. If she isn't a scholar, she met them on the road. Isn't that the way, alannah? A quare one for the books.

SYNGE: One can always tell when a young person has known a home in which reading has been encouraged. It is an activity greatly valued by our people, of course.

GRANNIE: An' who would those be, now? According to Trinity College.

[*He looks at her.*]

GRANNIE: 'Our' people. Who is that? In your own considering. The quality out in *Kingstown*, is it?

SYNGE: Well, the people of this country. We are all of us inheritors of a beautiful place . . . are we not? With its heartaches, yes,

and its terrible injustices — but our hopes for greater brother-
hood and forgiveness —

MOLLY [*interrupting*]: Could we not be talking of such serious
subjects at supper, John, please.

GRANNIE: It's well for them has a 'country' when the rest of
us has debts. Faith now, I'll say it to the landlord and he knockin'
for the rent. 'Hold your hour my little maneen and forgive us
the arrears for I'm a citizen, not a tenant, Mary bless yeh.'

MOTHER: In the name of Holy God, must we have politics at
the table? There'll not be a minute's luck in such a house.

SYNGE [*sincerely*]: . . . Please forgive me, Mrs Allgood . . . The
fault in introducing the topic was entirely mine, not Mrs Harold's.
I was forgetting my manners . . . I . . . intended no offence . . .
I'm afraid I sometimes overlook the wisdom contained in the
ancient proverb: *Ná glac pioc comhairle gan comhairle ban.*

[*The family look at him. What is he talking about?*]

SYNGE: The well-known Gaelic saying? 'Never take advice
without a woman's guidance.'

MOLLY [*quietly*]: They don't have Irish, John. I'm after telling
you before.

SYNGE: Oh yes . . . I am sorry . . . Please excuse me . . . Wasn't
thinking.

[*A coughing fit besets him, becoming increasingly more violent. No
one else moves. Fade to blackout.*]

10

APPROACHING BLOOMSBURY

3.07 p.m.

Lads in Edwardian drapes and peacock-feather waistcoats and they eying me, a relic of the past. 'Cosh-boys', they call themselves. Look at that fellow there. Grease in his barnet and the aviator spectacles all black as a Sunday in Lent. But the street is crowded, Molly, there is nothing he could do. And don't be meeting his gaze for that's only seeking troubles, and if you seek them, you will always find them.

My son. In an aeroplane. Over northern Germany. Those who I fight I do not hate. Those I defend I do not love. Somewhere in the room all his copybooks from school. But we must not give in to weakness. The world is full of blessings. To be alive at this time, when the cruel war is over and nobody's son is being ordered to die, and if the manners are queer and the slangs are gone strange and the fashions eccentric and the music discordant, what matter, after all? It was surely always thus. The young must be permitted to come into their force. They do not mean to look at one so harshly, should not be misinterpreted. And if the rouge on the girls seems a little too flagrant and the sullenness of the boys unremittingly brutal, it must always be remembered by those who are getting on that they themselves once resisted their inheritance. It is how progress happens, Molly, through scepticism, impatience. And if the hems are growing shorter with every passing season — woe betide us with Muddy if we came home in *that* — and if they like their blouses lower-cut than used to be permissible, sure where is the harm, when you think? The beauty of their bodies is not something to be ashamed of. Aren't they better off that way? So much fuss, so much fear. Let them show what they have. God love them. More luck. They think it will save them, the poor lost lambs. And they think there is time to rehearse.

But the boys, all the same. You'd wonder about them sometimes. That rolling-shouldered swagger they affect in the street; their sneering at the police and the old. And they fighting the Jamaicans on Chepstow Road, not only with fists, but with bicycle chains, brick-ends, and then *bragging* in the doorways as you hurry past to Mass of the black man they beat last night. From where, these boasted hatreds? What is the victory? She enters Shaftesbury Avenue. Stops.

A constellation of scarlet light-bulbs across the frontage of a theatre.

THE ABBEY THEATRE OF DUBLIN PRODUCTION
DEIRDRE OF THE SORROWS
BY J. M. SYNGE
SEVEN PERFORMANCES ONLY

A shock. Yes. Didn't know it was on. Could someone not have written? Don't they know? A telegram, even? But they must have written, surely? Have they lost the address? Don't they know that I used to . . . ? But they can't have forgotten? No right to be jealous. No right to be hurt. Offence unintended. It is only a play. Doesn't belong to you, Molly. Property of the world. A shock, that's all. Probably lost in the post. For heaven's sake, idiot, they don't need your *permission*. Gather. Collect.

I am outside my mother's junkshop on a sunny day in Dublin, a parade of soldiers passing, their coats as red as month's-blood, a sentry line of breakfronts and battered old sideboards observing their progress down the quays. I am opening old compartments, searching for something – a lost letter? The black wood of the furniture is greening with age, the hasps and catches rusting, the thinning linings sundered. Coming on for dawn. I am in the bed beside Sara. Below in the street, a dog barks.

Do they think I am dead? Surely, someone in Dublin . . . But they can't have forgotten me. An invitation, a pass? She is *Maire O'Neill*, she was once his fiancée, we must find her address in London, we must honour old soldiers. Perhaps the first-night reception? Little speech of our gratitude. Presentation or token. Piece of Waterford Glass. Not even that one would necessarily *like* to attend, for an opening night performance can be over-excited, too keyed up, with the reporters and the critics and the ambassador and his wife, and an artist doesn't need to take a bow from her box, the whole house on its feet raising cheers to her past, and the gallery calling her name as the heroine directs the spotlight, and bouquets at the fall of the curtain. Who would crave that? Only a pathetic old failure. A swirl of damp wind strikes your face.

His photograph. There. In the glass case by the booth. And a poster of the leading lady. Don't know her. So young. And a notice announcing 'to interested patrons' that the eminent Professor Somebody of Something College Somewhere will give a commemorative lecture at the Authors' Club, Whitehall Court, on '*John Synge, his life and legacy*'. The director and some of the cast will attend. There will be an opportunity to ask questions following.

But why would they do that? What is to be asked? He was a man who could see *into* things – very ordinary things. A hat left on the floor of a café in Kingstown, a proverb overheard, an old fisherman mending a net: these, for him, were a kind of incitement. There are no answers other than that. He was not like the rest of us. Nor even like *himself*. His imagination, or soul, or whatever province of his mind was hungry for the sustaining rain of the world, would soak in the storms of his own haunted strangeness, and the berries would bloom, and they were what they were, and if the tendrils were peculiar, and some of them wild, the fruits were so shockingly luscious and potent that the thirsty were willing to savour the bitter for the sake of the concomitant sweet. He needed the very ordinary. He was a beautiful man. What more than this need be said?

The sort of man who makes you think the movement of foliage might be causing the breeze. Nothing was clear and everything was clear. Impossible, particularly, to know what he wanted from you. Perhaps he himself did not know. Looks that lingered too long, abashed glancings-away, and sentences that seemed in retrospect to have been calculated for ambiguity but at the time of their delivery sounded daringly direct. You would get queer intimations sometimes; maybe you imagined them: that the pain of wanting you and being denied had become an addiction, better than the pain of having you and becoming disillusioned, or better than the pain of having you at all. How could such a character be met halfway? Only by loving him. How else would you survive? His unpardonable faults, his crippling fear of happiness; you would never call him normal, he must be forgiven or left. What he wanted was a degree of powerlessness in you that was too much to ask, a surrendering without terms, then a withdrawal from the field, and the fact that he posed as someone immobilised by the blaze of your charms was merely a subtler mode of domination.

'If I asked you to be my wife?' But what did it mean? Some would say you were a fool to have tolerated all of it so long. But you would say: I made my choices.

And on another day, you would say it was enough to have had hours and afternoons; to have been a perpetual mistress, an understudy. It should not have been enough. But it was. And perhaps, in its way, it was also a liberation. The lonely island of the wifely years. The scrubbings with the nailbrush, the torn hopes darned, the shilling eked from the housekeeping and hidden away, the leavings reheated, the silences over supper, the clock watched late and the joint sliced thin – like being buried alive together in the same coffin of politeness. It was not my lot. And I ought to be grateful. It was not what I wanted with him. Honestly.

Snow begins to fall on Shaftesbury Avenue. Passers-by gape upwards in delight or in worried-looking awe, or they hurry in for shelter beneath the porticoes of the theatres where the touts are already gathering for the matinees. And you pass the Prince of Wales, where you played ninety-seven nights, many of them ending with the roar of your name, and where the stagehands grew so weary of lifting the curtain for your ovations that in the end they had to leave it raised. It was only a year after his death; the memory of him was still fierce in you, so that it could be termed not remembrance but communion. Still frozen at the point of glimpsing him in the street, in shop-window reflections, of sensing him behind you, of half expecting every post to bring a fulminating letter that reeked of his tobacco and his sepsis. Alone on the stage, taking bow after bow, you had one night happened to glance up at a box in the gods. *Always remember the poor, Changeling; they have paid, too – often what they could not afford.* There was a weeping man in a greatcloak among the shadowed dark drapes. You saw him as you watched, his frail shoulders shaking. You could not have been mistaken. You knew who he was. The theatre's ghost, the manager had explained.

> *When I was young, oh I used to be*
> *As fine a man as e'er you'd see,*
> *And the Prince of Wales, he says to me:*
> *'Come, join the British Army.'*

Sit down a while, Molly. Now you've had a little start. And nobody will object if you rest a moment on the steps. And *fuck them* if they do. Let them glare. Let them pass. Open up the bottle. No one will see. And if the pictures must come, girl, don't be trying to drown them. For they will come to you anyway, in disguise if they have to. It is one thing knowing him taught you.

And what do they mean, his queer, florid stories? Does anyone have to ask, in the end? Every time you have seen a production in which you were not yourself appearing, a truth has struck you about what is missing from this otherworld of peasant grog-shops and holy wells and hamlets and strands. What is missing is their author. And yet the absence is a presence. Better to have a director put his sickbed on the stage, in the midst of all the violence and the rainstorms of language. *Show* him in the deathbed, face the colour of ashes, drowning in the ether they prescribe for pain. That is what they are about, if they are about anything at all. About having to live inside a body as its geography corrodes: its viaducts, scaffoldings, passageways, canals, its fissures and canyons, its boglands and airstreams, and the eternity possessed in the cranium. About wanting to live, when you know death is close. Withering to be loved, when to love is so hard. Holding to the creed to the last, dying minute. Knowing that everyone is a changeling.

—*Don't die, love . . . Don't leave me . . . I beg you . . . Don't die . . .*

Sydney Parade station. Your black train delayed. Two clerkish men in bowler hats examining the track. Taking measurements with plumb lines. Comparing fat notebooks. An engineer with a theodolite figuring a reading on the far platform. A tragedy the previous evening. A middle-aged mother and she attempting to cross the line. Drink taken, apparently, the unfortunate creature. Sinico, her name. Husband a sea captain. Rumours of a man involved.

Seapoint, Monkstown, the stern, tall houses, lime-washed, many-windowed, presentable. The governesses in the gardens, ecstasies of rhododendrons, and the knickerbockered children pushing hoops. A woman seated at an easel on the pier that leads to the coal harbour. Couples strolling lazily and the white-coated sailors, and your nervousness making everything melt into everything else like ices on a plate in summertime.

Four black horses, plumed. Three funeral carriages. Observers making the sign of the cross. Kingstown Harbour to your left, the sea and the yachts, and in the wake of a little trawler the gulls whirling crazily, as panicked and taunted as your thoughts. Should you have brought her a gift? Chocolates? A book? You notice, from your window, a flower-girl on the platform and you beckoning her over and reaching for your purse. 'Take the sweet williams, Miss, they're the best for lover's luck.' And he waiting for you now, his mother, their stares. Glasthule station approaching, the trundle and rock of the train. Not too late to turn back, to hurry across the footbridge, return to the noisy city and the safety of the greenroom, away from this appalling quietness. You could say you fell asleep or felt suddenly unwell. He is always so kind when you are unwell.

And he skulking in the shelter as you alight from the carriage. He looks nervous, is smoking, as he approaches from the turnstiles, a threadbare varsity scarf double-knotted about his neck despite the morning being hot enough for coatlessness. Haggard, yellowed, since his last operation, his eyes flicking about uncertainly as though loosened from their gimbals. You notice the tremor in his hand as he lights a Turkish cigarillo off the one he is about to finish. The scalpel cut him open. Fingers probed inside him. A tiny flake of tobacco adheres to his upper lip and you want to reach and remove it but you're afraid of his reaction. It is as though he is waiting for a first-night performance, his mien is so wild with anxiety. He doesn't kiss you, of course, only removes his crumpled hat, like a man greeting a female cousin who has suffered a recent bereavement.

'Reckoned I should meet you in case you got lost.'

'I wouldn't have, but thank you. Is everything all right?'

'You are a little late. We need to hurry. I say, Mother doesn't much care for wildflowers. You don't mind awfully if we get shut of them?'

He takes them from you and pushes them into a gap in a hedge.

'You need only be yourself, Molly. You are not to worry about anything.'

His reassurance sluices apprehensiveness through you.

And suddenly you are in his house, having looked at nothing on the way, not a rock not a bush nor a tree nor the road nor a garden nor a servant in a window.

'Molly, this is my mother. Mother, may I present Miss Allgood.'

'How very pretty you are, Miss Allgood. Do you always wear spectacles?'

'No, ma'am, only for reading. I was reading on the train.'

'I see. Do you intend to read now?'

And there are remarks as a maid accepts your macintosh and hat, about the warmth of the weather recently but the coolness of the evenings, a feverishness that is going about, much worsened by exposure to the pollen of wildflowers, the regatta at Kingstown, the pleasantness of train travel, and the elegance of an eighteenth-century pier glass that badly wants silvering, the only conversation piece in the hallway. Seeing yourself reflected in it beside the mother of your lover, shockingly, suddenly real.

And we're going into a drawing room, which is smaller than you'd imagined, and less opulently carpeted and furnished. A bay window embrasure gives out on to a sun-dazzled garden, which a walnut tree consoles with shade. The floorboards creak slightly as you move towards the centre of the room. The fire has been carefully set but isn't lit. A portrait of a stern-looking man in preacher's drabs above the inglenook; in the background a rocky field and an expanse of grey sea and overgrowth in a ruined grey garden. An uncle, he murmurs, when he observes you looking at it. He is smoking again, cupping his hand for the ash, and you wonder why he isn't availing of the hearth or an ashtray, and you notice that he hasn't shaved today. A key on a looped string around his neck like a medal. His britches are too loose, full of patches, ancient mud-stains. It doesn't matter how he dresses now. He is too sick to care. His face is a death mask waiting to be moulded. Appearances are losing importance.

'Is that Scotland, John?'

'Where?'

'The place in the picture?'

'It is Inishmaan, one of the Aran Islands. He was a minister there. He is remembered by the people with great fondness.'

He half turns towards his mother, controlling a wince as he does so, fingers moving to the wound in his neck.

'I was saying that to you, Mother. About Uncle Alec and the islanders.'

'Were you, Johnnie? Oh yes. I suppose you must have been.'

She is examining the cruet suspiciously. Her pince-nez is tortoiseshell and her hair is so beautifully white.

'Yes,' he continues. 'They loved him. It's rather touching. On one occasion, Molly, I was summering on the island and a local type approached me from the under-pier. Been mending his old trawl-nets or something of that sort. They do wizardries with a needle. The old men, especially. Oh yes. You look surprised. But their handiwork is quite remarkable. Anyhow he happened to notice me wandering by with my violin case and camera. He said "God bless us, sor, you are a Synge, or I know nothing of the world." Do you know, it had been forty years or more since he had laid eyes on my uncle. But he perceived the familial resemblance immediately. Remarkable.'

And you wonder what to say to this. It is obviously significant to him. The old woman is silent but has a way of colouring her silences. Something about the table evidently displeases her; she keeps approaching and coming away from it, peering intently at the condiments as though they, like the islanders, are about to be photographed for posterity.

'Now Mother, don't be a fusspot. It is only a cup of tea. There is no need to use the table; we can be more comfortable in the armchairs. For pity's sake, let the cutlery alone.'

And you sitting in to your places and he strikes a small Chinese-looking gong and his stare touring around the room as it clangs. Almost instantly, as though the listener has been waiting outside the door, the tea is trayed in by a small, slightly stooped young woman who says nothing at all as she places it on the table but glances at you assessingly in a way that is not quite resentful, being faintly cross-hatched with glee.

Someone's footsteps upstairs are distinctly audible. And the old one shaking a napkin and spreading it on her lap.

'Miss Allgood, would you care for a cake or perhaps a cucumber sandwich?'

'I am not very hungry, ma'am, thank you.'

'It would be a pity to waste food. When there are people in want.'

'One of the cakes, then, ma'am. If you please.'

Droplets of steam on the cover of a water-pot. When the old one begins to eat it is in a suspicious and deliberative manner, like a taster in a medieval court.

'Your teeth are so straight, Miss Allgood.'

Is it a compliment?

'Thank you, ma'am.'

'I always think it agreeable to see teeth so very clean. One sees it too seldom nowadays. Particularly in Glasthule.'

'I'm sorry, ma'am?'

'The dental imperfection of the villagers is one of Mother's rather ongoing preoccupations, Molly.'

'I should hardly term it a preoccupation to wish they would act sensibly.'

'What a darling old fusspot you are. I wonder they ever smile at you.'

'It is too often asserted that the eyes are the window on the soul, a grotesque sentimentalism and not even true in my experience; but the teeth are most certainly an indicator of the condition of health generally. This has been solidly established. There are reliable authorities. One wishes they would take it to heart.'

'Who, ma'am?' you say.

Her pausing a moment, apparently in the belief that an insect has invaded the room and is hovering over the table. 'People generally, I expect.'

'Particularly natives of Glasthule,' he says coolly.

What class of game are they playing? Is it your presence that is permitting them to play it?

'I happen, Miss Allgood, to hold to the view that cleanliness is next to godliness and that both are to be desired. Ireland, unfortunately, has a long road to travel. One reads of the poorer orders and despairs. The Gorbals, I am told, is if anything slightly better. The Gorbals is a place in Glasgow.'

'Yes, ma'am.'

'My son Samuel is a missionary in China, as Johnnie has no doubt mentioned from time to time. It has often struck me as an irony while reading his letters that the basest pagans in the world at least know a little of common hygiene. Would that we could say the same of some who are nearer. The Dublin slum is a very Calcutta, I am told.'

'Toothbrushes are no doubt what is required,' he says. 'Mother is getting up a fund with some of the other dowagers of Kingstown to provide them to the poor of the Liberties.'

'You may mock,' the old one responds. 'But it would be at least a way to show willing.'

'For us, or for them?'

'For both, if it comes to it. There is nothing wrong with encouraging individual responsibility rather than an expectation of continuous charity, which can only weaken character. Indeed,' she adds loadedly, 'this is a lesson many of us might profit from.'

He takes a sandwich apart awkwardly and examines its contents, touches his fingertips to his sweat-sodden, limp moustache as though suddenly remembering it's there. An elephant-foot umbrella stand in a corner looking dismal. Inside it, a golf club but no umbrellas. Close to the opened window, a stack of old newspapers in a stream of dusty gold light. Nothing is said. Cups plink on their saucers. You are frightened by the wordlessness, the strange heaviness of the teaspoons, the rustle of your skirt as you shift.

From the garden, the clipping of shears, rhythmic, diligent; from the distance, the whistle of a train. The clock placks solidly, adjusting its ratchets. You look at him quickly. You look at his mother. The subtle transmission of family bondedness. It is something more, and something less, than similarity of gesture, sameness of accent, physical resemblance. It is that they seem versions of one another, differently aged simulacra, or some multi-headed animal escaped from a myth; people who do not have to speak to one another more than once or twice a week to know exactly what the other is thinking. And you can see, in that moment, that to love him will be even more complicated than you thought, for it will be to love *all* of them, not only the old woman, but to find unity and common ground or at least contiguity with everyone who sits around that delft-loaded table and everyone who ever did. It makes you terribly afraid, for to love him alone is so demanding. But you can see that they, too, are trapped by their need for you, that only by your being with him can the family that loves him be saved from its own irrelevance. The trawler is in the water but they are not in the wheelhouse any more. They are out in the waves. Does the old woman sense it? Wisdom is reputed to come with great age. Is she wise enough to see she needs rescue?

'Are your parents living, Miss Allgood?' It is asked with the coldness of perfect courtesy.

'My mother, ma'am, yes. My father died and I a child.'

'That was a hard burden. For your mother and for you.'

'It was, ma'am.'

'The children's father passed many years ago. Time does not mend. We are commanded to acceptance. And we must abide, of course. But I may tell you, Miss Allgood, that I feel his absence every day. As a wounded person might feel an amputation.'

'God be good to him, ma'am. I am sorry for your trouble.'

And do you remember what happened then? The tears in her eyes. And you forgave her for everything. She was old and so frightened. She hadn't meant to hurt you; it was only that she was afraid. Her face pale and wrinkled as parchment.

'What a dear child you are. Thank you for saying that.'

You thought about the little trawler breasting bravely through the breakers, steaming out beyond the Muglins towards the herring-banks of Howth. How wonderful to be on it, cold and alive. To be anywhere far from this room.

'I imagine it must be difficult to have lines by heart, Miss Allgood. It is hard enough knowing what to say when one is saying it oneself, let alone to memorise and repeat the words of another.'

'It can be difficult, ma'am, yes. It is a matter of training.'

'Training?'

'Well, practice. Repetition. It becomes a matter of habit. If you say a thing over and over it goes into your brain.'

'Somewhat like scriptural texts, if you like,' he says. 'Indeed, one often thinks of the Bible as a collection of stories. Rather remarkable hero, at that.'

No reply for a while from the old one, who stares hard at her plate, and when she speaks again her smile is beautiful as a ghost's.

'Johnnie says these things to hurt me, Miss Allgood. As a way of seeking attention.'

'Mother – I did not mean any – I was merely –'

'The Bible is the word of the eternal and terrible God. It is the foundation of what little is decent in the sordid history of our species. And when the gaudy illusions we idolise are dust in the wind, its truths will be all that remain.' Her voice is frighteningly steady, modulated in its tones. His face has turned the colour of violets.

'Forgive me, Mother, truly. I was speaking without thinking.'

'Yes. That is your principal talent.'

You are aware that you are trembling. She turns to you stonily. 'I am afraid I was brought up with certain views about the theatre. No doubt they would be considered old-fashioned by younger people today. But we are what we are. Is that not so, Miss Allgood?'

'Yes, ma'am.'

'Yes. And we always shall be. There it is. Now I wonder if you would forgive me, Miss Allgood, but I am a little tired on a sudden. I assume you shall see Miss Allgood to the station, Johnnie, will you? Forgive my son's manners in not rising as his mother makes to leave the room, Miss Allgood. But perhaps you are accustomed to his forgetfulness.'

'I . . .'

'It was most interesting to meet you, Miss Allgood. I wish you a pleasant journey home. Perhaps your family would like the remaining cakes? Please take them if you wish.'

'I hope we meet again, ma'am.'

'Goodbye.'

———————

A blear of rain suddenly, and a bitter, earthy smell. Schoolboys in sky-blue blazers and indigo shorts, as though their uniform was designed by a colour-blind pederast. Past a line of London plane trees, some with branches half wrenched from their trunks like amputations hideously botched. Beggarwomen are watching a council workman with a saw. He rends at the shoulder of a thick, fallen bough, rips the shockingly white sinews with his heavy-gloved hands. Buses and a coal truck inch through the sleet. Hailstones drum on the hood of a perambulator. You see the museum, austerely Greek, as you cross by the post office, and you are thinking of Mr Duglacz, his mild, lined face. How pleasant it will be to have his company again.

And the letter is in your pocket. Today it will be sold. A piercing guilt takes you; it is as though the piece of paper is a child who is about to be abandoned to an orphanage. It almost seems to whisper: *Do not put me away.* But what choice have you left? It is only an object. You remember what it says; you are not selling that. What it says isn't saleable anyway. It is what he would have wanted. He was not sentimental. The idea that you would be hungry and cold would have hurt him to the quick. You listen for his forgiveness as you stand in the street and it comes to you in the stillness of the snow on the railings. We must do what we must. We did not make the world. If we had, it might well have been worse.

The afternoon smells of fog; you sense it coming from the river as it used to do in the Thirties, before London was at war, rolling in off the estuary like a yellow dream of fog, obliterating your very hand before your face. It frightens the old people and you felt for them, then. And they would live to know the blackout, its terrors. They had hardihood, so it seemed to you, they had come through war before, but blackout must have terrified them even more than did the Blitz, for a blade of light from a window would be treason. A morning when you awoke to find every front door on the Terrace had been plastered with handbills of a swastika bearing the slogan DEATH TO JUDAH. Who had stolen through the preternatural darkness, risking everything he had, through the ice-wreaths of cold and the cordite-scented air, to paste his filth to the walls of your street? To the hydrants and the gateposts and the Belisha beacons and the motor cars, as the bombers throbbed over the city. You yourself are old now, yet fog doesn't seem to matter. And blackouts don't matter either – they come in many forms. Of course, age can be forgotten, or success-fully not remembered. But lately that is harder. There is always a mirror, and you are never alone when you look in one.

The ting of the bell and then the particular and immediate restfulness of places where old books are gathered. The propri-etor's ancient Labrador is asleep in an armchair that was rescued when a gentlemen's club in the Strand was bombed. You wander an L-shaped aisle of second-hand poetry: the tattered paper spines and faded leather bindings. On millboards on the gables of the mahogany shelves, the pinned-up notices of Leftist study groups and meetings, patchworks of bleached old postcards. And the subject-headings written in his scrupulous cursive. Socialists and Socialism, Sociology, Spain, Sexual Happiness and Marriage, including Birth Control, Family Life, Suffragette Movement, Stalin. A poster of a black fist clasping a white one, the watch-word beneath them in mimeographed capitals: *The Internationale Unites the Human Race*. Mr Duglacz is not at his tome-laden table in the back of the shop; there is a young man instead, speaking quietly into the telephone, and there are several shabbily coated housewives browsing the overstuffed stacks of remaindered or jacketless romances. The portrait of Marx with its scarlet Cyrillic slogan, made poignant rather than ludicrous by the addition, many years ago, of an edging of Christmas tinsel around its broken ebony frame. The aroma of vigorous coffee arises like a blessing and over the door the embroidered sign reads 'Go in Peace'. What a beautiful place to work. It would not be work at all. You wonder if it might be possible that he would need help; an assistant? Even for no money, it would be somewhere to keep warm. But no. It would be too much to hope for.

Out of the dust comes a recollection of your daughter's sixteenth birthday: a book Sara sent as a gift. 'To my darling Pegeen from your auntie in Hollywood – tell BORING Mum to let you visit. Will introduce you to DIVINE Gregory Peck.' *The Illustrated Lives of the Great Composers.* Beethoven with bloodied rags protruding from his ears. Bach at an organ, keyboard littered with manuscript. Drunken Mozart being hefted through Vienna in a wheelbarrow. The laughter at the birthday party as they studied the strange pictures. Silly Sara never had a clue regarding presents. But Pegeen so touchingly kind when she wrote back to thank her. There are times you truly think your daughter the most admirable person you know. Wasn't easy for her, either. Saw a thing or two, poor kid. Listen to you – 'kid' – and she a middle-aged woman. This morning she was teething in my dreams.

You drift over towards the glass cases where the rare volumes are displayed, and the autographs and signed photographs of the famous. There is a letter from Abraham Lincoln to an Irish-born general, a menu initialled by Napoleon, a postcard from James Joyce to his brother, a fine first edition of Wilde's *De Profundis* almost illegibly signed by its author. *Cartes de visite* and love letters; an attempt at a sonnet; the magnificently etched cornucopia of a medieval psalter's frontispiece. How could such things be for sale? What are their truer stories? These foxed and stippled novels with their *ex libris* labels and insignia, their scrawled dedications and assertions of lasting love. It is suddenly as though the phantoms of the sellers are present in the doorway, glancing regretfully over their shoulders, guilty money in their hands.

'Might I help you at all, madam?'

'Is Mr Duglacz about?'

'I am Mr Duglacz,' says this ludicrously handsome youngster, his flop of sandy hair falling loosely over his brow. There are holes in the elbows of his donnish pullover and he looks as though he needs a bowl of soup.

'Excuse me, I meant an older man.'

'You are thinking of my uncle. I am Michael, should have said.'

'Oh but how nice. The famous Michael. You went to Cambridge, I think?'

'That's right. Few years ago now. Just after the war.'

'And you were decorated for bravery unless I am greatly mistaken?'

'More a matter of luck than anything else. Right place at the right time, that's all.'

'I see the resemblance to your uncle. Particularly about the eyes. It is remarkable, actually. I am delighted to meet you.'

He smiles so broadly that the creases in his cheeks would hold a shower of rain. What a sweet, infuriating face, like a grubby little boy's. 'All the men in my family look like brothers, I've been told. The women are not so alike, don't know why. Was there anything in particular you were interested in at all, or just browsing?'

'No, it's nothing tremendously important. Only a little manuscript I'd been meaning for some time to have valued. Well, to be honest, it is something I'd be content enough to let go. Seems a shame to keep it to oneself when a proper collector would treasure it. It is an autograph letter from the Irish playwright John Synge.'

'Oh I'm terribly sorry, Miss, we're not acquiring just now. We're rather over-stocked at the moment, as I'm afraid you can probably see. And to be frank, we're sort of moving out of the manuscript line. We're an unimportant little bookshop in the end.'

'Oh. Oh I see. I quite understand. Well, no matter at all. No matter. You're quite certain you wouldn't want to take a look? It's a nice little curio. It was valued several years ago at thirty guineas give or take. But one wouldn't want to quibble. For cash, one could accept twenty.'

'Rather too rich for our blood, I'm afraid. You might try Christie's or Sotheby's? I know a good man at Sotheby's. Should be happy to ring him up and make an appointment for you, if that would be of any help? They're planning an auction of literary collectables next summer, so I'm told. Rather think it's where most of ours will end up.'

'I would be happy to accept less, of course. Say fifteen pounds. Or ten. It's only that it's been on my conscience, keeping it all to myself. And so I woke up this morning and do you know what I thought? If old Duglacz would have that blessed nuisance of a thing for five pounds down, I would just as soon allow it to go.'

'Really, thank you for thinking of us, but we'd be unable to take it.'

'Yes of course. Well, there we are. No difficulty at all. And so your uncle is not here at the moment? Is he expected presently?'

'Oh dear – you hadn't heard. What an idiot I am. I'm so sorry to have to tell you that Ernie passed away in August. He had been ill for a short time. Cancer of the lung. He was very brave, as you can imagine. Tremendously brave. To the very last moment he was laughing and joking and writing notes and little letters to his friends. We all miss him terribly deeply. We're just carrying on here as best we can.'

A bus pauses outside the store, emptying out a gang of horse-playing schoolboys who puck at one another and throw caps in the puddles, a whirl of dirty-faced happiness.

'I have shocked you. Please forgive me. Won't you sit down a moment over here? May I offer you a handkerchief? Please don't cry.'

'I am so sorry for your loss, Michael. Please excuse my being upset.'

'It's quite all right, really. We know how people felt. He had so many friends in the business and in London generally. He was a wonderful person, so courageous and kind.'

'He reminded me very much of a man I once knew in Ireland.'

'Who was that?'

'Oh, it doesn't awfully matter. A person I knew when I was younger. Thank you for telling me so gently and considerately. I mustn't take up any more of your time.'

'Forgive my dreadful manners, I've not even asked your name.'

'It's O'Neill. Miss O'Neill. I used to come in and out sometimes.'

'Not Miss Allgood, do you mean? The lady from Dublin?'

'Yes.'

'Oh, but my uncle spoke of you with great fondness. We tried to find you for the funeral. We wanted to write to you. Couldn't rummage up your address. Would you forgive me just a moment, Miss O'Neill, there's something in the back which Ernie wanted you to have if you happened ever to come in to us again.'

He rises and goes into a curtained room behind the table, returning after a few moments with a small buff-coloured envelope on which someone once placed a cup of coffee.

'Sorry about the stain. Don't know how it happened. Things have been a little upside down about the old place as I'm sure you can imagine. We're still finding our feet. It's my cousin and I, by the way, from now on. Her name is Rebecca. Not quite sure where she is just now. Won't you come in and meet her, too, some day if you're passing?'

'Of course. I should be honoured. But the envelope – what is it?'

'I don't know, I'm afraid. But he wanted you to have it. Please won't you call in to us any time you happen by? Now if you will excuse me, there is some paperwork I sort of can't escape from attending to. We're short staffed today, I'm so sorry.'

The museum grey and stately as you stand in Russell Square. Buses growl through the smoke fumes and the snow. A stone urn containing pampas grass in the window of a shop and a clerk hurrying by on his way to the Tube wondering what it is they sell there. He barely notices the old woman near the telephone box on the corner, the schoolboys not far from her trading football cards and sweets, the tranquilly uninspiring grey sky over Bloomsbury, the tremor of the old woman's shoulders as she reads.

Dear Miss O'Neill

A little note just to tell you how much I have enjoyed your company over the years of our friendship. I'm afraid I'm not so well. I've thought of ringing you up. They've sent me to this chest-hospital which is like something out of Dante. Well, it's not so bad as all that. They buck you up nicely. Can't be easy for the nurses and doctors but they're very fine people. So young, full of liveliness and brave, bright talk. Food's not too ghastly; not that I'm eating much at this stage. Bit of fear now and again and of course regrets. Roads not taken and so on.

I'm not a fellow for scenes or speaking out his mind. My late wife, may she rest, used always to chide me for not saying a thing out. But that is a man, I suppose. But I did want to tell you something, which I hope will not distress you – that I thought of you in many ways as fondly as the sister I never had, and, if I am honest, and I hope it will not offend you when I say it this plainly, as an even dearer and more special friend. It was an honour to know a lady as beautiful and kind and lively. And your lovely spirit and gaiety for life. Everything you ever said was so full of common sense, and yet charity, too, and feeling for people, and understanding. So much so that I often thought to myself: 'If only everyone in the world were like my dear Miss O'Neill, we wouldn't be in the pickle we are in.' I used to greatly love a day when you came into my little shop and our nice long talks and happy joking. Books are so wonderful, aren't they, how they bring people together. I think they are the best part of us, really – books and music. And courage. My assistant, Mr Boyers, would often rib me about you. He used to term you my 'sweetheart' and 'best girl' and so on. He retired the other month and has gone to his daughter, who is married in Truro. Anyhow; there we are.

I'm afraid I don't believe there is much in store for us on what is sometimes called 'the other side' but if there is, and who knows – I have been wrong many times! – I have made a little commitment of a spiritual nature to be with you all the days of your life, if I can be.

Goodbye, my dear Miss O'Neill,

With my sincerest gratitude,
Your loving friend
Ernest Duglacz

11

ST MATTHEW'S CHURCH
RUSSELL SQUARE

4.03 p.m.

Agnes beatae virginis
natalis est, quo spiritum
caelo refudit debitum
pio sacrata sanguine . . .

The nave is cold and dark. Candles burn before the statues. The
odour of beeswax and incense. You are trying to pray for Ernest
Duglacz but the praying is hard, and the words of the prayers
turn to steam. That gently intolerant, scrupulous, irascible, eter-
nally Luddite old bookseller. He regarded the portable typewriter
as an instrument of the devil, believed in sealing wax and quills
and ornate sans serif the way others believe in Christ. No prayers
exist any more for such believers as these; their credo is a thing
of the past. But you try. Yes, you try. Perhaps attempting it is
everything. But strange pictures come, which you don't understand. The night the flying bomb fell on the street parallel to
the Terrace, the queer *whirr* in the moments immediately before
it struck. Sara in her costume when the two of you were in a
picture. Sara in the limousine to Elstree. Mr Hitchcock was the
director. It was a great chance, she told you. Really, you would
have to stop drinking.

And the incense or the odour of the beeswax polish raises a
chapel in New York, on the East Side of the city. The rich, heavy
wood of the serried lines of benches, and the purple of the
confessional curtains. And high in the rafters, the carved faces

of men and women, cut there by the boatwrights who had fash-
ioned the timberwork on the corbels. The images of their people
back in Ireland, it was rumoured, though nobody knew if it was
true. And one of those graven, imperturbable faces always
reminded you of an uncle who went away one autumn to pick
a harvest in England and never came back to Mary Street. Mercy
for Ernest Duglacz. My dear, dear friend. You look up at the
altar through the mote-filled beam of light. Mercy for all the
departed.

And you are remembering a wreath of lilies before a plaque
in that church, for the Irish boys who died in the Civil War. The
fighting Irish. Heroes of Gettysburg. Champions of brotherly
freedom. Sara had no time for 'all that auld talk'. They want the
Irish to build their railroads, fight their wars, kill their Indians,
whose land was robbed off them for nothing, Sara said. Then get
soused and die quiet in some gin-shop, she said. And that's the
great plan for the Irish. The way some Americans go on, you'd
swear no Irishman ever did anything bar shooting someone in
the head and spouting the rosary. She liked being mischievous.
It was one of the reasons you always loved her. She saw the world
differently. Her own woman.

The third time you came to New York, America was about
to go to war. Recruiting officers were waiting on the waterfront.
You and the other actors had watched some of the boys sign up
to fight, as though they were joining some fraternity of revellers
on a spree. Not a minute in America, like foals with the stag-
gers, pucking one another, joshing, moon-eyed with exhilaration.
A lad Sara had taken a shine to, Michael English from Ennis, had
led two of his cousins to the tent in Castle Gardens and asked
the Yankee corporal for a uniform and a gun, for he wished to
prove himself for the Republic of liberty. *Tis a tiger you're looking
at here, boss. I'll kill a thousand before breakfast.* It had seemed strange
to you – to come all this way in the hope of a new life, only to
fight in another man's war.

You didn't understand the war in Europe, its causes, its

purposes. Sara had tried to explain it to you, but you suspected she didn't understand it either. You suspected that nobody did. Her eyes were sea-green and they shone like dappled water. She adored America. She would make herself a home here. If you'd half a pick of sense, you'd do the very same, she told you. Jesus God, was she bossy. Dear Sara.

Her hope was to make that home in a German or Italian neighbourhood in New York, for Germans were hard-working, proud, staunch Americans, and Italians so beautiful to look at. Her children would be Americans. It was the freest country on earth, the land where everyone married whoever they wanted and if anyone didn't like it, go hump. How little she knew, but how lovely her ignorance. Sometimes she spoke in contradictions.

You think of her now. My difficult sister. Maybe she is in Paradise today. God help the poor angels, she'll be ordering them about, getting them organised into a trade union before she's done. There is a wedding in progress in the chapel near the transept. The party is small, no more than a dozen guests, but the bride and groom, who look anxious and thrilled, are as magnetic as a wedding couple always is. The groom is a soldier, his uniform pressed and neat. The bride fidgets with the hems of her sleeves. Two elderly women are observing, taken by the spectacle. 'In't she beautiful,' one of them says. 'Pretty as a postcard.' The fumbling for the wedding ring. Avuncular laughter from the Padre. You are an old lady watching a wedding.

It was the way he had looked at you sometimes, in his dishevelled little bookshop: an expression of such kindness, of hopefulness and courage. His gaiety was a sort of currency, self-replenishing, always new. You weep, wishing not to, wiping your tears with your wrists. And the bride and the groom, alerted by your quietly echoed sobbing, turn from the side altar and stare at you a little resentfully. You cross yourself and move away, towards the doors.

A memory whispers up, of a time you were playing in New York when the child of one of the costume-girls died of meningitis. The woman was from Galway, her husband from Clare. You and Sara attended the wake out of duty or sympathy. Nobody else from the company was free. The funeral was to be held early the following day, for a longer period of mourning would be unwise, the undertaker said. He spoke with the practised diplomacy of all his profession, in euphemisms, sidelong looks; in silences. Flowers would be useful to have in the room. Lilies, if possible, for their aroma is heavy. Better for the casket to be closed, he had murmured, when the deceased was so young, and so thin. You and Sara were silent, as though guilty for something. And mainly because there was nothing to say.

You watched as they draped the ancient mirror in the parlour, as the country people back in Ireland prepare for a waking; for at the hard time of life an old custom can seem important, the practice you might mock at the easier time. The few dollars the father had managed to raise at the pawnshop on 7th Street were spent on food and drink for the mourners. There must always be tobacco at a wake, the father had insisted. A wake must be done with propriety.

Was he trying to help his wife? Did he think it what she wanted? Or somehow did he want it himself? He had borrowed chairs from some of the neighbours, placed them carefully about the parlour, efficiently, like a waiter preparing a function, never once glancing at the terrible object in the corner. His face was slick with sweat.

They filed into the parlour quietly, as though trespassing on a privacy, the women clutching rosary beads, the men with hats in hand. It was as though they were waiting for something important to happen: some sacrament or a revelation produced by their solidarity, their sitting together in a room. Some of the callers were neighbours in the tenement building; others nobody knew very well. Men from the fire station where the father drove a wagon, you assumed, for one or two of them seemed to know his name. Police officers, stevedores, navvies: all Irish, and a man who was an organiser of some sort for the Democratic Party, and another, from the Ancient Order of Hibernians, which was said to have offered a little money towards the funeral. And others who had insisted on condoling in Gaelic, as though the vowels of the old language could heal. And the German and Italian women who lived in the tenement coming in, in twos and threes, or some of them alone, speaking quietly in their own languages, which the mother did not understand, or in broken phrases of English, or saying nothing at all, but sadly shaking their heads and touching the mother's hand because conversation was impossible now. How it must have hurt her to be condoled with, for there was nothing to say, no matter the language or the kindness lying behind it. How you wished for her that they would all go away.

You sat together in the room, the women around the coffin, the men in a huddle by the kitchen. Perhaps there was a priest but you do not remember that. The firefighters bowed their heads. Some wept. You had been sick that morning. It was the year the drinking worsened. It was as though you could hear the mother's thoughts. *That is not a body. That is my child. Why are all these people in my home?* Candles burned down. The visitors murmuring. The mother was told the child had gone to a better place. A place where there is no suffering, where the poor are loved and honoured. It was how the people in Mary Street used to talk about America. A paradise of honey and milk.

> *O come to the land where we will be happy.*
> *Don't be afraid of the storm or the sea,*
> *And it's when we get over, we soon shall discover*
> *That place is the homeland*
> *Of Sweet Liberty.*

And you recalled the waking held for a neighbour's girl on her last night in Dublin. Her father and mother and the gathering of relations. An uncle singing 'The Twang Man' in a corner of the house and then a man with a melodeon, but he wasn't good. 'Get up with me, Bridget,' said the father, late in the night, 'and face me in a step. Will you do that for me, girl? For likely it's the last dance we'll ever have in this world.' And the girl and her father had danced in the kitchen. And in the morning she had left for the steamer at Kingstown, with a couple of shillings and an address in New York: an agency placing Irish girls as maids of all work in the houses of the wealthy of Manhattan.

Dear mother. More mourners arrived and tobacco smoke purpled the air. The mother couldn't write, her parents in Ireland couldn't read, so it was you and Sara who helped her write the letter, as best you could, and someone back in Ireland – the schoolmaster, was it? – would read it aloud to her people. It would be the voice of some elderly schoolmaster that would pronounce the terrible words of the letter: that a child who had lived only five months in this world had lost her life in America. On the night of her funeral you would appear in a play. It seemed absurd and obscene. It seemed pointless.

My child is dead. Why can't you understand? There is nothing I want said to me now.

An old Connemara woman who lived in the slums of the Five Points had shuffled into the apartment, leather-faced, Iberian, clad in the ragged tweed shawl of her homeplace. She touched her forehead to the tiny coffin and began an ancient keening: a soft ululation, wordless at first, but soon widening into the *ochóns* and *bróns* of Gaelic. The German women stared at her. Many of them looked frightened. You and Sara were frightened too.

From outside in the street came the bawls of the vendors, then a shrieked obscenity, and the rattle of a cart. Rain spattered on the windows. The room was too full. The children were restless on the floor. And the main memory you have is of wanting to hold the author of that play, whose lines you would speak that night in New York. To see him again, just for minutes or seconds. But he was gone, as the child had gone.

And you leave the chapel now, into the cold light of London. Must be morning-time in New York and you picturing the busy streets, the workers crossing the avenues and the park. Children in the playgrounds. Someone ringing a handbell. Is there any freer city in God's wide world? Will you ever see it again? Or Dublin? A long time now since you walked Mary Street or the Coombe, saw the sea at Killiney or Dalkey or Howth. The word 'Kingstown' has vanished. It is now called 'Dun Laoghaire', a name foreigners find hard to pronounce. And you seem to hear him say it – Dunn Leary – Doon Leerah – as you cross by the gates of the chapel.

And perhaps to change the name is to alter the essence too, as a woman changes her name upon marriage? But maybe baptism means nothing, and marriage means nothing – perhaps they are only words. What has happened has happened and you will always carry Kingstown, no matter the name ever given it. And you are there once again, in a place whose name has gone, as you walk the dirty fog of Russell Square. In whatever cells of memory you haven't succeeded in destroying, you will always be there, old girl. It visits you in dreams and in strange irruptions of the day, the eternal Kingstown, its unease. On your left is the coal harbour, on your right the black belfries, and the slow train is empty but for you. Through the high ivied corridors, the tunnels and cuttings, past embankments of wilderweed and overgrown gorse that nobody can be bothered to burn. And it chunters again into Glenageary station and stops with a screeching of steel on steel. He is buried in Mount Jerome, with his mother, his people. Cruel, to think of it. His body corrupting. And the house looms up at you, grey, many-windowed, asterisks of gull-shit down its half-collapsed storm porch. You think of snow falling into the sea.

You have received a telegram at the theatre. His uncle needs to speak with you. That is why you are looking at the house.

I am alone in the hallway. Dark, wainscoted walls. The pier

glass that wanted silvering is gone. In an alcove, framed in bog oak, an ancient map of Kerry. Mounted above a dresser, his violin. And there are photographs of Connemara and the Aran Islands maybe: stone-filled fields, battered thatched cabins, coracles upended on dulse-strewn strands like beached sea-dragons in a dream. I am not thinking about the photographs but of the eye that framed them. The photographer is always in the picture.

The maidservant returns — but no, it is a different one, older, thinner, more tired. She looks like your mother. Striking, the resemblance. She gestures that you are to follow and you do as you are commanded, down a dark mildewed passageway lined with portraits of magistrates, hunting scenes, prints of portly boars. Past the doorway to a library lined with leather-bound tomes and a long black table stacked head high with papers. You can smell French tobacco, his must, his sickness. And suddenly, now, it is like looking at his face.

His uncle gazes up at you appraisingly. He is dressed all in black. Miss Havisham in the clothes of a man. He looks broken, dead-eyed, like his nephew near the end.

—Please be seated. He gestures. You do as you are told.

—You had an efficient enough journey from the city, Miss Allgood?

—Sir.

—The trains are not always reliable.

—No, sir.

—Personally one ascribes the difficulties to the agitators in the trades unions. The trains were far more punctual previously.

—Sir.

—I should have preferred for you and I to have this talk with a male relative of yours present, Miss Allgood. But there it is. We must rub along as best we can.

—Sir.

—I am to inform you that my late nephew willed a bequest to you, Miss Allgood. You are to receive a small annuity from the performance royalties of his works. I may tell you I disagreed with the proposition but my nephew would not be countered. I am of the unfashionable view that outside of a family one's income ought to be earned, not given. Nevertheless, you are to receive a sum of eighty pounds per annum. In full settlement and acknowledgement of your occasional assistance to my nephew. It should be enough for you to employ a parlour-maid or a person of that nature. Should you marry, that amount shall be halved. Do you understand?

—Sir.

—I think you have in your possession a number of letters my nephew would have sent to you. It is a matter for a later time. But I should like to acquire them for his archive. Naturally you would be compensated for any material loss.

—I would never want to sell them, sir. They are private.

—Quite. As I say: it is a matter for a later time.

—And my own letters, sir. The letters I wrote him?

—Yes?

—I should like to have them returned. There would be several hundred of them, I believe.

—A literary man's papers comprise part of his estate.

—But they were private, sir. They are mine. Not to do with his work. I should not like to think of anyone else reading them.

—I can set your mind at rest on that score. They have been destroyed by the executors. So as to protect the confidentiality of the friendship and its particular circumstances. It was thought, should they fall into unscrupulous hands and so on, that they could be vulnerable to exploitation or misunderstanding. I hope you will agree that this was the only correct course. At any rate, what is done is done.

—I –

—This is why one would have preferred you to have a male relative present. A male relative would be able to see that the executors have acted correctly. You will understand it yourself, Miss Allgood, in the fullness of time. Perhaps when you are married.

Perhaps when you are a parent. Would you like to see his books, perhaps? Now that you are here?

—His books, sir?

—Have you washed your hands this morning? Some of his books are rare editions and so forth. There is a visitors' cloakroom with lavatory at the end of the hall. Be sure and use the soap provided, won't you? Good girl.

The bed in which he sweated. That is what you would like to see. To sink your face into his pillowslip, touch his sheets, his clothes. But the upstairs of the house would be forbidden you. As you rinse your clean hands and come back through the hallway, you wish you were anywhere else.

—Miss Allgood – there is something further I have a duty to say to you. It is a delicate matter.

—Sir?

—I am speaking on behalf of the Synge family. For my nephew's whole family. It would not have been the intention to cause offence to you, Miss Allgood, in appearing not to have invited you to be among us at my nephew's funeral. It was felt that a private family service would be best. In the circumstances.

—In which circumstances, sir?

—In the circumstances of great sadness. A family closes its ranks. No offence would have been intended, and I have been asked to convey that to you most sincerely. If these things could be approached again, they might be approached with more thought. I would very much wish to apologise if we have behaved with insensitivity regarding your feelings.

Don't go crying now, Molly, whatever you do. You'll be back on the train in a few minutes. Look at him, don't be harsh. He is elderly and frail. He has suffered a loss, too. He is doing his best. The thing he wants to say, he doesn't have words for. It isn't his fault. He didn't write the lines. He is speaking them the only way he knows.

—My late sister – Johnnie's mother – she married for love. That isn't always easy. In the old days, these matters were regarded differently. There were many other considerations in the background of a marriage. The world is changing greatly, of course.

You look at the old man. It is like seeing your lover. The dark, pained eyes, the inhibited stance; the way he holds his beautiful hands. And you wonder what would happen if you ripped open his liar's face with your teeth. Nothing, probably. He would pretend not to have noticed.

—It might interest you, this collection of Mr Yeats's poems, Miss Allgood. I cannot affect to understand them, I am sorry to say. Some of the earlier ones are melodious enough. The swans and so forth. He is clearly a gifted rhymer. The music, I mean. But I confess that I have little feeling for these modern complexities in verse. Do you understand them yourself, at all?

—Some of them, sir. I know Mr Yeats.

—Oh yes. I suppose you would. Tell me, what is he like?

—Like a priest, sir.

—A priest? How queer. Figure of speech, do you mean?

—It is hard to express in words, sir. He feels things very deeply. He is a very great man. But I do not know him well. I only work for him at the theatre. I have played in some of his works. He would be a fairly changeable person. I am only an employee.

—Somewhat distant is he, then, Yeats? Head in the clouds?

—He has been extremely kind to me, sir, since your nephew passed away. Himself and Lady Gregory have been goodness itself. I don't know how I would have managed without their tenderness and help. My own family could not have done more for me.

—Would you like to have that book, then? As a keepsake and so forth?

—It's gracious of you, sir, but I have a copy of it already.

—Something else, then. If you wish. I have been authorised to offer you something from the library as a memento. Anything up to the value of five pounds or so. But we shan't quibble if it's a few shillings more. Only don't go too mad about it, will you?

—There is nothing I want, sir, thank you.

—The matter I raised with you previously, concerning my nephew's funeral arrangements and so forth. We approach these things a little differently from the Roman Catholic Church. I had intended to say that to you. We regard these things more privately. We are rather set in our ways. I suppose one would term it a tradition.

—Yes, sir.

—In your own faith – as I understand it from my Roman Catholic friends – a funeral is regarded as an opportunity for a very wide gathering of the deceased person's acquaintances; whereas in ours the approach is one of family and those with very close relationships only. Misunderstandings can sometimes arise as a result.

—There is no misunderstanding at all, sir.

—That is good. Thank you, Miss Allgood. I am glad that we have been able to have this little talk. It has put my mind at ease. At this difficult time.

—It's my opinion they're all the same, sir. One as bad as the other. And the sooner this heartbroken country is rid of all filthy hypocrisies of God, the better it would be for everyone.

—I can see that you are distressed. We can sometimes come to rash conclusions when we are upset by a loss.

—Yes, sir. We can. May I go now?

—I should like to express my gratitude to you, Miss Allgood. My nephew was a difficult man. Always very difficult. His temper was choleric. One had bright hopes, of course, but they were not to be realised. And now, of course, they shan't be.

—I cannot say I found him difficult. Myself, I mean.

—Nevertheless, he was. Poor Johnnie.

> *Agnes beatae virginis*
> *natalis est, quo spiritum*
> *caelo refudit debitum*
> *pio sacrata sanguine . . .*

You look at the clock on the post office gable. You must gather yourself, Molly. There is no time to mourn. The other actors will be hurrying through London now, in the tube trains, on foot, minds brimming with lines. You are thinking of your room. The cat staring at the window. You turn down Great Portland Street, in the cold.

12

BROADCASTING HOUSE

4.38 p.m.

The vast lobby has an ordered and brutal imposingness, like a battleship's stateroom designed by the politburo as a gift for the tyrant's birthday. You speak your name to the security commodore, who has clearly never heard it before and asks you to repeat it and then to spell it. He pages through his register of those who are expected today, occasionally glancing up to beckon through a messenger or someone bearing a pass or a parcel.

'And you are an actress, are you, Miss?'

'So I have been told.'

He looks at you uncertainly. Are you joking?

'An actress. Yes. I am here for the transmission of a play.'

'Lord, I don't see any Allgood, Miss. Definitely not.'

'I may be listed under my professional name – Maire O'Neill?'

'No, I don't have an O'Neill, Miss. Now that is curious. That *is* curious. By whom is the play in question?'

'It is by the Irish author Sean O'Casey. It is for the World Service, I believe. The piece is called *The Silver Tassie* – perhaps you see the title listed there? The producer is Kenneth J. Hartnett.'

'Ah yes. Indeed. Here it is on my list. You'll be wanting Room S–1, Miss, in the sub-basement – you probably knew? Transmission to commence at 1800 hours. I'll just telephone down to the greenroom and let them know you've arrived.'

'I say,' she attempts, 'it's a little like trying to talk one's way into Paradise, isn't it?'

'In which sense, Miss?'

'Well, St Peter and so on. You are the guardian at the gate.'

He grins at you good-humouredly. 'I hadn't ever thought of it in those particular terms, Miss. But I dare say we've our share of angels inside.'

Nice man. Handsome. Soldierly in his uniform. Pleasant to watch him dialling the number and speaking quietly into the receiver, a calming sense of properness and efficiency and order, and his neatness and his amiable decorum. Great improvement on *some* of the staff at the BBC. Fellow they used to employ to drive you home after a performance looked like a lavatory attendant's slightly stupid apprentice.

'You will have worked with Mr Hartnett previously I expect, Miss, have you?'

'Many times, yes. It is always a pleasure.'

'I'll tell you a thing about Mr Hartnett, Miss. He's a gentleman. And a professional.'

'Indeed.'

'Married to his career. I declare, that's true.'

'Quite.'

He guides you through the barrier and indicates the way on a wall map, despite you knowing every detail of the way already. But indulge him a moment. It's his job. Make him happy. *Over to the door, you say, sir? And two flights down? I'm most awfully grateful. What a saviour you are.* You go slowly, with care, for the steps are unusually steep, your hand gripping the banister as though a life-rail on a ship. Through the corridors and landings, past the heating ducts and stairwells and the women polishing the linoleum floors. Yes, you know the building well, have been here many times. Several nights, during the Blitz, you slept here. You enter the little basement elevator and it descends with a whine. You find the Women Artists' Dressing Room. It is empty and cold. You had been hoping there would be food. There is none.

You wait.

You think.

You look at the walls.

Photographs of famous actors in heavy wooden frames. Household names. Heroes of everyday England. A fire bucket in the corner, rusted, punctured, full to the brim with cigarette ends. An odour of lichen and eau de toilette. Coffee grounds collected in a cone of old paper that is actually the title page of a script. You run the tap several minutes but the water stays cold. It plashes on the metal of the sink. You bathe your hands and throbbing eyelids but the towel is too dirty, so you dry yourself on the hem of your blouse. Then you sit at the table. But nobody comes. And the strange thought strikes you that you are far under the ground; that beyond those walls with their smiling, posed portraits is the black, wet clay of London. Everything is quiet. You can hear your own heart. You are hoping that the peppermint has taken care of your breath. For a moment, you close your eyes.

Receive unto your love the soul of Ernest Michael Duglacz and may all the souls of the good through the mercy of God rest in peace this day. Blessed Mother, intercede for the soul of my broken John Synge, the soul of his mother, of my son, my father, of all who need forgiveness, of all who were hurt, and Jesus, Mary and Joseph assist me in my last agony and angel of God my guardian dear to whom God's love commits me here ever this day be at my side to light and guard to rule and guide, amen.

You cross the corridor to S–1. All the lights are off. Is it possible you have made a mistake?

But the porter would have known. It was there, on his list. You throw a switch – the room is flooded with hard, cold whiteness. There is the faintest metallic hum from the vents. You leaf through the script but the hunger is distracting. Often there is food at the BBC: a curled-up sandwich, a cake; a cup of tea. You had been banking that there would be something. Perhaps the girl has forgotten. Usually there is a girl whose job is to bring food. Is there a way of asking someone that would not seem impolite? Where has everyone gone?

Deep in your right ear a hard spangling of pain. Shocking. So sudden. Is it your eardrum or a tooth? Out of the wince, somehow, Yeats's voice comes to you. *If in doubt, speak the text. Do not gesture or flounce. Our purpose is not to entertain; it is the creation of beauty. Praise may be the result; it must never be the aim. Biddy and her Pat may go to the pantomime. Our quest is not that of the jester.*

What a silly he was sometimes, like all Great Men in that way. How very, very little he knew. Never done howling for solitude in his poems, but he forever jaunting to London and manoeuvring himself onto committees and *talking* incessantly and getting mixed up with women and writing letters about important matters to the newspapers. He'd no more stick a day of solitude than would a monkey without his troop. Fond old divil. And yet so kind.

Never saw the everyday, the warp and weft of a life, the forgettable conversations and meaningless glimpses few storytellers could include in a tale. Afraid of a drapery window, a conversation on a tram, an old man's non-sequiturs, a cat crossing floorboards. And yet, you have come to feel that those nothings *are* the story. Mahler, yes, but the cry of a newsboy; that has its music too. A woman walking hungry through snowblown streets. Is this not a drama worth playing? And where in the world is the sculpted Michelangelo that compares to a weary seamstress on the Tube? You are the daughter of a junkshop, a child of rag and bone, raised amid the tat no one wanted any more, the bric-a-brac and clutter, the ugly and expendable, but give the junk a little rub and you'll see your reflection. A bit of spit and polish works wonders.

Close your sore eyes, Moll. What do you see? A pretty girl in a tenement bedroom, bent over an old copybook she still has from Mary Street School. Can you make out the phrases she is secretly writing? '*Mrs John M. Synge – Mrs Molly Synge, Kingstown – Maire Synge-O'Neill – Mrs Synge.*' The poor smitten dote. The dreams you'd be swimming through. And if you had borne him a child – yes, there is still that thought sometimes – he would be middle-aged

now. You always imagine a son. Why is that, Molly, when he understood women so well? Catch a hold now, Molls, someone's coming.
Buck up. Am I laughing or crying? I don't know. Well, gather, Molls,
gather, and beam like the sunshine on a summertime fairground in
Kerry. Because it really wouldn't do to be letting down your guard,
especially when the door is opening.

'Ah, Molly, my auld pet and you radiance entirely.'

He shuffles into the waiting room, his left hand in a glove, his
right leaning hard on a walking stick. 'I had a little fall a couple
of weeks ago, made a royal hames of my ankle. Oh I'm fine, not
a bother, it's just a bloody nuisance getting about. Oh, but look
at you, how beautiful. You're growing lovelier with the years.'

'You tell such pretty lies, darling.'

A fond embrace is exchanged.

'I don't know how you do it, Molly. Have you a portrait in
the attic?'

'Get away, you outrageous charmer. I look like Methuselah's
mother.'

'We shall never be as young as we are today, my love. But —
is something the matter, darling? You look sad?'

'A little shock, Ken, that's all. I was just in town earlier seeing
to an errand or two and I heard a friend had passed away not
too long ago.'

'Oh my dear, I am so sorry. Anyone I knew?'

'No, a bookseller, a darling man. He was elderly and so on,
but still, just knocked me slightly. There it is.'

'Would you like a few minutes? I can let you alone if you wish?
I'd say go home but it's a tad late for me to find a replacement
at this stage.'

'You know me better than that, Ken. We always give the show.'

'You're certain now, Molly? You're up to the job?'

'Never funked a performance in fifty years, darling, hardly
going to start today.'

'Good girl, there's my stager. We'll have a little drink afterwards, you and I? We might trundle around to the Bunch of

Grapes for a bite of supper if you'd like. Richard might join us; I'd mentioned I was seeing you.'

'And how is my princely Richard? It's been too long, it really has.'

'Oh he had a little stroke a while ago but he's terrifically on the mend. Do you know we're twenty years together in January, isn't that an astonishing and ghastly thing? We're like an old pair of slippers, that's what he always tells me. I'll ring him up and we'll make a trio, if you're game?'

'Lovely, darling.'

'Now, before the others descend, there's the little question of the source of all evil. The usual rate would be two guineas but I went and said I can't offer that. This is strictly *entre nous*, by the way, not a word to the others. "This is Maire O'Neill," I said, "*the* Maire O'Neill, I simply will *not* insult an artist of her calibre," so I hope you can accept three pounds ten. You'll be paid in cash this evening, immediately we're finished the broadcast. And I've told them I won't stand for any of their pen-pushing nonsense, I'll be up to the comptroller's office with a blunderbuss.'

'Thank you, Ken; that will be useful. It was good of you to think of it.'

'We are privileged to have you, Molly. We don't see you often enough. And how is the beautiful Pegeen keeping? In the pink?'

'I do miss her now she's in Aberdeen; she was always my lovely girl. And her husband can be a little austere – we've never quite hit it off. Funny thing, like most convinced atheists one has come across down the years, he has rather a touch of the Reformation.'

'Ah.'

'Still, the chicks must flee the nest, and we have to let them go. They're living out of a tin of beans, of course, but she's happy, that's what matters. Tiny one-bedroom flat. Not much room for old Mum. We've to sort of shove up in the bed when I visit.'

'The boys must be getting a fine size? Do you know, I remember them as babies.'

'Turned seven in August, great gallumping galoots. But the sweetest pair of naughty monkeys you'd meet in a leap year's travel. I shall go to them for Christmas. Hope so, anyhow. If son-in-law hasn't barred me as undesirable.'

'And I noticed the Abbey are in town. You'll be attending the party, of course?'

'Oh, I mightn't bother really, darling. These affairs are such a bore. They bombarded me with invitations to this and to that, as you can imagine. A lecture by Professor Something of Something College Somewhere. Do you know, I'd just as soon stop at home with the cat and a book. All the hoo-hah rather gives me a headache.'

'Molly, you're a card. Oh, here are the others now. Mr Doyle I believe you know, and Miss Hargreaves and Peter Eglantine.'

'Delighted, Miss Allgood.'

'Deeply honoured, Miss O'Neill.'

'Lovely to see you again, Molly.'

'All present and correct, then,' the producer says amiably. 'Well I think we know what we're about, unless anyone's got a question? No? Good. Yes, Peter, of course. Just be sure of the tone when we get to that speech, give me a lot of colour in the voice and nice and sharp and clear, and really sing it strong in that lovely Welsh way, we'll keep a welcome in the hillsides, you know? Same with you, Helen, keep it crisp as a knife and really let me know what she's feeling in that little bit in Act Two. But that's teaching granny to suck eggs of course, you'll be wonderful, I know. All shipshape with yourself, Bob? Good man, that's the ticket. Anything else, then? Molly, you're all right? Of course you are, darling. Excellent. Well, I believe ladies and gentlemen that we will do our work well, and perhaps if you would do me the honour we'll just run through a couple of the cues. I have the finest cast in London and I hope that you will enjoy yourselves immensely and I have every confidence in your wonderful abilities.'

You form trios for rehearsal. There isn't time for a full run-through. An engineer arrives to see to the cabling and test-connect the microphone. Water is poured into tumblers.

The studio is thick with cigarette smoke, a great bluish cloud of it, floating up toward the lights and the gleaming steel ducts and the pipes and the soundproofing tiles. The heavy Roman numerals of the clock on the wall tell you there are less than thirty minutes to go. And your hunger is fading. Everything is fading. You are among people you understand. All is well. You turn and notice a golden-haired girl of about seventeen come into the room, accompanied by a woman who is clearly her mother. The girl is wearing a dark-green brocaded dress. Her pale face is freckled and hopeful. She is like a girl out of a novel of Somerset or Wessex, as heartbreakingly lovely as an English cornfield in August. A necklace of amber stones. Green ribbons in her hair. If a boy kissed her lips in a summertime orchard, he'd smell forget-me-nots and apples and sweet william and sweat and he'd remember it every time he heard bees. She is holding a satchel and looking at you intensely. She purples as you meet her limpid eyes.

'Mr Hartnett?' says her guardian, in an apprehensive voice. 'We're not interrupting proceedings, I hope?'

'Oh, Molly,' says the producer, 'this is Elizabeth Collins and her stepmother, Olivia. Elizabeth will be working with me soon on a production of *Romeo and Juliet* we're doing. She is going to be our Juliet; it is her first leading role. Sort of experiment I'm having a crack at; going to play the whole thing before an audience in the Concert Studio upstairs. Miss Collins is a great admirer of yours and I happened to mention you would be with us today. She asked if she could pop by for a moment to say hello.'

The girl comes forward nervously, her stepmother encouraging silently, and seems afraid to accept your hand. 'You're my absolute heroine, Miss O'Neill. I've read up on all your performances. In reviews and old newspapers. I can't believe I'm meeting you.'

'Why, you dear, dear girl. What a lovely thing to say.'

'Elizabeth saw you when she was seven in *The Islander's Revenge* at Crawley, Miss O'Neill,' says her stepmother. 'It's no exaggeration to tell you that you are the reason she wanted to act. Nothing we could do about it, her poor old dad and I. She's hoping for a place at RADA. We're very proud of her.'

'Well, work hard, dear, work hard. And who knows what may happen? You are pretty enough for any role, but you must work like a demon too. And attend an actual production every chance you get. We mustn't only study. We must see.'

'And steer clear of the boys,' says the producer, with a frown. 'Brutish, malodorous goats.'

'Dad and I do our best on that score,' her stepmother smiles. 'But there's one candidate we've not managed to shoot down just yet. He's a nice boy, really. Poor Elizabeth is blushing. Better shut up or I shall be in trouble going home.'

'Oh as long as it's not too serious,' you say to the girl. 'Just have plenty of friends and nothing too tying. But I can tell you're a sensible young lady, as well as a beautiful one. I find the younger people extremely wise, I must say.'

'Could I dare to ask you to sign something for me, Miss O'Neill? If that would be all right?'

'But of course, dear. Of course. I should be absolutely delighted.'

She reaches into her satchel and takes out a dog-eared paperback copy of *The Playboy of the Western World*. His story of a boaster, a peacock, a cosh-boy, a jolly roving ploughboy, a lover. Many lines are underscored. Tiny notes in the margins. A bus ticket doing duty as bookmark.

'It's my very favourite play of all time, Miss O'Neill. I'm learning Pegeen Mike's last speech. As one of my audition pieces for the Academy.'

'That old thing,' you say, as you inscribe its yellowed flyleaf. 'Such a fuss it caused at the time. And when you think of what's going nowadays.'

'They say he wrote the part for you, Miss O'Neill.'

'Oh now, they say lots of things.'

'It's such a romantic story.'

'Isn't it.'

'Molly was the prettiest girl in Dublin,' the producer says gently. 'And the sweetest, kindest heart. And the loveliest eyes. Every man in the town was smitten with love for her. Every last one of us. Always.'

'Now Kenneth, you exaggerate.'

'Not by much. Not by much.'

'I declare you'll have my head swelled if you don't quit your absurd flattery.'

'We have taken enough of your time, Miss O'Neill,' the girl's stepmother says. 'It's been most awfully good of you. We appreciate it very much.'

'Have you any last word of advice you could give me, Miss O'Neill?'

'Oh, you don't need advice from an old squawker like me, dear. Only speak your lines clearly and be sparing with movement. Some of the younger actresses nowadays tend to rather jitter about, when there's really no need; there's a great power in stillness. And always love the audience, even when they're tough on you. And earn your chances. And take them when they come.'

'I find the movement part of it hard when I'm actually on the stage. Remembering the cues, I mean.'

'Do you know, in my day at the Abbey, we used to have a giant chessboard painted on a great sheet on the floor – an old mainsail it was – someone bought it from a wrecked ship – and by God you were given your square and you'd better be stuck in it until the moment you were told to move. And woe betide you if you landed up in the wrong position even slightly. Oh my word, you'd have the lard cut out of you before you knew it.'

The sort of warm, courteous laughter you love ripples around the gathering. You caress the girl's face briefly, tell her again she is pretty, but to pay attention to her schoolwork and not just the stage, for a career can be brief or may never happen at all, but an education can always be leaned on.

'Now we'd want to be getting ready,' the producer announces

mock-firmly. 'This will have been a lovely experience for Elizabeth, to have met a true great such as yourself, my dear. It will be something for her always to remember.'

'Goodbye then, Miss O'Neill. Thank you so much for taking the trouble.'

'Wait now a minute.' You reach into your pocket and take out his letter. To look at it a last time? But no need. No need. You know what it says. You could never forget it. You hand it to Elizabeth Collins, who reads it quickly, eyes widening.

'But it's from him,' she says. 'This was written by Synge.'

'Yes, it was. It's rather ancient. I was very young when I received it – not very much older than you. He was a bossy old coot, as you'll see from his tone. But he gave me the wisest guidance I ever received in the profession. *Permit the words to lead you to the heart words come from.* That is the finest advice of all. Because it's loving.'

'How wonderful. I'm shaking. His actual handwriting.'

'He was a great, great man. I would like you to have it. As my gift at the start of your career.'

'Miss O'Neill – I couldn't possibly. I really couldn't possibly.'

'It's out of the question, Miss O'Neill,' the girl's stepmother says.

'I would like you to. It would honour him. Please permit me to insist.'

'Miss O'Neill, I couldn't, really. Just to have seen it is enough.'

'It is an old tradition in our profession that a gift from one of us to another must never be refused, particularly when a performance is about to begin. You will bring me a great blessing if you take it, Elizabeth. Look after it for me, won't you?'

Tears fill the girl's eyes. 'I can't tell you what it means to me.'

'Put that in some old book and take it down from time to time. And say a prayer for me when you do. Have we a bargain?'

And it is there that Death comes for you, in that unprepossessing bunker from which the waves reach all over the world. Death finds a way down the labyrinthine corridors, like an odour of winter fog in the city of London, like a forest child who left a trail of crumbs to pursue. Past the turning reels of tape, the windowless offices, the clerks in ashen corduroy, a secretary bringing coffee, a messenger-boy with envelopes, a maintenance man sorting spanners, a correspondent wondering silently if there is anything left to say. Death drifts past all of them, for it is not their turn this evening, and he snuffles for the scent of his quarry. He sees you in the circle of actors surrounding the microphone, their eyes flitting adeptly from the pages to one another. The studio has been darkened – it is better for atmosphere – but near the microphone is a single lamp and it illuminates the faces. A man is producing sound effects with a selection of implements. Like the actors, he has a copy of the script.

Death listens to the words. He has heard them before. He too has a copy of the script. He is not impressed by artistry, is far beyond catharsis. He crosses towards the circle, looks calmly in your eyes. Such a shame to take you now, but a cue is a cue, and Death has his own role to play.

You are halfway through your third soliloquy when the pain begins in earnest: softly, subtly, like a rumour of pain, but then suddenly blooming violently in the floor of your abdomen, and you press through it, thinking it will pass, as it always has before. The other actors look at you, sensing something is wrong, but you wave your pages abruptly, do not want to pause or demur when the end of the scene is in sight. You are Maire O'Neill. You do not kill a scene. The show will go on at all costs.

And the pain comes burning harder, finding a way through your veins, into nerve endings you have forgotten you ever had. A girl hurries from the booth and stares at you, transfixed, like a woman looking at a frightening apparition. You don't know who she is. An assistant? A secretary? She shimmers and hazes in your sight.

'Are you all right?' she mouths. You nod, still speaking the speech, shushing her away with your script. The soundman brings a glass of water and stands by your side; your colleagues eye you fearfully but you concentrate on the microphone. It is now the only thing that matters in the room and in the world; it seems to be growing larger or wider or smaller, or changing its dimensionality in some other way you can't name. The leading man comes in with his reply; you know he is slowing his lines, creating time for you to sip the water, become collected. Every text has an elasticity, like a symphony or a song; in a crisis it can always be found by the experienced. The water tastes of dust. You stare at the ceiling. You spiral your hand at the leading man, encouraging him to accelerate the speech, for the hour available is limited and must on no account be overrun. And in you come again, finding the words a kind of lifebuoy. Hold fast to them, Molly. The welter will pass. Let the ocean thrash around you, and the breakers rise to mountains, but *never* let go of the text.

You can see that in the booth Mr Hartnett is on his feet, speaking urgently into a telephone, looking worried. He pushes his fingers through his hair and gapes at you as though lost. You smile back *Don't worry*, gesture for him to sit. You have a sense of pushing Death away; as one would banish an unwanted admirer at a dance you never wanted to go to. India is listening. The words must be spoken. Ireland is listening. Canada. Hong Kong. Children glancing up from homework, couples seated by fireplaces, old men alone in cold rooms. And they will not be betrayed. It is not in you to stop. Death will have to wait until the closing soliloquies, for it is the ambition of every member of your profession to die with the boots on, and to be taken before the end of the show would be shameful. And so you utter the lines and wait, and the cues are taken up, and you feel Death recede resentfully into the cracks in the floorboards. It is not time, after all. It was only a rehearsal. He has departed to gather his forces.

'Molly darling – what happened?'

'Just a touch of indigestion, Ken. Heartburn. Nothing more.'

'It looked like serious pain. Are you quite all right? . . . Molly? . . . Look at me? . . . I have told them to fetch a doctor. Won't you come and sit down a moment? No, you must . . . you must.'

'If there was something to eat, darling? . . . Just a little something small? . . . Silly fool, I forgot to have lunch . . .'

Across Brickfields Terrace, in the upper room of the bombed-out house, the light of your unknown neighbour is glowing. There is solace in seeing it. You know he is there. The cat is asleep on the floor near the cooker. Through the walls comes the voice of a man on the wireless saying tomorrow will bring a storm to the Orkneys. Humber. Dogger. Forties. Rockall. Fair Isle. Malin. Stornoway.

Ghost light. An ancient superstition among people of the stage. One lamp must always be left burning when the theatre is dark, so the ghosts can perform their own plays.

You stoke the fire and kneel before it, pull the blanket round your shoulders. It is almost midnight now. What a long, strange day. But a day full of blessings. To be alive – even this. To be sent home in a beautiful taxi from the BBC in London and the cost not even to be mentioned. The British *people* paid your fare. When they have nothing, nothing. And you stepping out of its blackness like the Queen of the Faeries. O did you ever think it, Molly, and you streeling around Mary Street knowing nothing of the truths of the world? A slight little brown-eyes; pretty thing you were. Your head full of nonsense and boys and old furniture and bits of songs you didn't understand. And the driver opening the door for you and handing you your carpetbag. And if only some of the neighbours had witnessed your arrival. But that is only vanity. You prideful vixen!

Cold night now. The wind in the rafters. Sacred Heart of Jesus, help the tramps and the drifters and the sleepers in the doorways of London. A long, strange day. You'll remember it. Yes. Sure, the day you didn't make a friend is a waste, so it is. From out on the street, the shrilling of the roughnecks. Oh you're not gone yet, girl. Not by a ways. There's a crack of the whip left in Molly Allgood.

Look closer at the fire, girl. Another little drink. Aberdeen for Christmas – your daughter, her twins. And on Boxing Night you might slip across to Fusco's and treat the children to a fish supper. Not be letting on your plan; just say you're away to the chapel, but come home with the cod and the sausages and the ray and the newspapers all sodden with vinegar. And Pegeen will be such a scold, *not be wasting your money*, but secretly she'll be delighted, and the children might sing. Bitter night now. Sit you in to the hearth. Oh, the warmth on your face, the red sheen on your glass – even on your fingernails, your skin. Lady Gregory is in the flames with white-haired Yeats. They look gentler than you remember them, so mild, so at peace. As though some layer of their earthliness had been washed away by time. All that tenderness they hid by giving imitations of themselves for so long – now visible in the shining coals. Augusta and William. Won't you call us by name? There is an old friend we would like you to meet.

The cover of the *London Daily Echo* one morning next week will have a headline about the murder of a police officer, Sidney Miles. Two cosh-boys, Bentley and Craig, will be charged with the crime. Christopher Craig is sixteen; Derek Bentley will hang. The sort of terror that garners outrage and questions in Parliament; men will write plays about it one day. In the late edition, a small article appears on page eleven. Nobody will ever write a play about this.

WOMAN UNCONSCIOUS

Last Tuesday, constables and firemen broke into a boarding-house room in Brickfields Terrace, London W2. A severely burnt elderly woman was found unconscious on the floor, having collapsed into the fireplace where she had evidently been burning books, having no other fuel at hand. Foul play is not suspected. A number of empty bottles were in evidence. Residents of the house did not know her name. It is thought that she was originally from Ireland and may have worked for a time in the theatre. She had been intemperate in her habits and was known to have approached passers-by for assistance. Anyone with information is asked to contact Maida Vale Police Station. It is believed that she was either widowed or unmarried.

13

PARK PRUETT MENTAL HOSPITAL
HAMPSHIRE, ENGLAND
November 1952

. . . Streetcar named Desire. Beautiful name for a play. *American* title if ever there was. Everything in America is blared, vivid: yes their scenery, the way they feel, their sousaphones and skyscrapers, their steak so steaky, their apples the size of grape-fruits, the iron-jawed chatter of their factories and taxi-men. Only an American would write a play called *A Streetcar Named Desire*. An Englishman would entitle it *A Bus Called Passing Interest*.

Dorset. Cumbria. Coniston Water. The moorlands of Yorkshire. The Medway towns. King's speech on the wireless. Muddling through. Brown soup. Watered beer. A bunk-up in a doorway. Little helpful hypocrisies that keep everything going. Snobbism deep in those who have nothing. Kindliness. Bravery. Hyde Park in a mist. Dirt under fingernails. Shakespeare's face on pub signs. Wordsworth. Cider. Sandbags. Contraceptives. Notting Hill Gate. Broadgate. Billingsgate. 'Ham' in the town names. Toffee-apples. Pleasantness. Brown paper and vinegar. Sadness. Fog. Best people in the world. English and Americans. Tragedy and Comedy. Twins.

Peaceful. Yes. The sisters come and go. Hear them mumbling I'm here a week. Don't know if I am. And they giving me injec-tions sometimes. Think that's what they're doing. And the pain all swallowed up in an eiderdown of drowse and the clock on the wall does be ticking.

Night-time now. Pretty Jamaican nurse comes on at midnight.

Hear her singing quiet as a wren as she's coming and going. Isn't a man in the whole world but wouldn't fall for her if he heard it.

> *Ah do do Kitch, don make mi cry,*
> *Ya know I love yuh*
> *Yuh playin shy.*

Sweet Pegeen the other evening. Or maybe it was dawn. But I couldn't speak couldn't move. Felt sad and she gone. Coming back tomorrow. So like Sara, her eyes. You'll be all right Mam, you'll be all right Mam, and a drawing from the twins of three galleons on the sea, the *Nina* and the *Pinta* and the *Santa Maria* and Columbus with a feather in his cap. Had frightened her. My appearance. Well she hadn't been warned. Molly girl, a nice pancake you're after getting into now. No beauty beforehand. But Jesus help you now, girl. Can't feel my face for the bandages. Like a mummy.

Mr Ballantine come this morning. Nice, soft man. O the flowers and the chocolates and a *True Romance* and a card. Well he wasn't to know I've no use for them now. Asked him: *Ted, why are we here?* He goes *I'm not a religious man, Moll.* I said *No, love, what I meant was why are we in fucking Basingstoke?* And he laughing into his hands. Nice, soft man. Told me I was brung here from St Mary's up above for there's the best man here for the burns. You'll be right as the mail, Moll. More lovely than ever. We'll throw a knees-up at the World. My Ellie's home from Canada. You remember my daughter Ellie? Got a baby on the way. Couldn't really see him. Recognised his voice. Heard him and he leaving and he whispering to the matron.

—*How long has she got, love?*
—*A few days perhaps.*
—*Let me know. About the arrangements. I'd like to see to things proper.*
—*You're a relative?*
—*No, love. We was friends.*

Woman in the bed across from me does be coughing, spewking.

Hard to close my eyes. Lids burnt. Ointment on my arms, my legs, my breasts. Can barely put a sheet over me. Three screens around the bed. Pictures like a film. Make a little story of them, pass the night hours. Won't show me a mirror. Matron knows best. At noon on an April morning before Adam was a boy, here's this doxy leaving a cheap hotel, the Prince Regent in San Francisco, and she walking the eleven long blocks through the leafed-out streets to the grand old Grand Central Station. Well, let's see; what's on her mind? And she trudging and thinking. Her husband and her sister and the other actors are waiting. *Let them wait*, the rip thinks. *Good enough for them to wait.* Holy Moses the cheeky mare. Thinks she's Cleopatra so she does. High Queen of Mary Street. God love her.

So what can she see, Moll? What does it all feel like? Give her a scene worth playing, why don't you? Well, there's this flat heavy heat after descending on the hilly city. So tiring to walk in the beautiful scarlet shoes and God between us but she's a bit hungover. Yes, Molls, she is hung-over, no point in saying she isn't. Apple blossom drifting on the hot air of 3rd Street through clouds of fly-filled pollen. And you'd clutch it in your hand like confetti so you would. And its powder on the silk of your glove. Then the darkness of the station so cooling, soothing. The players drinking iced coffee in the concourse café. Can you see them? There they are! They're beckoning.

America is not her country – she was born in Mary Street, Dublin, when the dinosaurs roamed Phoenix Park and the groves of Chapelizod, and they lumbering the Atlantical forest connecting Inishmaan and Manhattan and their eyes as gentle as giraffes'. Lived a few years in London, now and again in New York. Lower East Side mainly: cheap the rents there. Life of a strolling player, wouldn't know where you'd awaken. But a professional engagement is after taking her to this Pacific city where she has played many times, oh many times. Her husband is a good actor and he's not a good husband. There he is, foostering around among the younger women of the company, flirting with her sister, with the costume-girls, the waitresses, and he pulling dimes from their curls and scarves of laughter from their lips and every inch of him the jolly roving ploughboy.

The country is not at war but there's a rake of kitbagged soldiers and their neatly dressed sweethearts all pretty as a parcel. O you wouldn't be up to the lipstick and the rouge and the powderclouds and the scent and the bonnets. And a Stars and Stripes flag the size of a tennis court draped on the gable over the gates to the platforms. Silk enough in it for fifty dresses for the beautiful sweethearts, and a star on the bosom of each.

And up comes a recruiting sergeant and he approaching her sister for an autograph. Always the same: oh modesty personified. Who, me? Oh how kaind. One can eaunly do one's best. *Sign the fucking thing, bitch. Don't be blushing and fanning yourself and trying to string everything out.*

And here's Moody out of the crowd and the stony old kisser like a president auditioning for Mount Rushmore. Moody is her dresser for this tour; a curious profession. She tramps around America with actresses and dancers, works cheap, is often hired, says little. She's after being along to Meeting for it's Ash Wednesday morning, and although Moody was born in Connemara in the same year as Moses, was a Catholic in her girl-hood and she kissing the beads, she now holds to a vigorous breed of shout-aloud Methodism long popular in the American south. There's nobody knows her age. Four hundred and seven. Lived in Louisiana one time, the voodoo queen Moody, and more lines on her face than on the map of Auld Ireland; she's like a fingerprint with eyes and a gob.

So let's see. Them's your characters. And what happens next? Where are we going, Molly? Something needs to happen. And if only the pretty nurse would come in with the injection. Jesus, my soul for a drink. Well, they board the long train, Moody hefting the luggage – and she coming and going, going and coming – and seeing Madame into the *First Class compartment*, if you don't mind, where cooled white towels have been provided in stacks, and the arms of the purple, calfskin seats all edged with the trims of grubby lace.

'New York *City*,' calls the neat conductor. (Did any of this *happen*, Molly? Aren't the dates incorrect? Sure it's only a story. What matter?) Let's call him a tall, grey man, nice and spruce in his bearing, like a steward on one of them liners, the Cunard or something, and the pleats of his sky-blue uniform pants pressed so sharp they'd cut you if you mocked him. His hair white and short, in these soft snowy curls, and the buttons on his coat glittered so golden with the polish you'd swear they was the eyes of the saints themselves and he whistling Thomas Moore through his beautiful white teeth it would be a pleasure and a privilege to be bitten by.

> *Believe me if all those endearing young charms*
> *Which I gaze on so fondly today . . .*

Well, into the compartment slowly, with a proprietor's air, or maybe like the curator of some queer auld museum nobody'd be bothered to visit any more. And he switching on the reading lamp with this bamboozled expression, as though he's not sure how it got there or what exactly it does. Then he turning to Madame and Moody with this forbidding auld face that seems at odds with the hospitality of his words.

'You ladies are welcome this morning. You got everything you want?'

'What is your name, my handsome fellow?' Miss O'Neill asks abruptly.

'Virgil, ma'am.'

'Thank you, goodly Virgil, you are a stout-heart and a hero. Now fetch me a fearsome Bloody Mary and see that I am otherwise undisturbed. Oh, and Moody will take a cordial of some innocuous description, devoid of the spirituous essences. She becomes violent when drunk. There have been unfortunate incidents.'

'I ain't allowed sell you no liquor, Miss. Not till we're running. That's law in the state of California.'

'Permit me, if you will, to clarify one matter for you, Virgil. I do not give two living damns for the state of California. A Bloody Mary this very minute and don't stint with the electric juice or I will know. Be off with you to the bar. Run along.'

The conductor eyes Moody, but Moody looks away and she busying herself unpacking a valise. Madame's fraying nightclothes and other nocturnal requirements she begins arranging on the berth-side table. The conductor, as though not wishing to observe such a dispersal (he was married one time and once was enough) turns heel and quickly leaves the uncomfortably hot compartment, sliding closed the heavy door behind him. Moody continues at her duties, working quietly, methodically. She is accustomed to making the best of intimate spaces; indeed her dependant often says it is her only talent. Outside on the track a beggar boy knocks on the window, a mask of pitiable hopefulness on his doleful face. Moody, without a word, draws the shade on the daylight and his thankfully muffled blasphemies.

'I suppose my sister has managed to board without being engulfed by her admirers?'

Moody says nothing. It is taken as affirmation.

'What a relief that the Police Department did not have to hose back the throng. Or beat them down with truncheons, as usual.'

'Take your medicine this morning?'

'Balls to my medicine.'

'Ain't gonna funnel it down you. You know what the doctor say. Seem to me like you need it but if you wants to be ornery, you fire on ahead and die.'

'You'd like that.'

'Yes, I would.'

'You are the devil's very handmaid.'

'Been times I get to thinking that's true.'

'Leave me,' commands Madame. 'I wish to rest up.'

'Where in the Hell would you like me to go?'

'Sit down, then. You're rocking the boat.'

And as the train jolts away – goodbye, San Francisco – Old Moody is reading Leviticus. You close and rub your eyes but your eyeballs creak. Like a rusty old gate in Mount Jerome. And you raise the crinkled blind to a scene of almost miraculous tedium. The wet brown wheat-fields extend to the horizon, only here and there a barn and after a while, near a town, an enormous black water-tank on stilts. DUBLIN OHIO painted on the cistern. Three farmhands gaping up at it, and they scratching their heads, as though it has only recently landed there and they don't know what to do, or it sprouted like a gargantuan mushroom. One of them swivels towards the train as it decelerates and passes and you notice he has a rifle in his hands.

You give a pull on the bell-cord but the conductor doesn't come and you begin to feel anxious, full of darkness. A half-empty tumbler of vodka on the table. It wants ice but you drink it down anyway. The conductor appears in the corridor, rocking fluently on his heels. Virgil, his name. Strange scenes out the window. The stillness of the back lanes around Mary Street, the market. A cartwheel on the wall of a blacksmith's forge. And walking now. On the Lower East Side. Onward, through the cacophony of Orchard Street New York, past pedlars and stall-holders, through clusters of hawkers, past the windows of Schubert's butcher shop, past the little German beer hall where carters are unloading clanking crates. And the pictures do be blurring like the spokes of a wheel. Where is the nurse? I am thirsty.

Embrittled, scooped-out, you walk as in a dream. Your eyes are weary. You are burning. Strange languages swirl around you like flutters of streamers: tongues of Saxony, Bavaria, Piedmont, Prussia; faraway places and wandering peoples. The smells of strange food. Spices you cannot name. From the embrasure of a window comes the sound of rabbinical singing, for a boy who loves Jehovah lives in that room. And there, on the corner of Stanton and Essex, stands the little Florentine pedlar, with his ribbons and combs. This city with its hundreds of thousands of immigrants, its parlances, its musics, its impenetrable slangs, its countless deities, its ghettos and rookeries, has nothing to say to your grief. A black woman is selling strawberries: people say she was once a slave. Everyone in this neighbourhood has a story behind them. So does Miss Maire O'Neill.

Every second Tuesday morning, quietly as a rumour, she leaves the small apartment, which is on 8th Street and First, and hobbles over to Christopher Street, to the premises of her doctor, whom she calls 'my alchemist' or 'Ludwig'. His name is not Ludwig, nor is he even German, but she has convinced herself, wrongly, that he looks like Beethoven. She is the kind of woman who persists in the face of hard evidence. It has caused her much grief, this trait.

Quarter after nine. Correct your watch by her, gents! The bell of St-Mark's-in-the-Bowery gives its single leaden clong – and here she comes crossing by Second Avenue and 10th, accompanied by old Moody, her dresser. Moody is ancient and slow, a skeletal piece of work, has on spectacles of bottle-black glass, which make her appear like a blind woman. There is no doubt who is the employer and who the servant, even when Moody walks in advance, as she usually does, for Miss O'Neill has been trained to communicate with the body as well as with words. One might think she is an old woman but she is not yet forty. Some years ago, back in Ireland, her fiancé died. Their love affair was difficult, secretive.

An incident last winter, in which Miss O'Neill's ankle was broken, is responsible for her laborious gait. Slowly, unsteadily, as though burdened, she shambles, disregarding the streetcars and the bawls of the newsboys, the clank of shutters opening, the lines of singing schoolchildren, her pale, unblinking gaze indomitably fixed on the shifting horizons of downtown. Past the fruiterer's, the grocer's, the entrances to the dives, the little five-and-dimes, the ironmongers and hobos. Her skirts so unfashionably long that the passers-by do not perceive that she is wearing a man's carpet slippers, unmatched.

Miss O'Neill dresses in her finery for this fortnightly appointment, in her Strass Paste jewels and feathered chapeau, in a threadbare velvet cape she wore eleven years ago in a production of *Wuthering Heights* at Philadelphia. Her gloves — ebon-black, the lace long sundered — are made of the skin of a fish. A first-night gift from the poet William Yeats who had admired her in one of his plays. She is carefully made up, black lines around her eyes and a dusting of glitter in her curled, greying hair, and pan-stick, white, with the *faintest* hint of blue, for a slight touch of blue conceals wrinkles.

The storekeepers know this curious duo of old and often trade bantering rumours about them. They are sisters, or cousins. One of them was jilted at the altar. The tenement room they share contains only one bed. Moody is 'the man', it is whispered. They are wildly rich. They are abysmally poor. Miss O'Neill was once the mistress of a famous theatre critic in Germany, or in Prague or Vienna or London. And Moody, some say, is the oldest woman in New York. She murdered a wicked priest in Louisiana. The shimmers of whispers, the storekeepers nodding or raising their hats, and this morning it is so hot, a steaming Manhattan July, and the men are sweaty and red. Look at them. Dear Jesus. The sufferings of their wives. Imagine them naked. Sweet Mary.

Dr Millstein, a Muscovite, has the old-school courtliness of a country physician in a play. He is bearded, well turned out — his late wife was English — and he moves among his bell jars and stethoscopes sombrely, as though they radiate religious significance. He offers tea and small cakes. He is proud of his samovar, the only object he brought with him when he fled the extremists, he says sadly. They talk for a while about nothing and everything: the news, or young people today. His profession, like Miss

O'Neill's, is a matter of appearances, fidelities as well as great knowledge. He considers himself a sort of artist, and who is *not* an artist in that city of immense verticalities? These little rites fulfilled, he rinses his hands carefully and injects his only Irish patient with the elixir that brings tranquillity – he pronounces the word *trankvilidy*.

Millstein is famously, forbiddingly expensive, attending all the least tranquil of Manhattan's numerous actors, and other ladies and gentlemen whose sensitivities are onerous, but it is years since the question of the root of all evil was last raised between Miss O'Neill and himself. Perhaps he does it as a charity. Perhaps her tranquillity is payment enough. Or perhaps there is something in the picture we need not be told plainly, for every female member of her profession has on occasion been asked for the nothing about which there is much ado.

He injects her, dabs the pinprick with a bundling of gauze, then measures the pulse in her stick-like wrist, making note of its count in a small leather notebook he keeps by a bust of Mozart. Oh, a great man entirely for the notes is ould Ludwig and a maniac for the Wolfgang Amadeus. All this is done quietly, his eyes on the grandfather clock, his brows moving curiously as though counterpointing its plack, and Moody like a gargoyle in the corner. 'There was pain, Miss O'Neill?' He always asks if there was pain, and always she answers that there was none, although in fact there always is. Sometimes he bends low as he gauges her blood pressure, the strap around her arm, the egg of his bald skull, and he mumbles almost silently, in Russian. His nurse, a beautiful black woman, comes in and out with documents, which he signs with barely a glance. 'You are feeling well, Miss O'Neill? The qvietness is coming now?' She can hear the rattle of streetcars, the calls of the newsboys, the whining of a violin from the apartment above the surgery – the neighbourhood is not what it was. His syringe is carefully placed in a small silver box. He touches his fingertips, briefly bows. His politesse.

'*Lyubimaya. Do svidaniya.*' Goodbye, my beloved.

Thus becalmed, assuaged, she returns to her apartment, which is noisy in the daytime in a way that used to bother her; but we accustom to anything, as she often says to Moody, who looks at her almost violently, the old viper. In the street below the window, the people come and go and often there is the explosive ruckus of a cockfight. Miss O'Neill is put to bed, for the injection makes her weak, and sometimes even weepy, though less so lately – and she finds, on those afternoons of opiate dreams, that a presence comes out from backstage.

The smell of his tweeds, of a French tobacco he used to favour. The sea is here too, its ammoniac headiness, and the crunch of his boots breaking mussel-shells. A wave sucks lustily on the pale brown stones. There is spray in his beard and his hair.

I see him walking near the lead mine, pointing to its chimney. I am climbing its spiral in the wrench of a hurricane, wet leaves flapping around me, and his murmurings, coaxings. The distant hoots and whistles of the tugs on the East River. I am turning into the city, my body a map, its capillaries laneways, my heart is Times Square. Last night I dreamed I was a storybook with my pages still uncut. A poor yoke nobody opened.

I am dressing, with the assistance of Moody, who has prepared hot tea and lemon, for soon it will be time to go. The walk will be arduous. The director can be difficult. It would not do to keep him waiting.

Moody has marked up a script, underscored the lines of dialogue. The part is that of Gertrude in *Hamlet*. It is a role I never understood but such a confession cannot be made at any audition for you'd be shown the fucking door in a moment. Moody warns me to be good, on best behaviour. The role represents a last chance.

The afternoon is sunny, so painfully sunny, and the walk to 42nd Street takes time. On the corner of 30th and Fifth, a streetcar accident has attracted a crowd, and out of the huddle steps an elderly policeman who could only be from one country on earth.

—Excuse me, Miss? Begging your pardon. But is it yourself? Who I think?

—I am Maire O'Neill. Do I know you, Officer?

A look of preposterous satisfaction illuminates his face, which is round and pleasant and sore-looking around the chin, as though he shaved himself too closely or once had an illness that chronically afflicts the skin. He salutes and offers his hand, but then, as an afterthought, wipes it bleakly on his lapel, before holding it out to you again.

—I've seen you many times, Miss. You're the finest actress in America. There's none could hold a candle to you so there isn't.

You will spin this out, for it will irritate Moody enormously. And the best way to prolong it is to say nothing at all, for if you remain silent he will have to keep talking.

—I seen you Adam's years ago in that play about the ploughboy killed his da. What's this is the name of it? You were mighty in that play. Myself and the wife nearly died laughing so we did. Hand to God I nearly bust myself laughing.

—You are gracious. Thank you, Officer. You are an Irishman, I think.

—From Mayo. Michael Mulvey. I had the pleasure of meeting you before.

—Oh yes?

—You were in Wicklow one time. When the world was only made. On your holidays, you were. In a cottage by Glencree. I was stationed down in Annamoe and didn't I meet you on the roads. A cup of tea you gave me and we chattering like the wrens. You were the most beautiful girl I ever seen.

—We are late, Moody mutters.

—Don't rush me, bitch.

—We are late.

—I am dealing with my public!

The theatre is cool, pleasantly dark, like a church. The stage is in half-light, almost bare. Carpenters and their lads sawing

———— 220 ————

quietly in the aisles. A girl distributing sandwiches and coffee. Gilded stuccoes and velvet seats and the sheen of the chandelier. Up in one of the boxes two scrubwomen are working, dusting at the cretonnes of the drapery. And from the gods unseen, at the very top of the house, comes the warble of a man singing a ballad self-mockingly, his mellow, faltering tenor far better than he pretends, and the dull, flat jeers of his fellows.

> *Brave manly hearts confer my doom*
> *That gentler ones may tell*
> *Howe'er forgot, unknown my tomb,*
> *I like a Soldier fell!*

You ascend the steps to the stage, test the angle of the rake. The auditorium is cavernously large and deep. It will be important to project but your training has prepared you: throw the voice like a ball; aim to hit the back wall. In backstage you glimpse a prompter repeating lines from a soliloquy in a monotonous burr to his assistant. A stagehand is unwrapping rapiers; a boy polishes their blades. A woman who must be the costume-mistress is measuring an enormously fat man, her tape around his waist while he puffs on a cigar and natters of the Brooklyn Dodgers.

—Molly, how have you been? I wasn't expecting –

—Good afternoon, Christopher, it is agreeable to be working with you again. I am sorry we are a little late. I was detained on the way. Fellow who'd seen me in a production – you know what they're like. Sign this and sign that and the dear knows what. It happens every time I leave the house.

—Molly –

—But to business. To business. I have never understood Gertrude. You shall have to advise me very closely. The text I find confusing. The rhythms, the metres. She is not one of Shakespeare's best women. But we shall find the truth of course. We always do.

—Gertrude has been offered. I'm sorry, Molly. I auditioned someone else Monday.

Moody is staring. Nothing is said. The director peers bleakly at his hands.

—I need a servant for Act Three. I can pay the union rate.

—I do not play servants, Christopher. I think perhaps there is a confusion —

Faces turn to look at you. A carpenter pauses. Backstage, the soliloquy ceases.

—Molly, I'm going to have to ask you to lower your voice.

—I shall sue. Do you understand me? I will finish you in this city.

—Don't speak to me like that, Molly. *Who in hell do you think you are?*

—I am an artist trained by *the Fays* at the Abbey Theatre of Dublin, the greatest national theatre *in the world*, sir. The first of its sort ever to have existed. It was born before my country took her place among the nations and its birth helped light her way to whatever measure of freedom she now enjoys. *I knew* John Synge. I knew *Augusta Gregory.* William *Yeats* gave me praise as he accepted the Nobel Prize. Is it a scrubwoman I am to be? A walk on and off? I have filled this auditorium more times than you have filled your disgusting face. *Am I now to be insulted in this manner?*

—You're drunk, Molly. Go home. Don't let people remember you like this.

—You odious little leech, do you slander Maire O'Neill? That will cost you dearly, sir. I have witnesses. Witnesses! Perhaps your own mediocrity causes you to assume that everyone else is grubbing in the sewer with you?

—*Here's ten bucks, get off my stage before I call the police. And never come back. You hear me? Get out. You washed-up fucking drunk!*

You are standing in the train corridor, light-headed with hunger, looking out at the lights of Chicago. *Molly* he whispers, behind you. *My changeling?*

He is swaying at the forefront of a ragged silent fellowship of the boys and men who loved you. They are white-faced, wordless, every man jack of them, hatless, ghostly, in dumb show. Little Patrick Counihan, the scene-painter's apprentice. Hutton, the coal-heaver. Blackmore, the plumber. Willie Pearse, the actor, and he riddled with bullets. Johnny Howlett, his fierce beauty, his arsenal of mimicries; the strut of him down Francis Street like a prince's through his kingdom, a confetti of compliments swirling around his face and he blowing them out of his path with a pout. Died at the Somme when the poisoned gas swallowed him. Black bunting draped from the tenements. Mair the critic, and Sinclair the actor: both have the lustrous sadness of archangels. And then — so strange — those you don't recognise at all. Here comes one in a beautiful suit, a portly man but muscular, like a one-time varsity oarsman who later became a barrister. He gazes at you shyly, beads of tears in his eyes. Was he someone in the audience, who came night after night? And a poor boy of the slums, who looks fourteen or fifteen, offering you — what is it? — an apple core? His hands cup it delicately, as though it is a precious jewel of Araby or the flame of his own lost life.

You shuffle away from the window, begin walking the train, and you sense them following but at a respectful distance. You pass passengers who are sleeping, or eating, or talking. Your son and your daughter, both asleep under blankets. Up ahead you see a bridge and its approach makes you feel relief, for you know the pursuers will evaporate when the Missouri is crossed. Like all ghosts, they are afraid of water.

It would be good to have a drink. Just to soften the edges. Your husband is looking weary, playing poker with two strangers. He gapes up at you unsmilingly. He needs to trim his moustache. He turns to his companions, both of whom are a little older.

—Gentlemen, may I present to you the other half of my soul.

The carriage rocks gently, a boat in a swell, and the whiskey in their glasses slops. One of the gamblers covers his tumbler, then licks the pads of his palm, then sucks his fingertips one by one.

—*You are an actress, Miss O'Neill?*

—*That is correct. Mister . . . ?*

—*O'Keeffe, ma'am.* He tips his homburg. *James O'Keeffe at your service. Commercial traveller. In paper and religious articles.*

—*You are courteous, Mr O'Keeffe. You are a Southerner, I think.*

—*I have that honour, Miss O'Neill. Jackson, Mississippi.*

—*I have never played in Jackson.*

He grins.—*I have.*

You allow it to pass. The flirtatious dog.

—*But excuse my manners, Miss O'Neill. May I offer you my seat?*

—*Thank you, Mr O'Keeffe, but I am unaccustomed to card tables.*

—*Of course.* He nods.—*Pleasure deferred. I hope to run into you again some time.*

You are alone in the dining car. Presumptuous, bold oaf. The moors of north Wicklow at dusk through the window and the fog bringing lights on in cottages. Gorse burning on the Sugarloaf. O the fire is flaring hard. I am covered in butterflies of pain.

Pegeen is holding a soap bubble between the tips of forefinger and thumb. And now you become aware that the dining car has only three walls. Beyond the space where you imagined the fourth is the darkened parterre. Shadowed heads of the audience. Everyone watching. The ushers like statues in the doorways.

There are eras of every life that have a carapace about them, a scar grown out of the woundedness. We gaze back on them as though they had meaning, contained intimations of future things – the seeds of the very subsequence we are now in a position to see. It is tempting to persuade ourselves we suffered a kind of illiteracy – we could not read the runes because we were young, or green, or undiscerning, or blind to the consequence. But that is not the truth, or not the whole truth, unmediated; for we sensed, even then, that this framed time must end and that all would be changed from this out. But we were adrift in a maelstrom of human feeling; already it was too late to swim. And we must somehow have wanted it, preferring the storm to the harbour: the hurts, the shattered feelings – the hurts to others, too. We are innocent of nothing we chose. It is my act of contrition. All our lives we do battle in the manacles of our mothers. But even the shaken chain has its music.

There was once a holiday in Wicklow. We saw the bones of an old ship. His gazetteer said that it had been wrecked in the time of the Armada. It was black as his hair. There were seals in the water. Strange cries had been reported from the hulk late at night. But that day, there was only gull song.

Come here to me, Moody. Sit down. Hold my hand. Let us listen to the train, my old love.

14

BROMPTON CEMETERY
LONDON
ENGLAND

MAIRE O'NEILL
DIED NOVEMBER 2ND 1952
SISTER OF
SARA ALLGOOD
DIED IN HOLLYWOOD

Epilogue

OLD LETTER FOUND AMONG
HER PAPERS, UNMAILED

Duane's Inn and Grocery,
Near Carraroe, Cashla Bay,
Connemara,
Galway

24 July *[year not given]*

Dearest Tramp,

I am after writing out your name and looking at the page a
hundred years. I amn't sure I should go on at all or if you'd
like a line or two from your bad old penny. So how are you
keeping this weather and you without me up in Dublin? Are
you fading away like the morning dew? I hope you won't be
thick with me for writing and you buried in your auld play like
a miner. Tis midnight in Connemara and I can't find the
morphine. Downstairs they are at the drinking and the singing
of sad songs. They live only for pleasure, the stony, grey
islanders, and the dark, deep sup of the blackness. It's said
there's a storm coming. No one seems to care. An hour ago a
girl was singing 'The Lass of Roch Royale'. And everything
went still. O, as still as the air. And you came drifting in and
sat down by my window.

I was thinking about the night in Cork when that old drunkard was singing it near the market. Do you remember his hands? They were like gnarled bits of bog oak. We were going somewhere, or coming home – was it after the theatre? – and there was a fellow too old to be begging and he collecting money in a cap. And a dog on a rope with a scarf around his neck. And yourself – big auld Soft-heart – were crying.

> *The sun would dry the oceans wide;*
> *Heaven should cease to be.*
> *The world will cease its motion, my love,*
> *E'er I'd prove false to thee.*

It was good to get your letter in Galway. You're a lovely old Tramper. Don't be fretting yourself about anything at all, little tinker – of course your stubborn girl understands your wanting a little month on your own and when your play is all written it's the happy outings we'll have, with the holy help of God. Meanwhile I have Sally here to mind me – though she's not so sweet as yourself – and coming here for my lessons will soon have me speaking the Irish like a natural, native nun. That last was the charmingest letter you ever sent me yet. It'd be lovely to talk to my Tramp and hear his voice again. You are my greatest little pet. I love you.

So is your play sending you mad? (Write me a BIGGER part than Sally's.) I've an awful ocean of time here – I hope you don't mind my plaguing. The post is only collected twice weekly down here – only once in the wintertime. It must be beautiful then. Easy knowing I'm a blow-in, saying something so stupid. I'd say November's hard here. And January worse.

The lessons are the hardest purgatory any girl ever had. We've this room in the guesthouse, quite small but it's pretty and the bed is bigger than the one we're in at home. There's a view of the sea and the cliffs. The smell of the turf is lovely. You can hear the terns in the morning, it's a beautiful sound. Mrs Duane says you stayed here yourself in the late fourteenth century, one of the Augusts you were down on your own. It's nice to stir in the bed and hear the waves if it's rough; that roar of the pebbles surging like billy in the breakers. I made friends with her daughter Mary who is twenty, same as me. She is a right piece of mischief. All the boys are sweet on her, so Sally is deadly jealous as you can imagine.

They'd a wedding on yesterday in the chapel back the way and it was a sight for sore eyes to see the bride arrive in by rowboat with her people – she is from Aranmore Island – and her chap strolling out of the bogland like a vision. She was carrying her shoes as she came up the boreen below and His Gills whistling 'The Coolin' in her wake. Coat over the shoulder and the paws in the pockets, as carefree as a cornerboy on a saunter. I am reading The Importance of Being Earnest. It's making me laugh. Aren't they the right pair of unholy bitches when they start – the two girls? They make Sally and me seem like saints entirely. (I KNOW it should be Sally and 'I' – I wrote 'me' to vex you.) The way they go on stays in your head after you close the script. As I can always hear my Tramper, and his kind, soft words, even when he's far from me. Because I love him.

So all is good and fine. Musha, we can't complain. I keep thinking I see you. It's the queerest thing. Yesterday it rained when I was down at the cliffs on my own and I could see you taking off your coat that evening you brought me to the Shelbourne and the way you draped it over your arm and reached out to shake my hand same as you were meeting me to offer me a start waiting tables. And rain in your hair. I don't know why I'd remember that. Sure it's mad I am after going entirely, dear man, a wusha, bedad, and begob.

I've been practising my blessed Irish the livelong day so you will be proud of your girl when I see you again. And I like the way they do be talking in English as well. 'A dumb priest never got a parish' being the Mary Duane way of saying: 'I'll ask you any question I want, my buckshee.' O Tinker but you'd want to have seen her in the fine frock for the wedding yesterday – and she ordering around the potboys with extraordinary cursings and half the bucks of the islands with their tongues hanging out for her. At the end of the night she was dancing a step with her father. He's a prince of a man, like a dolmen with limbs; they say he can pull a furze bush out of the ground with one hand. Could my Tinker do that? With his teeth!

Oh, I wrote a love poem the other night with Sally. Here it is:

> *A Protestant bishop called Synge*
> *Decided to kiss a nun's ring,*
> *So he stripped off his mitre*
> *Which so did delight her,*
> *She soon was anointing his thing.*

It's *exquisitely* fine, isn't it? Will you show it to Yeats? (The poem I mean, not your thing.)

Well, how is Dublin and your work? Has it got you in a straitjacket? Well, see you get a rest, you auld loon. A student lad who's here told Sally it's hot as the hobs up there. Mind yourself, won't you? You know how you burn. I was thinking of making an *[illegible word]*.

Well, what other tidings? They're still singing away downstairs. There do be a party of German scholars after descending here at the present time, some of them handsome young ladies of the yellowhaired persuasion, to the becrazement of the indigenous peoples. Ceilidhs do be held and the courting and the sporting and the pucking and the jockeying and night-rambling. This morning I was on the pier with Sally and her student lad when one of the fräuleins – I believe an archaeologist – went past us in a bodice of such a remarkable tightness that you could near enough make out what she had for her dinner. The boys will be all in educational mood and getting stuck into *Elementary German*.

Mother of Christ I hear the rain coming up the road like a

monster. Sounds a serious storm of wind, as they say in these parts. They're saying it could be a hurricane yet. Johnny Coyne loves telling the English visitors: 'A man who is not afraid of the sea will soon be drownded'. You'd believe it on a night like this.

You're right what you were telling me, it's beautiful how they speak. Rolling around the vowels in their mouths like grub. Though there's times it would give you a pain in your face. I mind you once saying they talk like Elizabethans. But maybe they only did that when they saw yourself coming, I'm thinking? 'Chrisht, here's that quare nighthawk down from Dublin – now quit looking happy and remember – Yr ſixſteen brotherſ emygrated unto Maſſachuſettſ in ye famine & ye reſt of uſ ate ſtoneſ & ſeaweede.'

I can see Inishmaan across the Sound if I filch a loan of Mary's da's telescope. Seeing it makes me think of my Tramper. It's myself would like to be walking and courting with you there, and kissing your knuckles and your eyelids. (Why am I telling you this? Sure, it fills up a rainy night.) I *would* like that, though. I miss you. I love you. Won't it be palatial altogether when we're married, Mister Millington? And they can all go and hump. And chew lumps off my rump. Come here to me till I tell you a little secret, Mister Honey – and you will think me a right schoolgirl when I tell you a silly fancy I had. There's this little cabin over on Inishmaan used to belong to a lacemaker, and it neatly on the sea looking over to America. Do you know the place I mean? By the north shore cliff. It's living there I'd fancy with my dear dotey Mister.

Well Sally and I went out there in a little steamer the other day with Mary and her brothers and some boys and some sheep and some goats and a cock and a postman. It looks pretty through the telescope at sunset but when you actually betake yourself over there it's a different state of affairs entirely. The gable's collapsed and the roof-beam's broken in two and a Sugarloaf of sheepshite in the lane. A couple of broken glasses was fairly much the only evidence of human occupation although when I foostered around in the rubble of what would have been the kitchen I found a couple of breakings of broken delft. Beautiful grey in the willow pattern – exactly the grey of your eyes. Pauric Danny – Mary's da – says you'd need a diviner to find water inside a walk of it and there isn't one on the island and it's a sultan's ransom to coax one over. So I'll probably just leave our little cabin of pleasures for the terns and the wildflowers. It's a nice picture to have in your head in Dublin.

We met an old woman called Mrs Flaherty. I think she was sweet on you. 'A *grave* poor man,' she kept saying about Your Scrawniness, with this faraway look on her face. 'He'd go *into* himself, do you know, and not come out the whole day. There's some men do be fierce for the going into themselves, God between us. He'd a type-writing machine. You never seen the like of it. But a grave poor sorrow of a natural man. And you'd see him going along the rocks there in the rain or the sun and the grief kindling away in the eyes of him.' She repeats herself, the old dote, the way old women do. Mary and the lads were good with her. I suppose it's as though stories are stepping stones when you're old, and you keep at the ones you know or you'd fall in. It was a prince of a blue day and this huge Italian sky, same as in a picture of the Mediterranean. There was this tall ship a few miles out. We watched till it disappeared. Below near the rocks there were these seals and a cormorant. The seals would send you a bit queer, their eyes are so human. Oh I went up to that little cottage where you used to stay every year. Funny old owl. Can't have been easy for you all alone. I wished I could have been there with you. Am I allowed to say that?

Well now, Mister Horn-Rims – I better off to my bed. Turn your back while I am undressing myself, you pirate! Can I tell you another secret? Do you mind that evening you took me to tea in the Shelbourne? I mean the evening you first invited me out. I can even remember the date. (Do YOU? Dirty liar – you don't.) When you took off your coat and put it over your arm and looked at me with the rain in your hair and your spectacles smudged? I wanted to kiss you. Amn't I awfully bold? Before we'd even said good evening or sat down at the table. You were burbling away about Yeats, or Paris, or something, and looking as grave as ten popes. I'd a feeling I would always know you — or that I'd met you in the long ago. It wasn't only that you were the kindliest man I'd ever seen in my life; it was stranger than that. Like weather. All the people coming and going and I couldn't even see them. And I was frightened too. I didn't want to fall for anyone. I was bringing a mended coat up to my Auntie Eleanor in Francis Street that night. And I wanted to tell her. Wasn't I mad? That's one night I didn't sleep, Mister. Should I hush up? You're right.

So anyhow. It's raining hard. There we are. What else? It would be grand to go walking with you tomorrow and catch a lobster or two. I have been eating like a carthorse. Sally says I am gone too stout like one of the seals, and I better not go bathing else I'd cause a tidal wave, the bad rip. There's a mirror in the hall downstairs, an old one, you know the sort, it says *Arthur Guinness* with a picture of a parakeet or some remarkably Irish craythur like that. I saw myself in it the other night – GLORY BE TO GOD. Funny thought struck me that my dear Tramp had looked in that mirror. I wanted to give it a kiss. There's flattery for you now! But that way I'd have been kissing myself. You will not have such a fancy for your girl if she becomes a great big article, I'm thinking.

So now, my old Millington Thrillington Moppet – I am solitary in my bed and that sister of mine is off up some hayrick with her student, and I'd lay odds I know what it is they're studying. Ho ho. And I have a famous piece of news entirely for Your Munificent Honour, which is that I wrote the scene of a play the other night. (Christ, it's thundering now; a clap like a BOMB just sounded to the south.) What started it was this old suitcase I saw in a junkshop in Galway a couple of mornings before the Queen of Sheba and my self headed out here: just this battered old yoke full of some dead person's belongings: old rosary beads and tickets and busted auld gewgaws and bits of almanacs and religious medals, and the docket from Ellis Island still pasted on the handle and a couple of dirty cents inside too. O Tramper, it was the saddest old suitcase a body ever saw. Well, all day the owner was in my head and who he must have been, or she. Anyways, I put an evening or two into making a play of it but then didn't I get frustrated and threw the hat at it. So I tear it and say BAD WORDS to it and fling it into the wind, but wait till you hear what happened: next morning I was out in the currach with Mary and her brother Alec hauling lobster pots and didn't I happen on a page of it in the water. As true as God! Soaked through, do you know, and the ink all smudged to buggery. But floating as though it wanted a last chance. So I fished it out anyways and into the apron pocket. And now it doesn't seem actually sickening bad when I look at it again. I mean it doesn't seem good. But it doesn't seem bad. I might work on it a few nights and see if I can give it a kick. I'm thinking I'd call it SCENES FROM A HURRICANE.

Do you reckon you might give it a read for me, my sagacious old nighthawk? The hero is a handsome man of the world and is inspired by yourself but I don't know if that would tempt you? (Cunning, amn't I?) Or maybe it would likelier put you off. (Ha ha.) It would be phantasmagorical of you to read it for I know you would tell me the truth of whether it is of any use, at all, or whether it is, conversely, a bucket of donkeypiss. Anyhow, the only reason I started it was you gave me the courage. And to tell you of my feelings. About you, I mean. For it touched something, that suitcase, took me a while to see what it was. Or maybe I just want to impress Your Bearded Eminence. How funny. Sure I won't actually set it alight on the chance I might hear from you again some time, ever, in my whole life, how is that? Would you not run away with me to California and I'll write it all up proper and play the whole thing to you some morning under a palm tree, in my nip? (Don't be giving me your priestly looks! Don't forget I know your secrets! O, it's the quiet ones want watching, as my mother does say. Don't you miss me at all, my naughty man? THEN WHY IN THE NAME OF GOD DON'T YOU WRITE TO ME?)

Saints' Mothers, it's barrelling down now, the gale of all gales. I should rightly go to my sleep and quit plaguing you. You'd want to hear the creaks and groans out of the roof this minute – like the masts of a ship in a hurricane. Did you know the stagehands in Shakespeare's time were sailors come home? Sally told me that. She has to know everything, of course. Sacred Heart, but it's gone quarter to four in the morning. How did that happen? Why am I asking you questions? Do you know?

I was thinking about when we quarrelled. You silly jealous lunk. I hate it when we quarrel. It makes me afraid you want to leave me. I'd no more go with another fellow – you are too silly a goose for words. I might play a little game of winks and bat my eyes but that is all. And I'll quit if you really do wish me to. The thought I'd make you unhappy, you blethering baboon, when it's myself is at your mercy and always will be.

And I HATE it when you say I'd be better off with 'some easygoing chap'. God it makes me want to scream the face off you, so it does. Some harmless nice fellow and his collars in a drawer and his mammy sewing him up for the winter. What would I do with him, when it's my crabby auld scrivener I only want? You say it for the devilment of maddening me, don't you?

Didn't I know it the moment I saw you, before you'd ever given me the time of day. Long before you ever touched me, or even I heard your name spoken. *Girls' nonsense*, I hear you saying. Never happens in life. Only in storybooks and songs. And the queerest thing of all is: I agree with my Tramper. I haven't hide nor hair of reasons for what's between us now. And if ever you

wanted to quit your impatient girl truly, and our little story had
to be stored away in a room that's only sometimes remembered,
that's still a room I'd want, and I'd go there now and again, like
some room in an old hotel on a seafront someplace where two
sinners did something they shouldn't. Do you mind what I am
telling you? It is the God's honest truth. Even if I never saw you
or heard from you again, you'd already have been the miracle of
my life.

I can see you rolling your seven-hundred-year-old eyes and
saying I make it sound a novel for dressmakers, you bittermouthed
aspish auld granny. But to find you in my mind at some moment
of the morning, to see some sentence in a script and wonder
what my Tramper would say to it, or to feel you glowing on like
a lamp in my head and know I'd sleep in your arms that night.
There's nothing in the world would ever give me the joy of that.
Nothing in the great round world.

You're forever at me to talk. Only I am sometimes afraid. The
things I should have told you when we were walking Killiney
Strand. Like that knowing you is the greatest blessing of anything
in my life and I can't think up the phrases and the fiery words
you have yourself, for there's not languages enough in all the
living world to tell you of your preciousness to me. And everything about you gives me courage I never, ever had and without
you I'm like a ghost drifting through some old house of a life
and there's nothing about you I don't love. You are so kindly and
good and wise and I love you and so patient and so loyal and so
manly. So now you know all. Can I send you this letter? Are you
reading it still? Am I mad?

When we marry, can we go to America and stay there a time?
That's if you still want me, my ploughboy. Wouldn't we be the
nice pair of ornaments in New York or Brooklyn or someplace?
To flit away from this rainy sadland and the gossips and the
dullards and the pokers-of-noses and auld maids. There's times
I think it will choke us. If only we could go. We would live to a
hundred and fifty! Do you think I could ever play a lead in New

York or Chicago? O my Tramper, wouldn't that be a pancake entirely. We'd be two fools with the laughter and we traipsing down the Broadway and back to some little flat in the midnight. It makes me weep with heart's joy when I think I have found you, and all the lovers' adventures we'll share. Do you know the way I have sometimes wept when we have been together alone, for all the pleasures you have given me have left me nothing else to do? That is how I feel this night. How I wish I had you here. I would measure your neck with my kisses.

God I can't sleep tonight. What is ailing your girl? Do you mind you asked me one time to sing you a song and I was nervous for I hadn't had lessons? It was the first day we ever spoke to one another – in Sackville Street – by the Post Office. But if you were here, I'd sing it now. Would you like that, old Millipede? Because the words on a page are only words on a page, but a song needs someone to love it by hearing. You told me that once; it was that night we were in Cork. An auld drunkard was singing it and not a soul of the world listening. But you and me were. And it's in my head now. And as long as I live, and no matter what happens us, I'll hear it every time I hear rain.

> *The sun would dry the oceans wide.*
> *Heaven would cease to be.*
> *The world would lose its motion, my love.*
> *Ere I'd prove false to thee.*

Well, it's coming on for dawn. I better go to sleep. Do you think I should send this, when you don't want interrupting? You're right: I shouldn't. But tomorrow I'm going to. As soon as the storm is over.

Whisht, I think it's lulling. Wait now, till I listen. Everything is quiet. Only the waves on the stones. It's little enough Irish I'll be learning today I'm thinking.

I can hear the terns calling. Beautiful sound. Come with me up to the cliff, and we'll watch them an hour? We won't say

Acknowledgements
and Caveat

I grew up about a mile from the old house where John Synge and his mother had endured their last years, a house that appears several times in this novel. As a child, I passed it often, was faintly afraid of it, often wondered about the stories it had seen. I thought of it as a slightly decrepit embassy of literature, a headquarters where brave things had been attempted, some magnificently achieved, but also as a hermitage of ghosts. On a wintry day it could be forbidding as the Bates Motel, or as Wuthering Heights in a rainstorm. But on a summer evening in that coast town of seagulls and steeples, a strange beauty seemed to glitter from its windows. To my parents I owe an acknowledgement for their valuing of books, their unlocking of the doors to that house. I thank my father, Sean, for his loving solidarity and his affection for the written word's possibilities. It was he who first brought me to a play, in Sallynoggin Parish Hall, an amateur production – I don't remember the author – but I can still hear the wolf-whistles that arose from the audience when the leading lady was kissed by her suitor. I thank my stepmother, Viola, for her loyalty and care, her wise counsel over many years. And I remember my late mother, Marie O'Connor, née O'Grady, who like my heroine had been a dressmaker in her Dublin girlhood, for bequeathing me a fascination with Molly.

It's to my parents, too, that I owe an inherited memory of the Edwardian Dublin words spoken by some of the characters in the book. My father was born in Francis Street, in the oldest part of the city, The Liberties. (His mother, like my leading lady, was an O'Neill.) And I pay tribute to the work of Professor Terence Dolan at University College Dublin, whose *Dictionary of Hiberno-English* is a treasure-chest of glories, an acknowledgement that the common speech of any society is sometimes more nuanced than its art.

Ghost Light is a work of fiction, frequently taking immense liberties with fact. The experiences and personalities of the real Molly and Synge differed from those of my characters in uncountable ways. Chronologies, geographies and portrayals appearing in this novel are not to be relied upon by the researcher. Synge and Molly did not holiday for a month unaccompanied in Wicklow; nor, so far as I know, did he express the wish to live in America. At least one meticulous scholar has contended that they had little or no sexual relationship. Synge's mother was a more complicated person than my portrayal. Molly's circumstances, although difficult in her later years, were not as depicted here. Most events in this book never happened at all. Certain biographers will want to beat me with a turf-shovel. Apologies to Yeatsians for my distortions of the great man and his works, and to scholars of Lady Gregory and Synge and Sean O'Casey. These giants often said they had fanned their fictions from the sparks of real life, renaming the people who had inspired their stories. The practice was sometimes a camouflage, sometimes a claim of authenticity. It was an option I considered carefully but decided against in the end, and so I dare to ask the forgiveness of these noble ghosts of world literature for not changing the names of the innocent.

The letters purporting to be from Synge in chapters 1 and 2, and Molly's love letter in the Epilogue, are entirely fictional. Other brief quotations from Synge's letters are authentic and are included in Ann Saddlemyer, ed., *Letters to Molly: John Millington Synge to Maire O'Neill*, but as with all acts of quotation not made by the original author, context can subtly change meaning. The reader in search of reliable material is directed to the following works and to the useful notes or bibliographies they contain: Elizabeth Coxhead, 'Sally and Molly: Sara Allgood and Maire O'Neill' in *Daughters of Erin*; W.J. McCormack, *Fool of the Family: A Life of J.M. Synge*; Andrew Carpenter, ed., *My Uncle John: Edward Stephens's Life of J.M. Synge*; R.F. Foster, 'Good behaviour: Yeats, Synge and Anglo-Irish etiquette', Anne Saddlemyer, 'Synge's soundscape', and Declan Kiberd, 'The making and unmaking of myth: Synge as anthropologist' in Nicholas Grene, ed., *Interpreting Synge: Essays from the Synge Summer School, 1991–2000*. The song 'Join the British Army' is an old Dublin ballad and is taken from the singing of the late Luke Kelly. 'The Silver Tassie' is by Robert Burns. 'The Heights of Alma' is a traditional Irish ballad celebrating Sergeant (later Major General) Luke O'Connor, who was born in Elphin, County Roscommon and was a recipient of the Victoria Cross for his bravery in the Crimea. The author of the poem sung by JMS in chapter 7 is unknown. A version by Lady Gregory, entitled 'The Grief of a Girl's Heart', appears in her collection *The Kiltartan Poetry Book* and is used powerfully in John Huston's film of James Joyce's short story 'The Dead'. Ardent Joyceans will have noticed that Molly's cat utters the same sound as does Leopold Bloom's in *Ulysses*, that a certain Dublin butcher may have had relatives in the London book trade, and a couple of other fleeting allusions. I thank the excellent librarians and archivists at the National Library of Ireland, at the New York Public Library, at the Abbey Theatre, Dublin, at the Lower East Side Tenement Museum, Orchard Street, New York, and at Trinity College Dublin.

My thanks also to my editor Geoff Mulligan, to Stuart Williams, Ellie Steel, and all at Harvill Secker and Vintage; to my literary agents Carole Blake and Conrad Williams at Blake Friedmann, London; to Jewerl Keats Ross, Silent R Management, Los Angeles; to my family, the O'Connors and Suiters and Caseys; to my friend Tony Roche for enduring my questions with such gentlemanly patience: he must be absolved from any blame for